Kismet 3:

When a Man's Fed Up

Kismet 3:

When a Man's Fed Up

Raynesha Pittman

URBAN Renaissance

www.urbanbooks.net

Urban Books, LLC
300 Farmingdale Road, NY-Route 109
Farmingdale, NY 11735

Kismet 3: When a Man's Fed Up

ISBN 13: 978-1-64556-049-4
ISBN 10: 1-64556-049-X

First Trade Paperback Printing June 2020
Printed in the United States of America

10 9 8 7 6 5 4 3 2 1

Distributed by Kensington Publishing Corp.
Submit Orders to:
Customer Service
400 Hahn Road
Westminster, MD 21157-4627
Phone: 1-800-733-3000
Fax: 1-800-659-2436

Dedication

On January 30, 2013, I was admitted to the hospital after a prenatal visit. My obstetrician said my cervix was dilated, and I would have the baby in a few hours, which was wonderful news to hear, but her timing was off. You see, I promised my readers *Kismet 3* would be released under my indie publishing house, Conglomerate Ink, on the 31st, and after making them wait years for it, I had every intention of keeping my word. The only problem was, how do you self-publish a book while in labor? It hadn't been typeset for e-book nor paperback because I was under the impression that I had at least another week before my baby was due to arrive.

Almost instantly, the contractions started kicking my butt as I began typesetting from my hospital bed. Once a ten-minute drip of pain medicine became my best friend, I passed out, only to be woken up by my doctor, informing that my daughter's heart was in distress, and they would induce me to push her out, or it would be off to emergency surgery I go. At 6:00 a.m. on January 31, 2013, after pushing for about . . . well, two minutes, which felt like the *longest* two minutes of my life, my beautiful daughter, Qui'Layah Chrisette, was born, and with her in my arms less than two hours after her birth, I originally self-published this book from my hospital bed as my readers congratulated the births of both of my babies on social media platforms.

With love in mind, I dedicate this book to my daughter and the beautiful experiences that came along with her birth. I pray she doesn't read this series until she's legally old enough to drink and that she doesn't mirror anyone in this book nor fall in love with anyone similar to these characters. I love you, Qui'Layah Chrisette, and this book I dedicate to you.

Prologue

Let Me Reintroduce Myself

Contrary to what you may think about me, I'm not a stalker, nor am I some ho-ass nigga that's ruled by his bitch. I agree that from the outside looking in, shit appears a little suspect on my part. That's because I've remained too calm, I've been too quiet, and I've wasted too much time trying to teach a dog-ass woman new tricks believing that I could tame that ho.

All I wanted to do was to teach Savannah how to find her worth on two feet instead of on all four. She was more than a cute smile and a good fuck, but I don't think she knows that. She was on that women empowerment, black girls rock, independent women, I am woman hear me roar-type of shit and had convinced herself that dick was the only thing she needed from a man but only after she realized she wasn't getting the kind of nut she was looking for from the women she was fucking. Her freaky ways and drive for success had her out here hoeing without a pimp and a corner, but in her mind, what she was doing in her bed was no different than what we men were doing . . . getting nuts and move on to the next.

Savannah was a lost cause, and I was probably the only donor willing to volunteer time into her charity because I could see her potential. It was buried deep inside of her, but it was there, and I've never been a believer of the saying, "You can't turn a ho into a housewife." I've always looked at it like the niggas who went around saying it didn't have what it took to tame the girl they were pursuing, so it was easier for them to come up with a slogan than to have to admit to their shortcomings. In truth, they didn't have the right recipe, or they were missing a few ingredients on molding the woman into what he needed her to be. I thought that with the right amount of love, teachings, and if she showed potential, that any ho could change for the better.

Then I fucked around and met Savannah's trifling ass, and she had me questioning it. She opened my eyes to a new breed of woman that resembled the crazed survival actions of a vicious female dog. Savannah wasn't going around eating her puppies like a dog, but the way she threw my daughter away for her own selfish reasons and destroyed the lives of others like she was a demolition crew wasn't any better. At times, I can't believe how I just sat back and said nothing while the dumb shit happened around me. That's the main reason why I felt the need for this reintroduction.

You get one shot to make a first impression, or so I've been told. Well, in this case, I'm asking for a do-over, because there's one thing about me you don't know yet. . . .

My name is Andre Burns, and I'm addicted to hoes.

Those twelve-step classes say the first step is admitting your addiction, so I've just accomplished Step One. Where's my chip? This ain't a cop-out, nor is it an excuse I came up with for making bad choices in women. I'm being real. The same way people get addicted to drugs or gambling by doing it once and enjoying the shit too much, that's how I got addicted to hoes. My addiction didn't just start when I met Savannah, either. On reflecting, I've always had this addiction. I just didn't recognize it for what it was until now.

Thinking back, it started when I got my first piece of the forbidden fruit. I had chosen a chick whose fruit had rotted and been damaged from excessive handling. In other words, I lost my virginity to a chick that had been run through by every high school-aged boy in Nashville's city limits. The list of handlers included a few of my close homeboys and a few niggas I didn't like. I knew she was letting everybody have it, but at sixteen years old, I didn't care. All I cared about was what I had heard about her, which was that she was a thick-legged cheerleading freak, and after a few hits of the blunt, she'd let you kill her throat and beat her cat. As a weed- and dope-selling virgin, I couldn't wait to get sentenced for murder one on her esophagus and a cruelty to animals' charge. I'd happily plead guilty to both crimes.

My closest partner back then and to this day, Mike had invited me to come flip her with him. He had been using his cousin's apartment on the eastside to hang out during school hours whenever the pressures of eleventh-grade schooling became too much. For Mike, this seemed to be every day. He went to Stratford High School with the chick, and they had been ditching school all week to start Mike's new side hustle.

Mike had always been an entrepreneur with a get-rich-quick scheme, so it didn't surprise me when he decided to make her his new hustle. Mike saw her spreading her legs for free and thought about all the money he could be making as her manager. He didn't like the word "pimp." It made him feel like a Memphis nigga, and everyone knew Nashville and Memphis niggas didn't get along. He started charging virgins and anybody else with items to barter, like Nintendo and Sega games, to have sex with her.

Being supportive of my friend's endeavors, I hopped the gate at Pearl-Cohn High School out west with my condom and twenty dollars in hand, ready to lose my virginity like all the other virgins my age had done. I had to catch two city buses and walk three miles just to get to her. I remember walking those three miles nervous as fuck, dick already hard, and thinking, she'd better be worth it.

When I saw the girl, my love for hoes was born as I instantly started plotting on getting her away from my boys to clean her off and shine her up to keep for myself. She was beautiful. She had her long hair pushed back out of her face so that you could know that hands down, her face was her best asset. I'm not knocking her body, but at sixteen years old, girls were either pretty or ugly. There was no in between, and that was judged from the neck up. Her skin was the color of roasted almonds, which went perfectly with her big, dark brown eyes. She did have a pig-shaped nose, but it was cute and made you want to pinch it if her lips would release your attention long enough. Everything about her mouth said, "Kiss me and fall in love." That's why her heart-shaped lips fit perfectly above her rounded chin. To top it all off, she had the Lexus car emblem on a charm around her neck, a true sign of luxury. I had never seen a bitch so bad in my life, and I knew I was going to step to her and make her mine. I don't have to tell you how it turned out in the end. Some folks are just comfortable in their own skin, no matter how funky and foul it is.

It's been fifteen years since I made that mistake, and I haven't learned my lesson yet. I'm sure you were hoping I'd leave Savannah's ass alone when I found out she gave my daughter away, and I was planning to. To be honest, I was done with her after she gave the police the letter I wrote her with my plans of turning myself in. Even though I wanted her to snitch on me so it could buy me a couple of days of freedom to get my affairs in order, there was a piece of me hoping Savannah would prove me wrong and hold on to the letter. But she didn't, so I said, fuck her and her good pussy.

Being in jail without a piece of mail coming in besides updates on my son from my mama made me think about her. Thoughts of her began to help me get though the day, so I sent my nigga, Ryan, lurking for me . . . and look at what he found out. Savannah was pregnant and hiding her pregnancy from the world. I wasn't sure if it was mine or not because baby girl was a freak, but she was ordering my favorite foods daily. I wanted to know and sent a letter to find out.

She wrote me back in her own fucked-up way to let me know that she had given birth to my daughter and given her away to the highest bidder like a car being auctioned. I read that part of the letter at least ten times a day until I was released, and although it's been years since I received it, I remember verbatim what she wrote. It said:

I am not a caring person. My only concern is me and what's best for me. Your beautiful eight-pound daughter, who looked just like you, will never know either one of us. I hired an out-of-country adoption agency to ship her off to her new parents two days after she was born. I know you don't believe me and will play a detective again, and that's fine, but the next time one of your goons finds me, they will see me alone without a child. I have destroyed all the records of the birth and my pregnancy to prevent you from trying to get her. You told me how you would have tried to get custody of your son, so I had to make sure I didn't leave you the option of getting her. If you still don't understand what I'm saying to you yet, let me make it simple. I am well paid and only use men for sex. Fuck a relationship, love, marriage, the white picket fence, and fuck the dog too. That shit ain't for me, and neither are you or your child.

Man, Savannah is hell for that one! She lied about the out-of-country shit, but she did find a way to make it damn near impossible to track my daughter down. How I allow her the right to have life in her worthless body amazes me too. Even after all of the blood, sweat, and tears she's caused me to shed, my hands still couldn't cause her pain. After snooping some more for signs of the whereabouts of my daughter, I realized Savannah was hurt and living with pain from her past. She wasn't born to be the bitch that she is. The life she was dished made her that way. And being the save-a-ho nigga that I am, I made getting my daughter and healing her heart my number one priority.

That's why I'm in the situation I'm in now. Since I haven't slapped the shit out of Savannah or snatched my daughter up and bounced, I'm out here looking like a pushover. What did y'all expect me to do, beat on her? Well, I can't. Hitting a woman ain't me. I've had a thought or two about wrapping my hands around her neck and not letting go, but that just means I'm human. I've even thought about snatching her scandalous ass up and shaking the shit out of her, but where would that get me besides back in jail? After all the bullshit I've allowed this woman to put me through, I still got hope I can make her change her ways, which is a true sign of my addiction.

You see, there is some meaning behind the shit I do and take from Savannah, so it isn't the addiction alone that has me biting my tongue. Please believe that I'd break a nigga's jaw for half the shit I've let Savannah fix her mouth to say to me. And if it were any other bitch, I'd have been gone, but there's something about Savannah's wretchedness that I can't shake. I'm stuck to her in a fucked-up way like a therapist to a seriously hurt patient. In the beginning, it was her looks that caught my eyes, her fast words that kept my attention, but above all, that goodness she got in between her legs with the vacuum suction head sealed the deal. I've never felt nothing like it.

I don't know why I'm always listening to my dick. It's the worst influence in my life. It always leads me in the wrong direction, like it's got a "nothing-ass bitch" GPS attached to it. When the head on my shoulders tells me, "Aye, Dre, she's a ho," the one in my pants says, "So what? Don't kiss her in the mouth and strap up, my nigga."

That's bad, and I know it is. The shit ain't safe, and that's sloppy living on my part, but I can't get my dick to listen. Hoes make it too easy. I don't have to wine, dine, or court anymore. I don't even have to spend cash on or time with them. All it takes is a show of interest, whether it's real or fake, and them legs go flying open. I ain't no mentor, so I'm not passing out self-esteem speeches. If it makes you feel better to hear me say, "Damn, baby, that pussy is good" than to hear me say, "Damn, baby, you're smart," that's some shit you'll have to work on by yourself.

I wouldn't say that I'm easily whipped. I'm just weak. I have a weakness for pretty things, and when I get them, I get addicted. Like any other man or boy, I like big, pretty trophies that say "first place." When I met Savannah's beautiful ass, it felt like I had caught a fifteen-foot, 700-pound marlin with my bare hands. I wanted to take a picture with her standing next to me, hooked to show off my prize-winning catch. I knew instantly that I was in the presence of the Most Valuable Player trophy, and I had to make her mines. If baby needed a little polishing up, I didn't mind giving her a spit shine.

It must have been all the weed smoke clouding my vision, though, and throwing my psyche off, because Savannah ain't shit. I should have checked out her shoes. One quick glance down, and I would've realized she was walking on toilet tissue and not the red carpet.

Baby has the potential to be priceless, but she prefers to have no value. I know it sounds backward, but that's how it is. Savannah walks around like the world is in debt to her, and she can do whatever she wants. It's time I show her that I don't owe her ass shit. Every move I've made has been on the strength that I love her. I thought if I showed her what love is and hit every spot that those random niggas she was fucking had missed, I could change her. I thought that with some home training and a display of Southern family morals, I could mold her into what I wanted her to be. I thought if I could get her to build a relationship with God, my daughter would have her mama, and I'd have my wife. That's what I get for reading a children's book on life. This shit ain't no fairy tale. But maybe there is still a chance for our happily ever after.

Part One

Dre

Chapter One

The Decision

"Open the fucking door, Savannah!"

I couldn't have been talking to myself, and I doubt the bitch went deaf after asking me to identify who I was as I knocked. The door never opened once I told Savannah that it was me, nor did I get a response from the other side of it. All I heard in return was my heavy panting from the workout I was getting from trying to get in that room.

I didn't know what else to do, so I kicked the door twice flat-footed with my back turned to it like a donkey, hoping to get a response. The sole of my booted foot stung and caused my toes to tingle from the impact of both kicks. The act backfired and left me irritated from the self-induced pain. I turned to face the door again, grabbed the doorknob, and twisted it as if it would magically unlock. But who was I kidding? I knew before I touched the knob it wouldn't open. It just felt like the right thing to do next.

The word "mad" didn't do any justice or come close to describing how I was feeling at that point. I was infuriated and seeing red. My foot was throbbing, my body was trembling uncontrollably, and my heartbeat sped up with more bass and depth to it than I had ever felt. The power in its beats made my pulse feel like it was on the verge of bursting every blood vessel in my body. An aneurysm was growing, I just knew it, with severe hemorrhaging and my death to follow. I had to take a second to laugh at my exaggerated thoughts. I can't believe how this chick had me going crazy, but fuck it. It is what it is. My normal rational way of thinking had flown out the window without a sign of returning. The fact that I had no control over being permitted to enter was driving me insane. All I could do now was keep pounding on the door and yelling, hoping she would let me in.

"Savannah, I said open the motherfucking—"

My yell was interrupted by the bell that alerted the elevator's arrival on the floor. I watched as the doors opened, heard the sound of someone pushing a button rapidly, and then watched the elevator door close without a soul getting on or off of it. I couldn't tell if it had been a guest or hotel staff from where I stood, but that didn't matter to me anyway. The unknown passenger or passengers weren't a big enough distraction to make me forget what I had been doing. Curiosity wasn't shit when it was up against my fury in the past, and today wasn't an exception. My focus was beating on the door until I was allowed entrance, and fuck everything and everybody else. I probably should have questioned that elevator's ghostly arrival and departure, but I was in a trance. My mind wouldn't allow my body to walk to the elevator and investigate. Getting in that room was my number one priority.

I yelled at the door again. "Open the door, Savannah."

How could a simple request take this long to play out? The delay in action was causing my body to have physical reactions. Now, my vision was blurry from the heat of my blood flowing through the veins behind my eyes. The dimly lit hallway wasn't making it any easier on my sight, either. All the color had gone, and I was left with black-and-white static. I looked around the hallway to focus on the sunlight that should be shining through the windows, but there weren't any windows on this floor. I double-checked my surroundings. I remembered this floor being brighter than this. I was standing in this very same spot less than two weeks ago. I had gotten high and was coating my throat from the weed smoke with a bottle of Rémy. I don't really remember what happened next. I just remember standing outside this door, ready to terminate that lawyer nigga Savannah was creeping with. I'm sure the lights had been a lot brighter than this.

I shot my eyes up to the ceiling and saw two of the track lights had been broken. I looked down and saw that there were small pieces of glass on the ugly mint-green carpeted floor. It must've been the detective in me or my criminal instinct that instantly made me notice that the security cameras were on the other end of the hall. If you got off the elevator with your back to the cameras and came straight to the door, you wouldn't be identifiable under these broken lights. That would make it easy to commit murder.

Maybe someone else wanted Royce's head as much as I did, or maybe Savannah had shown her face too many times around here, and the plot was to get her. I had to shake my head to clear that last thought from forming. I couldn't get caught up being Savannah's protector right now. She was fucking me over and wasn't opening up the door. I turned my focus to my rapidly numbing hands. I had to make myself remember that it was because of Savannah's creeping that my hands were swollen like I'd eaten too much salt. It was hard to make my hands out clearly because of the lights and my vision, but the tingling sensation in my knuckles gave away their condition. They were fucked-up. Both hands were busted and swollen. I didn't think I had knocked on the door that hard, but then again, I didn't care. I tried to ball my hands into fists and open and close them to revive the feeling in them, but anger was easing the pain and forcing my hands to feel numb. I balled my fists one more time out of frustration, cocked back, and hit the door with everything left in me.

"*Fuck,*" I screamed out in agonizing pain as a single tear made its way to the inner corner of my left eye. "Savannah, are you gon' open the door and let me in, or do I need to make my own key?"

I took my nine out of its leather holster, cocked it back, then I aimed at the electronic keypad on the door. My hands couldn't take anymore. I was tired of knocking and even more tired of playing these ho/snitch games with Savannah and her mama. I waited a few seconds more to give her an opportunity to respond, but she never did. That's when the reality of it all hit me. I had really changed. The old Dre—that wild, not-giving-a-fuck-ass nigga that I used to be—wouldn't have waited for a response. I would've shot the lock off the door by now, booted the motherfucka in, and said fuck being permitted, but luckily for Savannah, that side of me is in a coma now. It was knocked out by growth and the many nights I spent praying for change while I was in jail.

I had grown, but that didn't mean there wasn't more growing to do. All it meant was that I had learned to make force my last option instead of my first choice. I wouldn't let this shit have me sitting behind bars—Hell naw. I wasn't going to be behind bars over a bitch ever again. My baby mama Tasha had taught me a lesson in loyalty that I'd never forget. She turned key witness for the DA against me. That's an experience I never want to go through again, so growth from my last mistakes made me wait another twenty seconds. Hell, I even knocked three more times with my gun-free hand just to show off my newly found patience.

Finally, Savannah's voice rang out again. This time, the confidence she originally had in her voice was gone.

"Hold on, Dre, I'm about to open it, baby, I swear."

Her swear bounced like a check from a closed banking account because two minutes later, I was still standing on the hallway side of the door. There was nothing but the hotel's surveillance cameras keeping me from making my way in. Since I had already checked out my scenery and noticed the lights were as dim as they were, the cameras were becoming less of an issue. I was feeling tested. I felt like Savannah and her mama knew I wasn't going to come through the door without them opening it first. They both knew I needed to keep my distance from the law and that my freedom depended on me doing just that. Shooting down the door would cause the workers at the front desk to call the police. And even if I managed to get in the room and handle mine, I'd still have to allow myself time to snatch up the videotapes from security before making a run for it. All these thoughts started to overthrow my better judgment and join forces in attacking my ego. My manhood was on the line, but so was my freedom. That "I don't give a fuck" gene lying dormant inside of me had awakened from its coma and began provoking me to get in that room and handle mine the way I used to.

Ay, Dre, she probably in there sucking that fool up right now while you stand outside the door begging to get in like a little bitch. You're trying to get in the room and ain't nobody letting you in, not even her mama, and she supposedly on your side. That's why Savannah doesn't respect you now because you're always doing shit the soft way. What'cha do, my nigga, give up your boxers for a thong while you were locked up? Man, you better teach that ho of yours some manners, then turn that nigga into shark food, and if her mama jumped ship and is back on Savannah's side, give her ass an expiration date. Fuck yo' changes.

My thoughts were on point, but I couldn't allow them to get the best of me. I walked backward away from the door until my back was against the smooth surface of the off-white wall across from the room. I closed my eyes and tapped my gun on my leg to a tic-toc beat as I fought with my thoughts. Even though my blue jeans were a loose fit, I could still feel the strength in the metal as if my legs were bare. I had the power I needed to get in that room in my hand. I could also use it to gain the respect I was lacking from Savannah, but that would be taking the easy way out.

Like my pops had once told me, "Real respect is earned over time, not taken by force within seconds, son. Respect and fear are not the same things, Andre. You better learn that soon or die by the hands of those you thought respected you."

My father's words replayed in my head like a song on repeat. They were repetitive, and the exact warning I needed to remind me of my change. Mental pictures of me spending time with my kids as my father had once done with me began to play in my head like a slideshow. It was a fact that both of my kids' mamas were trifling, and I refused to let my ego-driven actions stop me from raising them. My seeds needed to be nurtured, and if their mamas weren't up for the job, I'd handle it myself. The slideshow I was watching of me being the perfect father to my children stopped abruptly as my inner demons gave it another go.

Think about it, Dre. Even if Savannah was in there fucking that lawyer nigga, five minutes was more than enough time to dress and answer the door. They're probably looking at you through the peephole in the door and laughing at your weak ass. I never thought I'd see the day that a goon like Dre turned bitch. You might as well go home if you ain't gon' try to get in that room, you pussy.

That was it. I was getting more upset by the second, and it was getting harder to keep my shit at bay. My father's teachings had faded out of my mind like they always did. My rebellion from him that started at the age of sixteen always sent me down the wrong path. I tried to convince myself that nothing was going on in that hotel room except for a mother blackmailing her daughter for money, which I was an accomplice to because a broke Savannah meant a dependent woman, or so I'm hoping, but that didn't help. I tried telling myself over and over again that Savannah's mama was in the room with them, and she was my ally on foreign soil.

Peaches was a general in my army now, and she would remain that way until she got her pay for services rendered. But if I were wrong, and she was in there double-crossing me, I'd make sure to ship her ass back to Kingston in a wooden box, toe-tagged up. Anger surged through me like electricity at the thought of it and caused me to aim my gun at the door again.

"Don't make me shoot this muthafuckin' door down, Savannah."

That was my last warning yell. Savannah's time was up. My thoughts had won. It was time to pull the trigger. I tightened my hand around the handle for a better grip of the gun, took two steps back, placed my index finger on the trigger . . . and squeezed.

Instantly, the door flew open, but the bullet wasn't the cause of it. Peaches was. If I hadn't been so anxious to shoot, I would have remembered the safety was on, and Peaches would be dead. She was standing in the door's landing, smiling from ear to ear like she just hit the lotto with no knowledge of how close she was to death.

My finger was still wrapped around the trigger, and my adrenaline was still pumping from the murder I had almost committed. I couldn't return the smile she gave me. I was on edge and had yet to find out what the delay was in letting me into the room. My gun was in hand and ready to spit fire if anybody in that bitch made a false move. I wouldn't forget the safety twice.

"Hey, future son-in-law of mines. I'm so happy to see you." Peaches's arms went spread eagle as she moved in for a hug. Once she made eye contact with my pistol, she froze in her stance. "Put that thing away, Dre. This ain't hunting season, and there ain't no animals indoors. Everything is fine, you crazy boy." She turned her head to face Royce after saying her last words and shook her head. If she were trying to put fear in his heart, she had achieved her goal.

Royce looked sick with fear. He was nervous and fidgeting. I decided to keep most of my attention on him because I learned a long time ago that a scared person would kill you. I wasn't up for being a scared nigga's victim. When our eyes met, Royce swallowed so hard that his Adam's apple sank into his throat and popped back out with the loudest gulping sound I had ever heard. If it weren't for the lack of smell, I'd bet money dude shitted on his self.

Royce's fear of me was well-deserved because looking at the clown from head to toe made me want to shoot him for doing his circus act with Savannah. Dude was a joke. I could tell by his dumb facial expressions. I almost flinched at him just to see if it would send him into cardiac arrest. I can't believe my bitch had pleasured this ho of a man. To keep me from putting my gun up and beating his face in, I searched for meaning in Peaches's empty words. She had said something about being my mother-in-law and rambled on about some other shit I wasn't listening to. She was trying to talk in code, but I read between the lines. The smile she greeted me with and her words were confirmation that our plan had worked. Savannah had given up her last dime for a shot at forever with me. She had chosen her love for me over money. Miss Independent well paid professional who prides herself on what she's accomplished on her own, put me over her banking account.

I can't lie. I was feeling good inside at the thought that Savannah did truly love me, but Peaches killed it with that "in-law" shit. She could have left that part out. She wasn't a mother-in-law of mine. How could she be when she wasn't even a mother to her only daughter, Savannah? She abandoned her children to live the life that was best for her and never looked back. Peaches wasn't a mother. She's a snake bitch that slithers on two feet instead of on her stomach that I decided to do business with. That coldhearted old ho didn't love anything except dead presidents printed on green trees, and her extortion and blackmailing of her daughter proved it.

When Peaches found out that Savannah was back spreading her thighs for every Tom, Dick, and Royce, she tried to sell me the information. But I wasn't about to pay for it because I already had it. LoJack had put me up on the game for free. I tracked Savannah's car to hotels when she told me she was headed somewhere else, so I already knew she was back passing out my goodies like Halloween candy. Her fight with ovarian cancer, that chick Keisha shooting her, then beating her ass for seeking revenge over childhood shit, and all the love I was showing her hadn't taught Savannah a damn thing. She was too comfortable with getting her sewers piped by multiple plumbers.

There was a time when I used to feel fucked up about looking at my woman as a ho, because if she was a ho, what would that make me? But it's the truth, and I got to call it as I see it. This wasn't the first time I'd stood outside of a hotel room that was occupied by my future Mrs. This is just the first time she's known I was there. I've had to fall all out of character to make this shit work between Savannah and me. I've acted like a police K9 just to see what Savannah was up to and got fed up with my role as a bloodhound. I would park my truck blocks away to hide behind parked cars to see what my bitch was doing. I wasn't about to wait for the truth when I could go out and get it. That's how I found out her mama was doing the same. I had Savannah's car tracked, so I knew which way she was headed, and I'd beat her there. Once I got there, Savannah would pull up, and so did a black Benz. It followed Savannah's Cadillac like a funeral procession. No matter which direction Savannah traveled in, that black Benz was always a car or two behind her.

I had originally planned on busting Savannah in the act of cheating, but I had a bigger job to do now, and that was to protect her from harm. She was still mine, and as her man, I had a duty to protect her. Savannah had done some unbelievable shit to folks in California, which gave them enough motivation to get revenge. Everybody involved in that Cali mess didn't get a life sentence behind bars, and the way California was going broke, they didn't have the funds to keep people in jail longer than they had to. Folks were getting released for good behavior left and right, especially first timers. I didn't want to tell Savannah this. I just decided to be an extra pair of eyes and ears and make the necessary moves to keep her protected. A car following her everywhere she went smelled like trouble to me, so I jumped on it. I got with Savannah's homeboy, Will, who's a Los Angeles county sheriff, to make sure none of the people she got revenge on were released. Once he confirmed they were still a part of the county jail's population or waiting on their prison stays, I decided to make sure nobody else would be out to get Savannah by getting friendly with her girl Stephanie.

I wasn't sure if it was going to work, but once I realized Stephanie was feeling me, I knew she'd be down to betray Savannah for a ride on this dick. Stephanie's big booty-having ass was sexy as fuck, and if Savannah had asked for a threesome, I would have drilled both of their pretty asses. But to lay Stephanie down in search of a nut, I wouldn't. I only did what was needed to get the information I wanted. Putting Stephanie on my dick's payroll was too close to home, and I knew that chick was too confused to be able to handle it. She was Savannah's flunky, and that's all she knew how to be. Once I got the dumb bitch to join Team Dre, I had her committing treason by telling me everything fucked-up about Savannah. All that time I spent with Stephanie and all the work I was putting in wasn't enough to uncover anybody else that would want Savannah's head. All I got was a long list of Savannah's past lovers, both male and female, out of Stephanie, and most of the names on the list were flings that didn't last longer than two weeks.

I was sure that the Benz following Savannah had a new hunter in it, but I couldn't uncover why she was the prey. I waited for the Benz to park, and normally, no one got out of it, but this last time I watched Peaches exit the driver's seat. She disappeared behind Savannah into the hotel, and so did I. I caught her hiding behind a newspaper in the lobby, pretending to be invisible as Savannah took a seat at the bar.

"How long you gon' keep following her, Peaches?" My voice had her closing the newspaper as fast as she opened it.

"What in the world are you talking about, Dre?" She laughed as if I said something amusing, then continued, "Who am I following? I'm just catching up on current events." Peaches tried to sound calm as she spoke, but my accusation caught her off guard, and the look on her face gave her away.

"Let's not play dumb. If I'm following her, Peaches, then I'm following you too, and your lying ass is reading the obituary section. You don't know anybody in Seattle." That's when I snatched the paper out of her hands and turned my volume all the way down, hoping not to catch Savannah's attention. "What do you want with her?"

Peaches, being the crook that she is, was worried about her surroundings, so she invited me to her room. She spent the first thirty minutes lying to me. She tried to use that "rekindle" and "rehabilitation" shit I put in her head back on me. She wanted me to think she really wanted a mother-daughter relationship with Savannah, but it wasn't working. She then offered to sell me information on the niggas Savannah had been fucking, but I already knew enough to get my own information on them. Twenty minutes later, I had broken Peaches down for the truth, and she was offering to split the money she was planning on stealing from Savannah with me. I couldn't knowingly let her rob Savannah, but I could help fix her money issues while I straightened out my bitch.

Three meetings with Peaches later, this plan was put in motion. If losing everything she worked hard for didn't wake Savannah's ass up, I'd have to let her stay asleep.

"Peaches, where's Savannah?" I said as I walked in the room, cotton-mouthed from thirst and yelling.

At that very moment, Savannah exited the restroom and handed her mama a cell phone. She had a look of disappointment on her face, but she wiped it off as she walked up to me and kissed me on my jaw. "Hey, baby, what's wrong?"

She tried to flip it like *I* was the one with the problem. She was smooth but not smooth enough. I could see the ashy tracks of dried tears on her face. I was glad to see the decision to choose me over her life's savings brought her pain. It was a sample of the payback life I had lined up for her for all the bullshit she'd done. It's good to know that Karma and I were in cahoots in making sure Savannah got back everything she dished out.

"That's what the fuck I'm trying to find out. What took you so long to answer the door?"

My words made her jump, or it could have been the sight of me holding my pistol in my busted, swollen hand. Savannah nervously turned away from me, looking for help from her mama, but she was too busy listening to the voice on the other end of the phone. I'm sure Peaches was listening to her pending transactions on her banking account and couldn't care less about helping Savannah at that moment. I glanced back at Royce. He looked at me and the gun, then turned to Peaches for help as well.

Savannah and Royce were scared shitless. I had them both running to Peaches for protection, as if she were a walking, talking bulletproof vest. A feeling of power rushed through me, and laughter grew in the pit of my stomach. My anger was still present, but it had collaborated with humor. My pops was wrong—respect and fear *were* the same things. Savannah's and Royce's actions proved it. I decided to make them sweat, all the while laughing inside at their asses.

"Who the fuck is he, Savannah? Is this nigga the reason you couldn't open the door for me? Huh?" I asked, hoping my voice would still sound angry. Then I pointed the barrel of my gun at Royce's head with about twenty feet of space between us. It was juvenile of me to play with my power, but I wanted to hear Savannah's lying at its best.

She didn't bite. Savannah continued to look at her mama for help as her heart pounded against her chest. Her breasts reacted to the pounding by hugging her black shirt and fluttering like a butterfly's wings. Royce was waiting for her response to my question with his hands covering his face as if they would shield him from bullets, but it became obvious Savannah didn't have one. Still protected, he focused his attention on Peaches again.

A smile reappeared on the face of Peaches. She hung up the phone, then approvingly nodded at Savannah before speaking. "Dre, I said, put the gun down. This is our lawyer, Royce Reed. He was here helping Savannah and me try to figure out how to get that nasty little background of yours expunged. Weren't we, Royce?"

The bitch nigga nodded his head "yes" faster than the speed of light, then stood up and extended his hand to me.

"How are you, Dre? I'm . . . I'm Royce Reed, your new lawyer. I was wondering when I would get the chance to meet with you."

I should have knocked his teeth down his throat for standing in my face lying. But then again, he was a lawyer, a career that paid him to lie. He was spineless, which made him the exact opposite of me. If this was the type of nigga Savannah was normally attracted to, then I know why she was interested in me. She was tired of dating bitches. Savannah needed a real man made from bone, muscle, and thick blood. This dude was watered-down gristle. I wasn't about to shake his hand. What would I look like getting chummy with the wimp who had been having sex with my woman?

I waved his hand off and said, "I don't fuck with lawyers like that. Y'all stay with a lie or two. So . . . Are you here to get my record closed for me? How much is that gon' cost me?" I slowly put my gun in its holster.

Savannah's face regained its color, but Royce's face remained the same.

Peaches walked in between us and faced Royce. "He's doing it for free, Dre. He owes me a favor, so I'm cashing it in on you. That's why I asked you to meet us here today."

Before Peaches could finish her sentence, there the punk went again, nodding his head "yes" and agreeing with whatever she was saying.

He opened his mouth again to talk. "Don't worry about all that, Dre. I'll get you all squared away for free. It's the least I can do."

Royce was right. After sampling my goods and using my fiancée as his blow-up doll, that *was* the very least he could do. Even a pimp would charge him more than a couple of hundred for a night with Savannah. I wasn't about to accept his help, because Savannah wasn't for sale even if she did make you want to put a price tag on her. My pride wouldn't let me accept a handout from him, and I'm glad it didn't.

"Don't trouble yo'self, Royce. I'll fix my shit on my own time. There's something about you I just don't trust." As I concluded my sentence, Royce's facial expression grew into a questioning one, and so did Savannah's. I couldn't believe what she fixed her mouth to say next.

"What do you mean, you just don't trust him, Dre? He's here to help you. I think you owe him the opportunity to try—and an apology."

I should have snatched her ass off the ground by her neck, then locked my grasp around her throat until she blacked out. What would make her think I'd owe him anything? *He* was in debt to *me* for nonpayment from all my pussy and time he's been getting. I'd never put my hands on a woman except to please or assist her, but Savannah had me ready to slap the shit out of her. She needed to learn where her loyalties should lie and to shut her mouth when two men were talking. It was hard to play cool after that, but I managed to bring Savannah back to reality.

"I don't know, Savannah. The nigga looks shady to me. He looks like one of them cutthroat niggas that would try to shake my hand after fucking you. You know what I mean?"

That shut her ass up and sent Royce to take a seat as far away from me as possible. Peaches was loving the live entertainment, and since she was the only one in the room who was truly winning, I decided to wrap up this show. "Thanks for trying to look out for me and all, Peaches, but I can handle mines. Come on, Savannah, let's go."

Savannah didn't move an inch. Her eyes were fixated on her mother as if they were having a conversation in Morse code using the blinks of their eyes. "Dre, baby, go ahead and go. I'll be right behind you. I just want to make sure everything is good with Mama before she leaves town tonight. I love you."

That was the first time Savannah had called Peaches "Mama" in front of me and truly meant it, but I didn't give a fuck.

"I'm not in a rush, baby. I can wait while y'all say goodbye. I'm glad to see y'all giving this mama and daughter thing a try. Maybe my daughter will benefit from it."

"No, Dre," Savannah blurted out. "We need some . . . ummm, mama and daughter *alone* time. You understand, don't you?" She tried to put on an innocent smile when she finished her last words. If she thought I'd leave her alone with them, she had another think coming.

"Hell no, I don't understand." I snapped back at her, then looked at Peaches for an understanding.

She looked lost back at me and didn't mind expressing it. "Savannah, we've already said our goodbyes. Go on home with your fiancé and start enjoying y'all's new life together with my beautiful granddaughter. I'll be in touch, and I still prefer you to call me Trisha. Peaches is for friends, and I've never liked the word 'Mama.' It makes me feel old."

Laughing at her final words, Peaches grabbed her package and cell phone off the table. She looked at the three of us individually and nodded. Before she made her way out of the room, she gave us a smile that I'd never forget. Now I knew what the devil looked like when he was having a good day.

Chapter Two

Never Saw It Coming

We made it home before the sun ducked off and let the moon do its thing in the sky. It wasn't quite sunset yet, but the redness of the day was beginning to turn burgundy, and it would only get darker. It couldn't have been a better time of day to start pleasing season. I had enough daylight left to get home and unwind with some foreplay before breaking Savannah's back in. I was ready to consummate my renewed relationship. I left all the bullshit that happened at the hotel back at the hotel. I wasn't going to bring that shit home with me.

When Savannah jumped in her car, and I got in mines, that Royce and Trisha shit was over with. I didn't know how Savannah felt about it, but I was done with it. While she drove home thinking about the money she lost, my mind was on my passenger. I wasn't in my ride alone. I was accompanied by freaky thoughts that made my dick harder than steel. He was ready to tear through my boxers and bust out of my pants to get inside of Savannah. I tried not to listen to him, but he was begging me to free him and stroke him now. I was seconds away from turning into one of them perverted niggas you hear about on the news. I thought about just stroking him enough to calm his overly hyped ass down, but that would only make things worse. We were out in public. I couldn't just pull him out and stroke him like the shit was normal. I was sitting in traffic on a busy Saturday evening with cars to the left and right of me. I wouldn't fall for his foolishness. Instead, I grabbed his hardheaded ass through my pants and mumbled, "Look, nigga, you gotta wait."

We had no choice but to wait because we both wanted to feel Savannah's warmth wrapped around us. I didn't like stroking my own shit, and he wasn't that fond of my touch. I only did it when it was necessary, and now wasn't one of them times. I was ten minutes away from the house; then we'd get some pussy.

Savannah didn't know it yet, but she was in trouble—in a good way. I was ready to give her all of me after all this time of just giving her enough of me. She didn't deserve the piping I'm capable of giving her until now. If she thought she couldn't handle what I'd been giving her in the past, there was nothing she could do to prepare for what she's got coming. I pushed my foot on the gas and cut over to the far right lane so I could be parallel to Savannah's car at the red light. When she looked my way, I rolled my window down, and she did the same.

"Stop driving like a granny and hit the gas, baby. I got something to give you when we get home." As the words came out of my mouth, the pounding in my pants got worse.

"What'cha got for me, Dre?"

Her question made her right eyebrow lift, and her eyes slant. Damn, my baby is sexy. I could've eaten her ass up at the light, but it quickly changed from red to green. If she hadn't hit the gas at the change of the signal, she would have heard me say, "This dick." I had to rub my pants before following her lead.

When she pulled in our driveway, I pulled in and parked right behind her, blocking her car in. She wouldn't be going anywhere anyway, at least not anytime soon. She got out of her car and smiled at me. I'm sure she didn't mean for it to be a sexy smile, but that's the way my dick convinced my brain to perceive it. I jumped out of mine, raced up the walkway behind her, and attacked Savannah before she could get her key out of the door.

"What are you doing, Dre?" Savannah said, laughing as I came up behind her and started nibbling on her neck.

"What does it feel like I'm doing?" I pressed the zipper area of my pants against her butt so she could feel my words, then said, "I told you I had something for you," as I laid combinations of licks and small bites on the back of her neck.

"It feels like you trying to start some shit; that's what it feels like." She moved her neck out of my mouth's reach, then continued, "I've had a long day, Dre. Can I get a rain check?"

Instantly, the throbbing in my pants stopped because I knew she was right, but my hardness hadn't gotten that memo. The head on my shoulders understood why sex would be the last thought on Savannah's mind, but not the head in my pants. He wanted to thank her for putting us first, and sending her to ecstasy was the best form of repayment. For the first time in years, both of my heads worked together to come up with a plan of attack. I left Savannah where she stood in the living room and drew a hot bubble bath. I threw in some of that lavender salt she liked to use when she wanted to relax and lit a few candles that she kept stationery in the bathroom. When the bath was drawn, I went back to get her. She was now barefoot, curled up on the couch, flipping through a magazine.

"Come on, let me help you relax some."

I reached out for her hands. She hesitated, then grabbed my hands and stood on her feet. I had her undress and get in the tub. Then I connected her MP3 player to the speakers in the house and played her "'90s

R&B jams" playlist. The first track on the list was "Butter Love" by Next. She sang along to the tune while I sat on the rim of the tub and rolled the perfect blunt in record time. I hit it twice and passed it to her, then headed to the kitchen to pour her a glass of wine. When I made it back, Savannah's eyes were already sitting low. I swapped the blunt for her glass and puffed away on it. I wasn't an R&B type of guy, but I did know the hits, and Savannah seemed to have everyone playing back to back. By the time Aaron Hall and Guy were halfway finished with singing "Piece of My Love," I was on my knees, sleeves rolled to my elbows, washing Savannah's body with her rag. I started at her neck, then made my way slowly down to her breasts. I encircled each one with the rag, making sure to lift them to clean the crease that hid under them. I lingered around her nipples and softly touched them both with the outside of my index finger. Her nipples responded to me by standing erect.

"Dre . . ."

I shushed her before she continued and motioned for her to listen to the music flowing through the speakers. I didn't know the song or the identity of the singer, but the beat was soft, and the words went perfectly with the mood I was in. I wanted to make love, and that's what the male singer kept reciting. I rushed my way down her stomach, then released the rag to squeeze my hand in between her legs. She tightened her thighs to prevent me from entering. I didn't like being rejected, but I accepted it and moved my hand down her leg to her foot. From right foot to the left, I messaged her feet until I noticed she had closed her eyes. I crawled back up her leg with my index and middle finger and tried to get between her thighs again. This time, they opened. I rubbed her clit for a little over a minute, then used my fingers to clean her opening and about three inches inside of her.

She purred my name and said, "I'm ready for you to get me out of this tub."

I grabbed her black beach-sized towel off the toilet, then picked her up and carried her to our bed. Once her body was dried and oiled, it was on. I was hungry, and it was time to feast. I made a meal out of her without resting my tongue until my hunger was satisfied. I made sure that every drop of her juices was caught in my mouth. The bed wouldn't get a taste. Since her legs were already on my shoulders, all I had to do was bend them back a little farther to slide in, and that's exactly what I did.

I dug deep with my first few strokes. Then I moved in and out of her like I was playing a violin, slow yet meaningful. Savannah had her eyes closed and was moaning softly. That meant I was hitting her wrong. I intended to make love to her, but I was doing it as if I were apologizing or making up for my wrongdoings. I hadn't done shit to her. I picked up my pace, and her eyes flew open. Then I beat it. For over an hour, I hit her like a drum being pounded with the palm of a hand.

"Dre!" Savannah screamed out breathlessly, still looking me in the eyes. "Did you pop a pill?"

I hadn't popped a pill, and she ain't never known me to pop one either. I was putting in overtime because I wanted to show my gratitude for her putting me first and to remind her whose pussy it was. I couldn't tell her she was being rewarded, so I blew off her questioning and quieted her up by covering her mouth with my hand and whispering, "Shut up."

She tried to move to make the beating easier on herself, but I didn't let her. "Bring yo' ass back over here. I ain't done."

I didn't want to hear her voice unless it was in moans and screams. So, what if this was her award ceremony? I hadn't forgotten that her creeping is what caused the shit in the first place. I flipped her over onto her stomach and pushed her legs up under her body until her thighs rested underneath her breasts. Changing the position was the only sympathy I was willing to show her. Now her butt was in the air like two mountains, and I planned on beating them down until they became hills. I know she was wondering what caused the change from sensual to a beast, but I knew the beast in me was what Savannah really liked. With my left hand, I snatched up both of her wrists like a handcuff and said, "Go ahead and bite that pillow, baby. Daddy gon' give you what you want."

She did as she was told with no questions asked, and I kept my word by forcefully inserting myself in and out of her like a Q-tip in an ear, twisting every time I got ready to pull out of her. I never completely removed myself from her warmth. I just pulled out far enough to cause her anxiety over my next deep dive. As she moaned her painful pleasures into the pillow, including my name, the urge to dig deeper came over me. I was in full beast mode and wanted to know how much she could really take without all of that fake moaning shit women trained themselves to do. She could save all of that "you're too deep shit" for another sucker. Savannah was far from virginity days, and I wasn't going to let her put on an act. Some women get in the bed and put on an Academy Award–winning show. Most of the shit they say and do in bed is rehearsed. It's Hollywood acting at its best. They've either practiced with the niggas before you, or they've summed up what to expect from you in the first few minutes of sex. Then they act accordingly. I wasn't about to let Savannah pull that shit on me.

Women have gotten too good at faking it. They can have a dick in them but be mentally fucking themselves. I call it mind over matter because it doesn't matter what you are working with as long as she can use her mind to imagine it's something better. She'll have you thinking you're putting in work, and the whole time, she's counting down for you to nut and get the fuck off of her.

Bitches used to have me feeling like I was King Dick before I caught on to them. Every time I heard them moan, "It's too big, Daddy," "You're in my guts, Dre!" or whatever other sounds they wanted to make to let me know I was causing damage, they had me feeling like a boss. I almost put a caution sign on my boxers. Then I realized the timing was off. I'd be about to stroke, and she'd be moaning and screaming before I even reached midstroke. Get the fuck out of here with that shit. I don't need an ego boost. I need a good nut. Since then, I'm in and out of it like a drive-through. If she enjoys me, cool. If not, fuck it. She just better hope that she gets hers before I get mine.

I didn't have to worry about all that acting with Savannah, though. I knew she loved my plumbing by what she *didn't* say in bed, but today, she decided to be as loud as she could. I thought it was acting for a minute, but I was wrong. I had tapped into something Savannah just couldn't handle. The deeper I went, the less she used the pillow. What once sounded like a bunch of undecipherable, smothered words now sounded like, "Aww, shit, Dre. You're in too deep."

Savannah voicing her limits didn't mean shit to me. I was ready to make new limits with her. The more she complained, the deeper I went. If I were really causing her pain, I wasn't about to stop. She deserved to feel some type of pain from me after all the shit she'd been doing. I was beginning to enjoy her yells even more. Savannah attempted to free herself from me again by crawling away, but I was stuck to her. When she climbed up the headboard, I was right there with her, constantly stroking. She was stupid if she thought I was going to stop. My stroke took no breaks even as our location moved, nor did my yearning to go deeper fade away.

"Where are you going, baby? You know you can't run from me. Take this dick. It's yours."

I whispered my words in her ear again, and like a chain reaction, Savannah's third orgasm came, leaving fluids dripping down her legs and her knees ready to buckle. Savannah had nowhere else to run. She was standing up in the bed on those unstable legs of hers with the upper half of her body pressed against the wall, and the other half jammed between me and the headboard. I continued putting in work until her legs gave way, and she fell back down to her knees. Then I prepared myself for the main event.

I let the liquid build in my mouth, then released it in a steady flow down her backside trail. She had never permitted me to enter her by her exit, but then again, I had never asked. I wasn't into anal sex. I'm a real man. I only wanted to penetrate parts that I didn't have, which was a pussy. I love looking at round asses, but their use in sex was only for slapping, spreading, and a place to shoot my business if I was in there raw. Penetration of it has never been a want of mine, but I could tell it was a want of Savannah's. Her exit sat open, and I could tell by the area around it that it had been touched before. Fuck it. It hadn't just been touched—somebody had busted it wide open. Since we were starting all over, I decided to make sure I was giving her everything she needed so cheating would be the last thought on her mind.

I didn't know how to approach it besides what I saw in pornos, but Savannah had no problem with walking me through it. It was like all the pain she was feeling vanished as she grabbed the hand I had parked on her ass. She put my hand to her mouth and sucked on my middle and index fingers up to the knuckles. It had only been a few hours since I busted them, and even though it was now early Sunday morning, we hadn't been out of the bed since we made it home Saturday evening. I planned to break Savannah's back for at least forty-eight hours. Taking time away to work on my fingers wasn't an option. The comforting feel of her soft lips on my busted knuckles healed my wounds temporarily.

Savannah then instructed me in a voice I ain't never heard her speak in. She said, "Dre, you know where I want you to put them. Enter me slowly and then twist your fingers once you get in there."

It was a mixture of Savannah's "in the middle of an orgasm voice" and her "Hit me from the back, Dre" demanding tone. Her words alone almost caused me to top off, but the curiosity of what would follow kept me leveled. I did as I was told, and she kept demanding new things of me. The shit was turning me on like Savannah hadn't done before. She was a seductress, and I was left seduced. She was bringing out the dog in me, and I was ready to mark my territory. Every time I'd ever touched Savannah, it'd been to make love or caress her body differently than them other niggas had. This was the first time I was ready to fuck Savannah like she was my bitch. I had the pink slip to her, and no one ever again in life would test-drive her. All of her demands, wants, needs, and all the other shit she was talking about got thrown out the window, and she was now a guest on Dre's Show. She was going to get it like I wanted to give it to her, and that was that. All of her longing for different feels from different niggas was over. It was time I left her with no choice but to be loyal.

I rested all my weight on my forearm in her back until her body collapsed under me. I traced the arch of her back with my tongue as I reached both of my hands under her to grip her breasts. Her nipples felt like small boulders in my hands, but when twisted, they felt like rolling marbles. Savannah didn't know what I was about to do, but she knew she was going to like it. The shaking in her legs told me that. I no-handed my way back inside of her and got a few more strokes in. Then I went for it. I dipped in her exit and pulled right back out of it. Instantly, I knew that anal shit wasn't for me. Maybe I wasn't high enough, or I should have been drunk. One thing I know for sure is that I'm leaving anal sex to them unsure or those triple-X-rated niggas and stick to head and pussy alone. The virginlike tightness of it was too much for me to stomach, and I refused to allow myself to enjoy it. I can't picture myself craving some ass. That doesn't even sound straight.

"Why did you stop?" She sounded pissed, and I knew the freaky bitch would, but I can't get on that level with her. She'll have to settle for some fingers from time to time.

"That ain't what I want," I said.

"But it's what *I* want."

"Naw, you ain't had enough of this dick to know what you want yet," I said, getting up.

I didn't let my dislike for mining her body for coal ruin the mood. Instead, I relocated our session back to the bathroom where her MP3 player was still spitting out the hits. I hopped in the shower and told Savannah to join me. I cleaned my pipe off for some natural sex, Adam and Eve style, not that Mike and Steve shit that I had just experienced. After three pullouts to prevent my eruption, I let it go.

"Oh shit . . ."

It was the first time since we made Sade that I went off inside of her. My knees felt like they would snap if I didn't sit down soon. I jumped out of the shower, water still running, body soaking wet, and lay across the foot of the bed to try to recover. Savannah wrapped us up in her towel, then straddled my limpness like a horse's back, and we fell straight to sleep.

We didn't wake up until Sunday night, dehydrated and hungry. I could feel it from the time I opened my eyes that something about that night just wasn't right. It felt like I had something important to do, but I couldn't remember what it was. I tried to ease my mind by smoking a blunt but didn't have a cigar to roll one in. I sliced my finger with the knife cutting up vegetables for Savannah's omelet that she later confessed she never wanted. I really should have gone to the hospital and gotten a stitch or two, but I used whatever I could find in the first aid kit.

After all of that, I got a text from my mama saying she signed Andre Jr. up to play football this year. He finally met the age requirements, and I'm on the other side of the map in Seattle, about to miss my son's first game tonight. I didn't think it could get any worse, but like a never-ending nightmare . . . It did. I got a voicemail from my boy Ryan back in Nashville, *"I don't know why you're unreachable at the moment, but I need you to call me back ASAP. You don't have time to put this call off. Call me back. You know who it is."*

The last time Ryan sent a message for me like this was on a night like this one. I'll never forget it because it was the same day I met Savannah. I was on my way to bring her some weed to her spot in Bellevue, Tennessee. I was less than ten miles away from her apartment when I finally got the text message I was dreading to receive. It was Ryan informing me that a warrant had been issued for my arrest. I knew the day was coming when I'd have to turn myself in and lie down for a while or go on the run. I had been preparing for it, but preparations were useless. How do you prepare yourself to face time in prison? There's some shit in life you just can't prepare for, and ten years in prison was one of them.

Before I could stomach that my time on these streets was numbered, my boy Ryan had sent one more text that read, Yo' baby mama gave you up. Get low, my nigga.

He didn't just tell me I was headed to prison any more, but that my bitch was helping to put me there. That made the whole scenario different. I would have dealt with facing all that time a little better if I was going because I got caught dirty-handed. It would be my fault for slipping. But knowing I had been voluntarily snitched on by somebody I loved—somebody that I one time planned on spending forever with and the woman I'm supposed to honor for the rest of my life for carrying my child—had me feeling sick. The thought of my bitch working as an informant, telling the cops everything she could about me for free, nauseated me. I had to pull over on the side of the road in case I needed to vomit.

I had told her too much and made her the protector of my secrets. My baby mama, Tasha, had enough information on me to have me *buried* behind bars. One minute we were together, strong in our relationship, and then we hated each other and went against each other the next. I thought Tasha was in it for the long run, but nothing lasts forever. I should have known she'd turn on me, and in the back of my head, I always did.

Tasha showed she couldn't be loyal every time we broke up. She'd have a new nigga in less than a week, and my son would become my mama's responsibility until the new guy broke her heart or cut her off. She was ready to drop her title with me and replace it with somebody else's before we could cool down enough to try to figure our shit out.

She had started being questioned by the police three weeks before I got that text message. So, I had a three-week notice, thanks to Ryan. I knew he was right about her deciding to work with the police by the words she said. For three weeks, Tasha would say shit like, "I wish you were back in jail so that I can have my man back" or some stupid shit like, "The only way I can trust you to be where you say you're at, Dre, is when you're in jail." She meant it when she said it. I could see the realness that lay painfully in her eyes.

I had an exit plan on getting out of the dope game, but I never thought I'd be forced to execute it. The part I don't understand is what the fuck I did to have her change up on me. I wasn't the perfect nigga, but I was close. When I wasn't practicing medicine via the streets, I had my ass home with her and my son. It was me who did all the cooking and cleaning while her ass sat on her throne of designer name bags and clothes, pretending to be something she was not. Tasha grew up with me in Jo Johnson projects. She didn't come from money, but she had no problem adjusting to it. I watched her taste go from five dollars Old Navy holiday tees to different designers' seasonal collections. There was a time when Tasha's gelled down ponytail was all she needed. Now, she can't step out without hair touching her ass.

I got that bitch out of New Balances and put her in Off Broadway heels, and look how she repaid me. My boy Mike told me he had seen her in the club a few months before that happened. She was with some nigga, smiling and grinning in his face like she was single, and I let it go. I told myself not to react off the words of others. If she were living funky, I'd smell it.

Breaking up with me would have been a lot easier, but that would have been too normal for Tasha. In all honesty, she was crazy. My mama said I made her that way, but I refuse to take the blame for it. I only did what she allowed me to do, and the cheating in our relationship went both ways. I started it, but Tasha made sure to finish it. Her mental health should have been under suspicion before

I got with her. She was crazy, and that's the truth. She found a way to cut off my visitation with my son while we lived under the same roof. How her crazy ass pulled that off I'll never understand.

"I put this shit on everything I love . . . Until you treat me better, you'll never see your son again. I bet my life on that," she screamed and then threw our son's bottle at me.

"Shut that shit up. You ain't going nowhere with my son. He's staying right here in this house with his daddy, and so are you."

"I never said we were leaving this raggedy motherfucka, Dre. I said you won't see your son again."

She told me I couldn't see our son and did everything she could to keep me away from him when he was lying in the bedroom next to mines. I don't know how she pulled it off, but whenever I was home, he was asleep, and if I decided to stay in the house for the day, he'd always get shipped off somewhere before I told her of my decision to stay indoors.

"You gotta move around to somebody else with the dumb shit. I can't see my son, but I'm supposed to keep giving you money and the dick? That ain't gon' work."

So, I cut her ass off and started fucking the streets. I watched my money triple in three weeks of not coming home. I'm sure she thought I was with another bitch, but that wasn't the case. I turned an eight-hour shift of grinding into a seventy-two-hour one. Money was stacking, but my son was suffering. He spent more time with my mama than he spent with his mother or me. There are just some things I'm caveman about, and one is a mother takes care of her kids, and they see granny on the weekends. Tasha had Andre Jr. with my mama Tuesday through Sunday and only had him Sunday night to Tuesday morning. Tasha ain't working, trying to work, or nothing like that, but she ain't got time for my son? Fuck that. I slowed down to take care of mines, and when Tasha saw that, she was ready to stay at home and be a parent too, which was cool, but I still cut her off. After the shit she pulled, my dick wasn't going to get hard for her. I'm not trying to be cold about it, but ain't nothing sexy about a woman who doesn't take care of her kids. And to top it off, it was my son. She was really cut off. I couldn't have sex with her if I wanted to. It wouldn't get hard, and I wasn't about to force it to.

Hearing Ryan on my voicemail now wasn't a welcoming thing, and I knew I had to call him back ASAP, but Savannah's needs came first again.

Trisha had left Savannah a voicemail saying, *"I love you, but fuck you."* She was thanking Savannah for not stopping the money transfer and wanted her to know that first thing Monday morning, she'd have her cash in hand. She told Savannah she could get with Royce to get her notebook and movies of revenge back, and she wished her all the best in life. Before the length of the voicemail cut her off, she managed to get out one last sentence.

"Oh, Savannah, you need to watch Dre."

That bitch Trisha was cold for that one. She gave her daughter a warning about me like I wasn't to be trusted. After all the shit Savannah had done to me, I felt like I deserved to plot against her. I was protecting Savannah, and Trisha knew it, but she turned me into enemy number one. I played it off like I didn't hear the message because Savannah had started dialing, and I knew she was calling the bank. When she verified she was broke by the pending transfer, she began stressing away. I hated to see her all upset over it, but she left me no choice. My heart was black when it came to it. If she wasn't cheating and living sloppy, her mama wouldn't have been able to blackmail her. I even went as far as to fuck with her about it.

"What's wrong, baby? You keep pacing."

Savannah quickly said, "Nothing, daddy, just thinking about work."

"What about work, baby? You look like you're stressed out."

"Um, just wondering how this shit is going to play out with Stephanie being back at the home office. That's all."

I knew she couldn't tell me the truth because it would convict her of sleeping with Royce. I kept asking her the same question to remind her of what caused all this in the first place. That little thing was too hot in between her legs and had caused her to go broke. I wanted that fact to marinate in her head the next time she thought about cheating or using sex to get revenge.

I'm not completely heartless, so I jumped in my Hummer and ran to the store to get some cigars. I wanted to get her mind off of it for a while, and weed had the most promising results. When I made it back home, we smoked, then hopped right back in the bed. I was drained, so we only went one round, which knocked us both out. If it hadn't been vibrating under my back, I wouldn't have known my cell phone was ringing. I checked the caller ID and it read International. It was Peaches calling. I slid out of bed to get away from Savannah and went to Sade's room before I answered.

"What?" I yelled into the phone but not loud enough to wake Savannah. "It's 4:47 in the morning here, Peaches. What the hell you want now?"

Peaches tried to pretend like she was shocked that she had forgotten about the time difference, but I could hear the lack of care in her voice as she continued the call. "Well, good morning to you too, Mr. Grumpy. I was calling to find out how my daughter was behaving. Is she the tamed animal you wanted her to be yet?" Peaches asked in between chuckles.

I wasn't in the mood to play with her. I was sleepy, and my body was tired. "What do you want, Peaches?"

She heard the irritation in my voice but didn't let up. Bullshit was still active in her voice. "I wanted to talk to my son-in-law and make sure everything was all right, Dre. How is Savannah doing? Is she holding up well?" Her laughter started back up, and the school-girlish sound coming out of her mouth had me ready to hang up in her face.

"I'm gone. I ain't got time for your dumb shit."

As I started removing the phone from my ear, I heard her yell, "Don't you hang up on me, bastard! Did you *really* think this was over?" I eased the phone back over my ear and listened. Her voice went from sixth-grade school yard to fairy-tale evil villain in a matter of seconds. "Dre, did you *really* think that I would let you plot against my child, and there be no repercussion? Tsk-tsk-tsk. So smart yet so stupid, aren't you, Dre?"

What the fuck is this bitch talking about now? I thought as my text message alert went off in my ear. I was too caught up in her words to check it. She had so much anger in her voice that I wouldn't be surprised if she were foaming at the corners of her mouth. I helped Peaches get Savannah's money. Hell nah, I wasn't expecting any repercussions or for her to have any animosity toward me.

"You see, Dre, men like you and Savannah's daddy fuck up a good thing by trying to tame it. You spend all that time and energy trying to change the unchangeable. You love us for what we are in the beginning; then after you label us as yours, you want to start changing shit." Peaches took a deep breath and made a noise that sounded like a growl, then continued. "You simpleminded bitch in loose jeans with a dick, you didn't break Savannah down far enough to break her cravings for other men. All you did was give her a reason to chase dick with a bigger dollar sign that's willing to share their wealth with her, asshole."

"Fuck you, Peaches. You don't know shit, bitch!" I shouted out at her, feeling at a loss for better words at the moment.

"No, Dre. It's fuck *you,* bitch, for thinking I was going to sit back and let you fuck over my daughter like her father did me. Don't drop the soap."

As her last words rang in my ears to the part of my brain that turns sounds into words, my doorbell rang, followed by three knocks on the door. I hung up the phone because there was nothing left to listen to but hysterical laughter from Peaches. As I walked over to the door, I checked my text message, and it read: 1 new message from Ryan. I didn't bother looking out the window or checking the surveillance cameras. I knew by Peaches's last words who it was. I clicked on Ryan's text message and unlocked the door at the same time. I was able to read: You violated, somebody gave you up to your PO before I was tackled down to the floor.

Once they saw the gun at my side, which was really my cell phone holder, I was beaten until I blacked out. The last thing I remembered seeing was Savannah's bare feet running my way. Can't believe I'm going back to jail over a bitch again. . . .

Chapter Three

A Piece of History

"Lord, I'm trying hard to be the changed man that I promised you, my mama, and myself that I would be. I've given up the fast lane to riches to cherish the riches you've already given me and continue to give me. I've repented for the sins of my past, and I try hard not to recommit them. I'm saved, but as of late, I haven't been acting like a saved man. I've sinned. I've knowingly sinned to cause pain to others so that I could find my own happiness. Going back to jail to sit down for a minute is man's way of punishing me. Although it kills me to be back in jail, I know my punishment for the sins I've committed is greater than whatever time man has planned for me. So, I come to you today to say, thank you, Lord. Thank you for hitting the emergency brakes on my life to give me time to reflect on the broken promises I've made to you and the hurt I've caused others. I won't ask for forgiveness right now because you know my heart, and the request would be in vain. But I will ask you not to give up on me. Watch over me and help me grow stronger in your Word. Father God, please continue to cover my kids, their mamas, and my own mother in your blood. I'm a work in progress, Lord. Sorry to have let you down again. In your powerful name, I pray, Jesus. Amen."

"That was a powerful prayer, Andre," the priest said softly, slowing raising his head. "But was it to impress me?"

"Why would I give a fuck about impressing you?" I snapped, causing the priest to look uneasy as he spoke.

"Well, your choice of words makes it sound like you wanted me to know that you have a relationship with the Father or like you felt the need to bring me up to speed. It's a personal relationship."

"I know that, but don't you Catholics like a confession?" He chuckled without responding, which made me feel the need to speak up. "Listen, I've only been locked up for a week, so I'm not running to God like most inmates do, and I didn't find religion in my jail cell either. I already had it. No matter where life has taken me or what I was going through, both good and bad, I made sure to keep my faith first. There isn't a Sunday or Wednesday that went by that I was not in church. Even if I had to fall in the closest church to where I was at, then that's where I'd be giving praise. I believe that everybody should believe in something, or they'll fall for everything and stand for nothing. Since I can't believe in the words of another man, including yours, I keep my faith strong in the Lord."

"Okay, so why did you request a visit from me? You seem to have it all together."

"Are you sure you're a priest? What kinda question is that? Do you not see where I'm standing?"

The priest took a seat at the foot of my bunk and stared at me. I was sure he played middle man to a lot of nonbelievers' calls to Christ, and I hadn't decided if I wanted to waste the energy convincing him that my prayer request wasn't that. A part of me wanted to tell him to get the fuck out of my cell, but there was something in his eyes that said more than his doubtful facial expression. I noticed it when he entered my cell. I wasn't comfortable with the prison sending a Catholic priest, but I tried to find comfort in him being black, and then I felt a connection. It was almost like a secret brotherhood headquarters were located in the depths of his eyes, and at that moment, I felt at home.

"Yes, I'm sure I'm a priest, but I've done a bid in your shoes."

"You've been locked up, huh? I could tell because you wear the pain in your eyes."

He shook his head. "No, I wasn't locked up. I was a cop just like you before I realized my calling. After dozens of arrests, some righteous, others, not, I went home feeling like the criminal every night. I came to a fork in the road, Andre. I had to decide if I'd take the bumpy road of doing good or that slippery slope of evil. It took awhile to decide, but I knew whichever route I chose, I'd have to give my all to, and now, I'm here, chatting with you." He stood to his feet. "You did say one thing I enjoyed hearing, and that was, thank you. Being here is a great reason to be thankful."

"I aim to be thankful for everything, even if it's waking up behind bars with a slab of metal for a bed."

"Waking up behind bars might have lengthened your days on this." He walked out of the cell and didn't look back as the guard locked it.

It was true, there are a million other places I'd rather be than jail, but I have to be thankful for regaining time which I never realized I was missing. It's fucked up that incarceration seems to be the only thing that can slow me down. It's a blessing in the pit of a curse that I had to have my freedom taken away from me to be able to clear my mind. It's sad, but that seems to be the only way God can get me to listen.

"Listen up, down the hall. It's mealtime. You are going to step out of your rooms on my two count, retrieve your meal trays, and step back in. It's that simple. If you don't want your breakfast, don't step out. If you have any questions, save them for med-call," the correctional officer's voice blared through the speakers.

Regaining time meant that I finally had the peace I needed to think about all the shit I put on the back burner for everyday living. I was temporarily relieved from all my daily duties for the streets. I could put my scales down, stop counting numbers, and put the safety back on my pistol. I didn't have to burn the extra gas driving around town to get all the bites nobody else wanted. I didn't have to ride through the hood, passing out fake smiles to niggas who were probably plotting on robbing me if they ever caught me slipping. I didn't have to be at all the local clubs on big event nights, making sure to step out clean with my dreads freshly twisted and styled to keep the bitches feeling me. Nah, there wasn't a need to show these hoes that I was still around and still on my shit. They already knew it. I could take a break from all that. I had made a name for myself and not just in Nashville. I was known from Clarksville to Bordeaux, from Goodlettsville to Inglewood, and you can add Hermitage, Antioch, Murfreesboro, and back. Hell, I even have welcome signs in other niggas' trap spots. Yeah, niggas know me. If they didn't know me by Dre, they knew me by one of the yellow whips I drove around the city in. And if they still wanted to act like they didn't know me, I'd make sure they did before I was done. They'd just have to wait, though, because my life was on a much-needed time-out right now, but I'll be back.

One . . .

Seriously, I've had more time in the past seven days to think about my life, my kids, and any future I could have with Savannah than I've had all year. The catch-22 with having time to think is doing too much thinking. I still had to serve my sentence before I could put all my thoughts and plans into motion. That's the part that will irritate the shit out of you, and irritation had already kicked in. I was ready for the states of Washington and Tennessee to get their shit together so I could be transported back to Nashville. I was ready to get my time and to start serving it. I had a game plan, and I was ready to execute it. All I needed to know was how much time they were going to give me for my violation. I knew I was facing a violation for leaving the state, and if Peaches didn't come up with some other shit to get me more time, that's all I'd be facing. I wasn't tripping about serving time for violating my probation. I wasn't supposed to leave the city, but chasing after Savannah's ass had me in Nevada, California, and Washington. I fucked up. That's my fault.

When it came time for me to face the judge, I wouldn't tell him, "Look, Your Honor, I was chasing after a bitch, and that's why I violated." I'd stretch the truth a little bit and make him believe my sole purpose was finding my daughter and building a relationship with her. With the right lawyer pleading my case, I might get off with six months or less. I couldn't walk in with a court-appointed public defender. They don't care about you or your case. They're just there for the money. But the real reason I couldn't walk in with one was because of my background. That's what really worried me about having a public defender. I didn't need the judge looking at my record and wanting to investigate how a felon like me keeps getting off with slaps on the wrist. I didn't need to be in the judicial system's spotlight. My goal was to stay low.

Two . . .

There isn't a sugarcoated way to say that my background was fucked in every way possible. With all the inside help I was getting, I could call my background cloudy, but with each arrest, those clouds were starting to disappear. The state of Tennessee knew about my degrees and the short time I spent on Nashville's police force. But for how much longer would I be able to keep that as all the information they knew? A lot of strings had been pulled to make my career look as if it had ended due to the highly publicized I-Team investigation of 2006. I couldn't let my mistakes uncover the truth.

The I-Team's investigation had uncovered more than 100 cases of people with criminal records becoming police officers in the state of Tennessee. I was supposedly one of those 100 with an illegal drug possession conviction before joining the force. It was made to look like I was fired at my two-year mark instead of being promoted to bigger and better things. The plan worked like we all assumed it would, and even my mama was convinced that her baby boy was kicked off the force over some bullshit. I'm glad that wasn't the truth because if it were, I would have never met Ryan. The truth was I had been scouted for an undercover position on the TBI's, that is, Tennessee Bureau of Investigation's drug task force. The bureau had traced me back to my father and knew I had ties to Nashville's drug trade. They were excited to know that I had ceased following in my father's footsteps and did the exact opposite of him by joining the police force. I had undergone months of extensive training in multiple areas from the best trainers Tennessee could offer. I even got flown around the country, all expenses paid, for some off-site specialty training. When I proved I was ready to take on my duties, they threw me back into the streets to hustle like I used to. The only difference was the TBI now supplied my supply and re-up money as bait.

They sent a shark to catch the sharks, and once I proved I could, they sent me after the whale. I had cracked a few midlevel drug dealers before, but none of my assignments compared to this one. I was ordered to go undercover to aid in the bust of the biggest drug trafficker in Tennessee's history. This was the same nigga that had my pops sitting behind federal bars for the rest of his life. My pops wasn't a snitch, and I guess he assumed that Big David wasn't either, but that wasn't the case. While Pops wasn't talking, Big David was in there singing. He turned on my pops, and since Pops still didn't snitch when he found out, I turned on him. I was six or seven at the time, and the way I saw it was my pops was more loyal to Big David than to his own wife and kid. I haven't talked to my pops ever since, but my mama does.

"Mr. Burns, are you're refusing your meal again?" the question came through the speaker.

When I was first assigned the case, vengeance consumed me. I was all for catching the fool who had broken up my household and left my mother brokenhearted. What I hadn't planned on or prepared myself for was being around money so large that I could retire before my twenty-sixth birthday. My team wasn't ready for it either. All it took was one year of making runs back and forth from Texas to Tennessee for Big David for me to learn all the details of his operation. I shared the information with my team and reported all my findings to my superiors. I used recordings, tapes, and hidden video to get the approval for the raid. Then came the day I would get to send Big David away to spend the rest of his life with my father in prison. Not only was I able to lock him up and throw away the key, but I also managed to stash 35 percent of the money we were supposed to be confiscating. I didn't plan on robbing him, but when they sent me in there to get the evidence with no eyes or ears, the temptation was too strong not to.

"I asked you a question, Mr. Burns."

It took a few months before the rumors started spreading about there being more money involved than we had confiscated. Big David had befriended a prison *guard and told him he had stashed at least $2 million more than what had been documented, and he was sure the TBI agents who arrested him had kept it for themselves. Our superiors didn't take his words lightly, and they conducted an in-house investigation. Nothing had turned up because I wasn't stupid enough to start flashing the money around, nor did I tell anyone on my team I had stolen it. That came two years later. I worked another six months, then planned my escape route to get out of it all. I knew the TBI was still keeping a close eye on me, so I gave them a reason to kick me out. I let them catch me selling small amounts of weed that I had bought from dealers we were investigating. I only bought a pound of weed at a time, which was $700 each time. I made sure to take the money out of my paychecks to buy it just in case they decided to track the funds. I knew they were watching me, but I also knew having a key witness to the crimes I was committing would seal the deal. So, I set up my baby mama to be just that. I let Tasha in on what I was doing and let her get some of my smaller sales. She didn't know anything about selling drugs, and I knew this. It was her test. I wanted to see if she would snitch if she got caught, or if she would ride for her man and take the blame.*

"Please believe me, this ain't my weed," Tasha pleaded as the cuffs tightened around her wrists.

"Funny that you say that because you're selling it like it's yours." The narcotics officer looked at his partner and nodded. They both knew the ten-dollar value of the sack they were arresting her for wasn't worth the paperwork, but scaring her into believing it would, would be priceless if they could make it work.

"There ain't nothing funny about it. It's nothing but nickel-and-dime sacks. That's all he trusted me with, and I have to give him every dime of the money I make selling it for him. I don't get a tip or nothing."

"Then why are you doing it? You seem like a smart girl. Why would you risk your freedom for somebody else and not getting nothing out of it?"

"Because that nigga is crazy. He controls every fucking thing I do. It's his way or—"

"Or what?" both officers asked in unison.

"Or my baby won't have shit. Do you know what a woman would do to make sure her baby is straight? We'd do anything a nigga says we have to do."

"Who is he? We need a name."

"Please, I ain't never broke the law. Look in your computer. I'm just trying to make sure my baby has a roof over his head and food," she begged.

"Who is he?"

"If I give y'all a name, will y'all let me go?"

Of course, she snitched, which allowed her to make a deal for three years of probation instead of serving jail time. Three weeks later, a warrant and raid were taking place for my arrest. I was sentenced to serve eight years when I finally turned myself in. I ended up serving eighteen months, two weeks, four days, seven hours, and thirteen minutes. I was released on six years of probation.

On the upside of all of this, I made my mama petition the court for full custody of my son by Tasha. She stated that we both neglected him and were unfit to raise him since we were drug dealers. She was granted temporary custody while Tasha completed parenting classes to get him back. Guess Tasha didn't have time to go to the classes, or maybe she just wanted to take the easy way out of her responsibility because she gave up her rights over him.

Just when I thought I was winning all the way around, I found out I was losing when it came to my new piece, Savannah. I had Ryan check on her, and that's how I *found out she was pregnant. Ryan had my back from the beginning and continued to have it even after I had been kicked out of the bureau. When he came to celebrate my release with me, I told him about the money I had stashed and where I had it hidden. Two minds were always better than one, and Ryan knew just how to get the money from my hiding spot to a safer location without getting caught. I took 1.3 million and gave him $700,000, although he didn't want a dime. Not because he wanted to uphold the law but because real friendship doesn't come with a price tag.*

That's why my violation was the least of my worries. I was knocked unconscious and wounded during the arrest, so I don't recall what the arresting officers said my charges were. I don't think Peaches could've uncovered my past, but there isn't any telling what lies she came up with. All I know is that I got my ass beat and woke up in the jail's medical ward.

"Mr. Burns . . ."

I looked up this time because the voice was coming through my door. The older Hispanic correctional officer was looking at me through the square in my door that they called a window. "You need to eat something today, Mr. Burns. I can't keep charting that you're not eating."

"I ain't hungry."

"Well, get hungry."

"No disrespect to you or the job you have to do, but I'm not hungry, sir."

At my words, I heard the door unlock. Usually, this would mean some type of disciplinary action was about to take place. Instead, I got more words.

"You have to eat something," he said, handing me a Burger King bag before continuing. "Take the breakfast sandwich out of the wrapper and pour the hash browns on the napkins so I can dispose of the holder." I looked at him, surprised, and he gave me a quick smile. "All law enforcement doesn't believe in beating down every man with dark skin and a cell phone clip, especially if he used to be one of our brothers in this fight. When you talk to Ryan, you should thank him for making sure that you're handled with care. You've done a lot to protect and serve, and if no one tells it to you anymore, know that you're appreciated." He took the proof of his kindness and left my cell.

"Noted, and I appreciate this," I said, holding the sandwich up. "I thank you and Ryan for this."

I ate the food, although, I truly wasn't hungry, because I instantly grew an appreciation appetite. In the medical ward, I had access to a free phone when no one else was on it. I waited for the phone to free up as I finished eating and then knocked on the door to be let out of my room for the first time in seven days. I called Savannah first to tell her I was straight.

"Hey, baby, how are you doing?" It was a dumb icebreaker, but then again, we had never held a conversation from jail.

"I'm fine. How are you, Dre? Are you okay? There was blood all over the floor. Wait. Why aren't you calling me collect? Did they let you out? Do I need to be on my way to come get you?" Savannah's voice was full of fear and excitement.

"I'm okay, baby. The blood is from the police busting my nose. They thought my phone clip was a gun, or at least that's what I've been told, and I wish you could come pick me up. I'm calling you for free because I'm still in the infirmary. Do you know what my charges are?"

"The officers said you violated your probation by leaving Davidson County or whatever it's called. He said you set up residency out of state without clearance. He mentioned something else about the failure to report too."

"I failed to report to who?" I yelled into the phone. "I had been up to the probation department and calling once a month from the day I was released. I was trying to find out who I needed to report to. The motherfuckas acted like they didn't know shit whenever I called and kept transferring me to a supervisor. When I talked to a supervisor, they said they would log my call as me reporting, and since I didn't have any mandatory drug testing, there was no need for me come to the office. I'll take the blame for leaving without approval, but the failure to report is some bullshit."

I calmed myself down enough to apologize and explain to Savannah why I was pissed. She didn't understand this probation/jail shit, so I told her, "I'll have my mama get with you on how to do some of it. You need to learn how to put minutes on the phone so I can call and how to sign up to visit once I'm transferred to Nashville."

Savannah didn't like hearing what I expected out of her at all.

"So, you expect me to write and visit you while you're in there?" she asked, and I didn't answer because I could tell she had more to say. "I mean, I don't mind talking to you on the phone, but coming to visit and writing letters . . . That's asking a little much of me, don't you think? I only wrote you last time because you sent a letter talking shit to me that deserved a response, but I never visited, and if you or anyone else asked me to, I'd say no. That's like going to the zoo and pretending the animals like their new man-made habitats. I'm going to have to pass on that, and besides, the police said you only violated for leaving the state without notice. You shouldn't be gone over a year. . . ." She lowered her voice and then said, "You can wait until you get out to see me."

"Fuck you mean I can wait?" Now I was pissed. "You think I'm asking too much of you? You wrote to me the last time I was in jail. It didn't kill you, and I'm not about to wait a year to see my fiancée. You better be the first person in the visiting line every chance you get. Who the fuck did you think you were talking to? That shit ain't optional if you're planning on being my wife."

She must have been in the mood to go rounds with me and to see just how mad she could get me over the phone.

"The only reason I wrote to you the last time was to fuck with your head. I wanted to rub it in your face that I had given Sade away. That was my motivation. I don't have one now, and if you're planning on making a career of being behind bars . . ." Her next words came out of her mouth so nasty that I should've called her a bitch and hung up the phone. "I ain't planning on being your wife."

"What?"

Where in the fuck is this shit coming from? I thought. A week ago, Savannah went broke to be my wife. Now, she was talking like she couldn't care less. Before I could question her on her change of heart, she was already apologizing.

"I didn't mean that, Dre, I swear I didn't. This shit is just stressing me out already. I'm going through too much at one time and need my knight in shining armor, but I can't have him because he's in debt to the Department of Corrections. I'm so sorry, baby."

"Then you should call that bitch you call Mama and thank her for telling on me," I spit back at her. Fuck her apology. She didn't have a reason to get that mad at me where she would say some shit like that. I knew she was stressed, but I also knew Savannah didn't know how to talk to a man. She was way overdue for a lesson in respect. *I* was the man, and *my* last word was final—*not* hers.

"We're not about to discuss this, Savannah. When I get settled and have an address for you to write to, I'll be waiting on my letters. Depending on how much time I'm going to get, I'll need to see your face, so you're flying to Nashville as much as possible. That right there is final. You don't have shit to say about nothing I expect my wife to do, and if you do, we can end this shit now. I don't need two captains on my plane. I need a copilot, so you better hurry the fuck up and learn your role, then play that bitch to the fullest, or I'm gone. I'm still your knight, baby, and I will protect and take care of you, but you got to show you can stand by me through the ups and the downs. Don't let stress send me walking, because I promise you'll never find another nigga like me. Now, can you do that for me, baby?"

Savannah hummed a quick, "Uh-huh," that I immediately shut down.

"Uh-huh ain't the way you answer my question. Can you handle being my wife and copilot or not, Savannah?"

She answered as quietly as a church mouse in a packed church on the first Sunday.

"Yes, Dre, I can handle it. I already said I was sorry. Forgive me and let it go, please." Then she changed the subject. Apparently, her pending questions became of more value than the lesson I was teaching her. "So, are the police right about how much time you're going to get? I hope you're not facing a couple of years because I can't go that long without you. How will the bills get paid if you're locked up? I mean, I have a little bit, but I opted out of medical insurance at work because, at the time, I thought they wanted too much a month, and I was never sick to use it. The hospital bills have eaten up my savings account. I'm about to be living paycheck to paycheck."

There Savannah went off into another rant of worrying about material things. I stopped her before she got worse.

"If you listen to what my mama tells you, you won't have to worry about the bills. That's what I'm trying to get you to understand. My wife doesn't have to worry about small shit like that."

Savannah sat quietly on the other end of the phone for a second, then said, "Dre, I don't have money like I used to. What didn't get spent in bills, I invested my future into something I believed in with the rest, and it seems like I won't make a profit from it now. To be honest with you, I'm broke."

She didn't know what broke was. She still had a couple of thousand in the bank and a full-time job that paid her ass good. I really wanted to fuck with her for making that "I ain't planning on being your wife" remark by asking her what she had invested in, but I left it alone. If she was riding for me, then no matter what my situation was, she was going to be straight, just like my kids. I had enough money put up for her to survive while I did this time. All she had to do was prove to be worthy of it first. I didn't care about her going what she considered to be broke for us. Now she needed to prove that she backed that decision, and if she had to do it again, she would.

Savannah said her next words so softly that I almost missed them.

"So, your mama got control over your money? You need to tell her to give it to me since I'm about to be your wife."

I heard her, but I wasn't going to respond to it. There wasn't a need to, because I wasn't giving her access to my riches until I knew she was the right woman to sit on the throne next to mines. Right now, that chair was occupied by the queen, who was my mama. You can call me a mama's boy if you want, but there ain't a woman alive that I'll ever love, respect, and trust like her besides my daughter.

Me and Mama Dee, as everybody called her, had been through too much, and every struggle we went through together made our bond stronger. When my pops first got hemmed up for selling and trafficking dope, I took over his in-town business to keep us afloat. I would hit the streets to make money, then give it to Mama Dee to handle the bills. That worked for about six months, then the lights went out, a pay-or-quit notice was placed on the door, then all my daddy's cars, clothes, and jewelry started disappearing—and so did my mama. She started smoking crack to deal with the fact my daddy was facing fifty years, which was a sugarcoated way of saying he was facing life. If my pops had known my mama was smoking rocks, he would have gone upside her head.

She was a strong woman until Pops got caught. She was making money in her own right as an RN at Vanderbilt Hospital until my pops signed her up for early retirement to become the queen of his dope kingdom. We went to live in the projects as a cover-up for my parents' unemployment to really needing the government's assistance. With Mama Dee being strung out, I had no choice but to hustle harder to catch up all the back bills. I had to keep a roof over our heads. I hadn't seen Mama Dee for like two months, but I was holding shit down and missing the hell out of her at the same time. I wasn't worried about her being dead or nothing like that. I knew she had pride, and her pride wouldn't allow her to be smoked out in front of me, so she dipped, and I respected her for it. Every time that monkey got too heavy on her back after that, she would dip.

"Mama, wake up. The lights got cut off again. What did you do with that money I gave you to pay the bill with?"

"It never made it to the light company. I owed a few people and thought I'd run across some more money before they came to cut them off." She sat up and began adjusting her clothes and put on her shoes. "I'll be back, baby, with the money."

"No, I'll get the money and get them cut back on. You just stay here, okay, Mama?"

"Okay, baby, I'll stay right here." I could tell by the look in her eyes she was lying, and her next words confirmed it. "I love you, Andre, and I'm sorry, baby. You won't have to keep handling my responsibilities. I promise you that this is your last time paying any of the bills."

"It's okay, Mama. Just promise you'll be here when I get back."

"I promise, baby."

I don't know if it was rehab or the church's doors because I never asked, but when she did come back after being MIA for six months, she was clean and back on her feet like her drug addiction had never happened. Now, *that's* a strong woman. If my pops was dumb enough to get caught and let jail keep him away from her, I wasn't going to be stupid and do the same. After two years of her off-and-on relationship with cocaine, my mama became my best friend, accountant, and my secret keeper. She helped me get into college and made me stop selling drugs and get a job. She made me flip my hatred for my pops and turn it into my career. That's how I ended up being a cop. Mama Dee will remain my number one girl until another woman proves worthy of her spot.

Savannah had a lot of showing and proving to do before I'd give her access to anything my mama was controlling. For her to even think I'd just sign everything over to her disgusted me. I had to get off the phone before I taught her ass another lesson about me. Then her next words reminded me that Savannah wasn't as hard as the words that she let come out of her mouth.

"I can't sleep another night in this house without you, Dre. It's been a week, and paranoia is driving me crazy. I keep hearing things. I need you here with me. I miss you already, daddy."

It was sweet of her to say, and I knew it was the truth. It wasn't safe for her to sleep in that house without me. I would have shipped her ass to Stephanie's house, but Savannah had killed that friendship, and now Stephanie was back in Atlanta. It was too soon for me to tell her what I had planned for her future. I went ahead and gave her a temporary fix.

"If you want to be protected, go to the Jeffersons, and spend time with Sade. If Memphis is back at your father's house, I'm sure you don't want to go there."

I was surprised, but she agreed with me and asked if I could talk to the Jeffersons about it. I told her I would call and tell them what was going on when I talked to Sade. I got her off the phone, so I could call then because I didn't know how much longer the calls would be free.

"I've been waiting on your call, my boy. What's going on?"

Either Mr. Jefferson had caller ID, or he could read the future because I never announced myself as the caller. I ran my situation down to him, and he agreed to move Savannah in for however long I needed her to stay. I didn't have to tell him to keep an eye on her. He had volunteered, and he assured me his shotgun and years spent in the military would keep her protected.

"I can keep her safe and protected from the outside world, but let's be honest. I don't think you, me, or anybody else can protect her from herself."

"You're right about that one. Let's just keep praying for change."

"I ain't stop praying for her yet. I've been praying since we picked your daughter up from the agency."

"I know this probably isn't the best time to ask you this, but you and your wife made an agreement with Savannah that if she ever decided that she wanted custody—"

"You can stop there. I've feared this day from the moment we agreed to the terms of being chosen. The truth is, I never agreed. The wife did. Sade was, or is, our first and only child, and I want to die knowing that. I love you like a son, Andre, but it breaks my heart that you are in the picture."

"Why is that?" I interrupted.

"You're not a fuckup like Savannah, who doesn't know what love is or how to give it. Sade has a parent who is fit to raise her now and doesn't need us. I don't understand why you keep finding yourself behind bars or what spell Savannah has put on you, but you're a good man and an even better father. My wife wanted to raise a baby from its birthday until the child was school age so that she could have that experience. She's done that with Sade, and she's told me that she's okay with you taking her if you decide to, but I'm not. I love her, and she's been my daughter for almost five years. Five of the most important years of her life, and I can't see myself giving up my child—not even to her real father."

"I'm not asking you to do that, nor would I take her away from you, but you're right. She has a parent who can and wants to do their job. I can't speak on if and when Savannah will come around ready to snatch her up, but I can promise you, she'll never be able to keep y'all out of her life."

"That's real nice, Dre, but I have to speak frankly with you. I'm not settling for a part-time, weekend position in our daughter's life, and if that's what you're planning to offer me, then you can kiss my ass. I'm telling you right now, I know you won't be a problem, but the woman you love will be, which means you will eventually become a problem too. If Savannah takes Sade away from us, I'd tell everything I know to anyone willing to listen and do something about it. Savannah's no saint, and she's not fit to raise an ant in an ant farm, even with supervision."

I couldn't help it. I had to laugh. His anger was just what I needed to hear to be sure that the right man was raising my daughter. I could tell he spared his words for me out of respect, but what he really wanted to say was exactly what I would say, and that's . . . I'd kill Savannah dead if she ever tried to take Sade away from me again.

"You just said everything that I need to hear, and that's exactly why the respect is mutual. By the time I get my shit together to be able to prove I'm better fit to raise Sade than you and your wife, she'll be getting ready to graduate from high school. All I ask is that you continue to welcome me in and out of your house when I please, as you've done since we met."

"As long as you remain the man that you are and continue to treat our princess like the princess she is, I don't care if you move in. Hell, you can move your next wife in too," he said, chuckling.

We chatted a little longer, and when we were done talking business, he put my baby girl on the phone.

"Hi, Daddy. Are you coming to see me today? I want to show you the butterfly I caught."

Sade never sounded sweeter. My baby's voice was the first piece of reality that made me realize I was about to do time behind bars. I instantly started missing her. Then my mind wandered over to my son. I wondered how he did with his first football game. I wondered if he was a natural on the field like his daddy, and if he wasn't, who would Mama Dee find to work with him. When I was done talking to my princess, I needed to call my boy, Mike, and tell him to step his uncle role up a notch and make sure he was on the field sideline coaching my son.

"Hello, Daddy, are you there? I asked you if you are coming to see me today."

I was brought back to reality by the sound of Sade's voice.

"No, baby, Daddy had to go away for a while. I was so excited about meeting you that I forgot that I had business to handle back in Nashville. I'll be gone for a few months, but I'll call and write to you every day, and I want you to write to me too, okay?"

I didn't want to tell her that I was in jail because I had taught Sade that jail was a place that they put those who broke the rules. I told her everybody in jail wasn't bad, but just like her, sometimes, good people get in trouble, and jail was their punishment. I didn't want her to think that being a father to her was breaking the rules.

"Okay, Daddy. I'll draw you a picture of my butterfly and send it to you. I named it Savannah, like my mommy. It's pretty just like her too. I put her in a jar to keep her from flying away and leaving me alone."

I was going to explain to Sade that caging beauty is a temporary fix, but she told me Mrs. Jefferson had already told her that. Whenever I get out, I think I'll need to get some knowledge dropped on me from Mrs. Jefferson as well. She seemed to know her stuff. I continued talking to Sade until I heard Mr. Jefferson tell her it was nap time.

Going to jail is not what my kids needed. They needed me, their father, in their lives, helping them with their day to day and helping them to build their faith. I should be the one tucking Sade in bed, and I should've been there walking the length of the football field rooting my son on and ready to fight refs for bad calls. It's not the

Jeffersons' or my mama's job to have to play mommy and daddy to my kids. Thoughts like these while you're behind bars will make you depressed. That's why I try to stay disconnected from the world when I'm serving time. The urge to call my mama and Mike about Andre Jr. disappeared. I'll make those calls tomorrow. I was only in the mood to tell Savannah what Mr. Jefferson said, then lay my ass back down with my thoughts. I tried to call Savannah to tell her to pack up and go to the Jeffersons, but the house phone went straight to her cell phone's voicemail. She must've already transferred the phone lines in preparation to leave. I waited a few minutes, then called her back, but this time, I called her cell phone. It rang three times, and then someone picked up.

"Hello?"

It was a man's voice, but the music was too loud in the background for me to pick up on to whom the voice belonged.

"Hello?" I asked, puzzled by the fact that Savannah didn't answer my call, but some unfamiliar man's voice did. "Who the fuck is this? Where's Savannah?" I asked, but I didn't receive an answer to either question.

All I got for a response was, "She's busy. Call back in an hour."

Then the phone went dead. My first thought was that the nigga had hung up on me, but as I attempted to call back, I couldn't get a dial tone. Before I could make it to the jailer to tell him something was up with the phone line, three of Nashville's sheriffs were walking toward me with handcuffs and shackles. They were ready to transport me home. The whole time I was being hog-tied and shackled up, all I could think about was who the fuck was answering Savannah's phone.

Chapter Four

A Pair of Queens

These last three weeks have been hard and almost unbearable. Every time I tried to focus on anything else but Savannah, my mind led me back to her and that same question: who the fuck answered her phone? She didn't have any male friends that lived in state, the voice was too immature to belong to her father or Mr. Jefferson, and her brother wasn't fucking with her because of Peaches. I kept pacing my cell from one solid grey metal wall to the next. No matter how hard I tried to sit still, I couldn't. My thoughts kept fucking with me.

It wasn't another nigga . . . It couldn't be another nigga . . . Fuck that. It better not be another nigga!

This girl really had me crazy over her. I heard love could make you turn that way, but this shit was becoming ridiculous. If I could just get to a phone, I'd be straight. Even if she said it was her other nigga answering, at least I'd have some closure and could move on. Not knowing anything at all was making my time feel longer and harder. I spent my first week, which felt like a month, in a one-man holding cell. I didn't have access to nothing: no phone, no pencil or paper to write with . . . nothing but three meals a day. I couldn't eat, not because the food was bad. I just didn't have an appetite, and when I did, I felt nauseated. I went to court that week but didn't see a judge because transportation got me there late, which pushed my next court date back for two weeks. My second week was a little better. I was moved into a dorm with thirty other inmates, and I was able to write. The first letter I wrote was for my mama. It was short and straight to the point. I told her where I was, gave her my next court date, and told her to visit me Saturday. I knew my mama wasn't the letter reader or writer. She preferred a face-to-face visit so she could read my eyes and phone conversations so she could feel the emotions in my voice. She didn't like letters because they made her jump to conclusions.

The last time I was locked up, she said, "You can save those letters you keep writing for your girlfriends. I'll keep money on my phone to hear your voice."

"It's like that, Mama? You don't want to read how much I love and miss my Mama Dee?" I teased her.

"No, I don't because I can't tell the mood or mind-set you're in when I'm reading them. Not knowing drives me crazy and makes me stress over you being in that cage. I'll wait for your call."

So, there wasn't a need to tell her how I was holding up on paper. She wouldn't believe it anyway. The next letter I wrote was to my baby girl, Sade. I promised to write to her every day when we last spoke, and I had broken that promise. I apologized to her and told her from here on out she'd be getting mail from me. The last letter I wrote was the hardest to write because I wasn't sure if the recipient was worth any more of my time, or if she wanted any more of it. I wrote her name at the top of the letter twice and erased it that many times. Then I stopped fighting with myself and let my pencil ask what I wanted to know.

Savannah,

I tried calling you before I got moved, but I was told you were too busy to come to the phone. Who the fuck was that answering? Keep that shit true, because I'm not trying to deal with the drama you love to keep yourself involved in. Write back and let me know what it is between us. If there ain't nothing between us, then it is what it is. Throw my shit out. I can replace it, and I'll have my car shipped here. You ain't gotta worry about hearing shit else from me. I can go through the Jeffersons about my daughter. If we straight, and I'm overreacting, then let a nigga know, and I'll apologize. Either way, you need to get with my mama ASAP about my whip being shipped or how to do this jail shit. Her name is Mama Dee, and she's a hundred percent no-nonsense, so come correct, or she will have no problem with checking you. Her number is 615-555-0103. I'll be waiting to hear back from you.

—Dre

I read the letter four times, looking for any signs of weakness. I couldn't let Savannah know how she was affecting me. Her playing hard to get and all these different niggas was making me sick. I wanted to walk away from her and just say fuck it, but I couldn't. I didn't know why walking away from her was so hard to do. I knew I loved her, and when she had her mind right, I could see her as my wife, but every time I felt like I was making the right decision about us, she made me change my mind.

"301, 302, 303 . . ."

I could hear myself counting off each push-up that I hit, but my mind wasn't exercising with my body. I was too busy thinking about her and wondering if she would ever change her fucked-up ways. I told myself that I would never let Savannah affect me again like she did in Washington, but there I was starting to feel sick again.

“337, 338, 339 . . . Fuck that, I was more than enough man for her ass,” I yelled, allowing my thoughts to come out of my mouth. But what I said was true. I am more than enough man for her, yet she had me feeling like I wasn’t. Her actions had me doubting myself, because why would she need another man if I was the full package? She couldn’t be that much of a ho. I had to be slipping somewhere, but every time I reevaluated myself microscopically, I couldn’t see any errors on my part. I provided, I protected, and I kept her more than satisfied in the bed. Could Savannah really be that hot in the ass that one dick, man, or whatever you want to call it, couldn’t satisfy her?

“368, 369, 69, 69, 69 . . .”

I counted the number sixty-nine eight times as I wondered if a sixty-nine was in Savannah’s plans for the night now that I was out of her way. See, this is the shit I don’t like. Jail always fucks with your emotions and leaves you feeling out of control. Now, I’m all worked up and feeling sick over her, and being locked up aided in my feeling this way. I’m a man, and feelings like the ones I was having were made for women. I don’t mean any harm, but that illness was structured for a female to go through. It wasn’t made for a man, because it forced us to deal with emotions that we normally didn’t give a second thought to. That’s why it was worse for a man to go through it. It fucked with our manhood and played with our minds. I never thought the illness would make its way to me because I was shielded with self-confidence. I’d passed out tissue box sentences to a few chicks, but I wasn’t ever expecting to receive one back. I was finally getting a taste of what I had put my son’s mama through. It felt fucked-up to be on the owner’s side of a broken heart that I should have seen coming. I wasn’t apologizing for cheating on my ex. All I was saying was that I understood what I put her through now. Karma is a bitch, and her address had to be the jailhouse.

"387 . . . Man, fuck these push-ups," I said as I got off the ground. I couldn't concentrate long enough to remember to count or what number I was on. *Who was that dude answering the phone? Are you cheating on me already?* I thought.

Even though cheating is expected of men, it didn't make it right for us to do, but sometimes, it was out of our control. We were outnumbered by women four to one. That meant it was three times as likely we would cheat. My stance on cheating was that it was more acceptable coming from a man than a woman. There was proof all over the world that backed me. For example, in some cultures, they entitle men to more than one wife. How many cultures do you know that allow women to do the same? None. Not one. And if it's going on in private, that's the way it's meant to be. It's not in a woman's nature to have more than one husband or to cater to more than one man. The same goes for a man. It's not a part of our nature to be inferior to our wives. That's a change in roles that will throw the whole family aspect off balance. A woman is made for a man, but a man is made for many women.

"Listen to Neanderthal-ass Dre."

Yeah, I'm on my caveman shit, but the shit I'm saying is real. Men fall on one knee and propose after we choose that right woman to be our wives. Yes, a few women were proposing out there, like Savannah proposed to me, but that's not the traditional way. The traditional way was to allow the man to honor you by his confession of love with the desire to give you his last name. Women nowadays were proposing because they felt like they'd earned it, but they get mad when the man didn't act like he was all into it. Don't get mad at me. Be mad at the truth. That just might be the same reason Savannah and my shit ain't flowing like it should. She jumped the gun, and I just went along with it. Damn, there goes some more shit I need to have a heart-to-heart with Dre about.

Once I gave my letters to the guard on duty, it seemed like my time got harder. Now, I had to wait on Savannah's response. I tried working out all week to get my mind off of the daily mail call, but that wasn't working. I was finally able to use the phone on Wednesday of my third week. I tried calling my mama to see if she had talked to Savannah, but she didn't have money on the phone to answer yet. I tried to call Savannah, but she had collect calls blocked on her phone.

It was Saturday morning, the end of my third week back in Nashville, and I still hadn't heard shit from anyone. Visiting had just started, and I hadn't been called to step out. After hitting a set of a hundred push-ups, I lay back down on my bunk to try to sleep visiting hour away.

"Aye, you said your name was Andre, didn't you?"

I had been awakened by my bunkie standing over me. He was a young guy, probably about nineteen or twenty. He was dark-skinned, tall, maybe about six foot three, and skinny. He had a high-top fade like everybody was wearing in Nashville. They called it a "Boosie fade" after the Baton Rouge rapper Little Boosie. Most of the niggas I saw rocking the haircut needed to kill themselves for walking around looking whack, but his fitted him. He tried to cover himself in tattoos to give himself a harder look, but his baby face with them soft, dark brown eyes showed that he had never been through any real shit in his life. Little buddy had just gotten himself caught up with the wrong older niggas. We hadn't had a conversation yet besides exchanging names. His was Montez, but he preferred to go by Tez. I had overheard him talking to his girl on the phone, though. He was in for some robberies he had played a part in. From what I heard in his conversation, he really shouldn't have been committing them. He was straight and didn't need the money, but he was trying to gain some status with the niggas in his neighborhood, from what I gathered.

"Yeah, I'm Andre. Who's asking?"

Even though I looked at him like he was a little nigga, I sat up on my bottom bunk. I didn't like nobody standing over me, and who's to say he wasn't trying to test me to gain some respect in here? As I sat up, he took a few steps back like he knew what it was, and then said, "I think they are calling you for a visit, man. That's the only reason I'm asking."

I thanked him, threw my shirt and shoes on, and then stepped out of the dorm room to the awaiting guards. When I walked into the visiting room, I was greeted by my mama's warm smile.

"Mama Dee, you can't be coming in here to see me, looking good like that. I don't want to have to beat up a nigga in here over you."

I turned my attention to the two older cats in the booths next to mine. They were checking the hell out of my mama like they were trying to memorize her for some late-night self-pleasure. I couldn't have niggas hitting their meat to thoughts of my mama.

"Boy, hush. I came here straight from Junior's football game. That's why I'm so late. I didn't have time to change."

"That's how you go to your grandson's football games?"

"I said, hush, Andre."

She was fussing but blushing at the same time. She must have seen them watching her too. Unlike my father and me, my mama's skin wasn't caramel or golden-brown. She was dark, but her black skin was smooth, like a cup of coffee served black. She didn't have any blemishes or scars anywhere my eyes were permitted to see, and wrinkles had yet to touch her skin. For fifty years old, my mama looked damn good in them tight-ass blue jeans and red, fitted "Nashville Cardinals" youth football shirt. I'm going to make it my business to burn the jeans she had on soon as I get out. They fit her fatless body too good and made her rump stick out. I didn't know what Mama Dee had been doing while I was gone, but it looked like she started walking or running a few miles a day. Her hair, nails, teeth, and neatness of her clothes showed she wasn't just fit, but she practiced and maintained good hygiene. She gave them old cats a reason to look, but I wasn't giving them a pass for it. I kept mugging one of the niggas until he felt the need to speak up to me.

"Man, you look just like your sister."

He tried to be slick with that old-ass line, but he was old so what else could I expect? Like I said, I wasn't giving out any passes.

"Pay attention to your visit, old head, and quit checking out my mama. She's married and ain't nothing you can do for her, you feel me?"

My mama hushed me up again, but this time more seriously. Old dude was right, though. We did look alike. We might not have shared the same skin tone, but I was her male twin. I didn't look like a female, nor did she look manly, but our likeness was off the charts. I had her thick, full lips, dark brown eyes, and long hair, just mines was dreaded. All I got from my father was his frame, color, and personality flaws. I mugged the old cat one more time and then turned my attention to my own visit.

"How's he looking out there on the football field?" I pointed at her shirt, proud to see that my son played for the same team I did at his age.

She looked at me like she always did when she knew I was upset, but she didn't say anything about it. She went with the change of conversation and answered my question.

"You know who his father is. My grandbaby is a natural. They got him playing running back, and he's burning up the field. Reminds me of when your daddy and I used to sit out there watching you. His team is 4 and 0, and that ain't thanks to nobody but Junior and that quarterback. His line doesn't block for poop."

"His line doesn't block for poop," I repeated mockingly.

It was funny hearing my mama switch out cuss words, but that was Mama Dee for you. It would take a lot to get her to cuss, and when she did, you'd wish she never had. We laughed and talked about the days when she was screaming for me to rip the field up in my cleats for fifteen minutes, and then she told me she had gotten a letter from my father. She knew I didn't want to hear about it, but that wasn't going to stop her from telling me what he said.

"You know the guy he's in jail over finally got caught a few years back, so your dad is thinking about appealing his case. He never told on the man. All he gave was a fake nickname, which, of course, they couldn't find the person to fit it. He said now all he had to do was say he didn't know his name but point the guy out, and the evidence would add up."

I gave a quick "uh-huh" just to show her I was listening, but I didn't care. What difference would it make? After serving all these years and leaving his family to struggle, now he's ready to snitch? I wouldn't get my hopes up, and I wanted to tell my mama she shouldn't either, but instead, I switched the subject.

"Mama, did anybody named Savannah call you?"

As soon as I said the name, Mama Dee's expression changed to pure disgust. I always knew the day would come when I'd have to introduce the two of them. I just always thought I'd have time to prepare Savannah for their introduction. When my mama opened her mouth, all hell broke loose.

"Yeah, the heffa called me, introducing herself as your fiancée." She paused and looked at me like she was expecting me to correct the lie Savannah had told her, but when I didn't, she continued with a frown on her face that was out of this world. "Who does Ms. Thing think she is calling my house like she's all high and mighty because she's educated? I could feel her turning her nose up at me like I'm beneath her through the phone, Dre. If the Lord hadn't been guiding my tongue, sister girl would have heard it. Where do you meet these floozies you call women? And I can't believe you fooled around and had a baby by this one. Or is that *really* your baby?"

I wish I could have lied and said I didn't know, but there was no question that Sade was mine. When Stephanie was telling me about all the hoeing Savannah had been doing before me, I got with Mrs. Jefferson and the doctor at the lab. DNA proved without a doubt Sade was mine.

"Yes, Mama, she's mine, and her name is Sade. That means she's yours too."

"Did Diane Nicole Anderson tell you she was yours, or did that girl convince you to believe it?"

"Who the fuck . . . I mean, who is Diane?"

"The only female you can trust in cases like this, DNA."

I almost fell out of my chair laughing and tried to laugh as long as I could, hoping she'd forget the question. The side glance look she gave me confirmed she hadn't, and I knew she wouldn't ask the question again without cursing me out.

"Diane confirmed it. She's mine, and if you saw her, you'd know it. She looks more like me than Junior."

"Junior doesn't look like you at all. His mama spit him out by herself. And you sure Diane was right? She said

100 percent without a doubt the baby by that . . . that thing is yours."

"Mama, you just said Diane was the only female I can trust, and you know she never says 100 percent. On paper, I'm 99.999 percent sure, but in my heart, there's no doubt that she is."

At my confirmation, Mama Dee took her eyes off of mine and closed them. In her Sunday praise and worship voice, she said, "Lord of all lords and King of all kings, I come to you today with my son and ask of you to cover my granddaughter in your blood, Jesus. She didn't ask to be given to her mama. She was chosen for her. I don't doubt your decisions or the plans you have in store for my grandbaby, Father God, but please keep her safe and protected. Lord, please strengthen my son's mind and heart when it comes to his choice in women and help to rinse that evil Jezebel desire away from him—"

"Mama, say amen." I had to cut her off because she was about to go overboard with it. I don't know what happened between her and Savannah over the phone, but I knew now wasn't the time to tell her how Savannah had hidden the pregnancy from me. Nor was it the time to tell her that foster parents were raising her granddaughter, that's for damn sure. Mama Dee looked surprised that I stopped her in the middle of her prayer, but she knew she was about to overdo it. She crossed her left leg over her right, folded her arms into her chest, then leaned back in her chair and stared at me with an evil look on her face until I spoke up.

"Mama Dee, you already know you're my favorite lady in this cold-ass world. Don't look at me like that. I know she's a handful, and I'm working with her on that, but did she say anything else?"

Rolling her eyes up to the ceiling, she said, "Ms. Thing had a lot to say, like how you told her I needed to pay all her bills and how when she comes to visit you in Nashville, we should have lunch somewhere that has a five-star rating instead of me cooking her dinner like I offered. She said she would be getting a hotel because she wasn't gon' dare stay at my house like I offered because I lived in East Nashville, and she didn't care if the rich were moving in. It would always be the hood to her. She said she wasn't about to get robbed or shot for you or me. Then she told me how I needed to—"

"Okay, Mama, okay." I felt like I needed to wave a white flag to get her to stop ranting. "I get your point, and I will talk to her about the way she talks to you, Mama. Thank you for not going off on her and cussing her out. She doesn't know who she's playing with."

"She doesn't know who she's playing with, and you should make it your number one priority to let her know that I'm *not* the one. I'm good with God. I'm sure he'd let me slide on one sin, especially if I was sinning to hurt a devil."

I laughed a little because my mama looked like she was ready to fight. I hadn't seen that look on her face since Tasha had busted the windows out of my car and had put all four of my tires on flat.

"I know you're hotter than fish grease at the church's fish fry, but, Mama, did she tell you anything to tell me, like about my car or anything else?"

"Yeah, she did." She unfolded her arms, a sign that she was calming down. "She told me to tell you it was somebody named Memphis answering her phone when you called. She said he popped up to apologize for that stuff with her mama or something like that. She claims he didn't know you were in jail, or else he wouldn't have hung up on you. Then she said she was moving in with him and her dad and that you could call and ask him if you don't believe her. Hell, I don't know what she was talking about or who Memphis is, but I don't believe her. I got a bad vibe from that girl, and you know I ain't wrong when I have them feelings, Dre. You don't ever listen to what I got to say to you about them floozies anyways, so I don't expect you to listen now, but are you sure this is the woman you want to make your wife? I just don't see you on one knee, begging this woman to be your wife. I can't believe I'm going to say this, but I'd rather see you married to Tasha. At least we know what to expect from her crazy butt."

I ignored her question about marrying Savannah, not because she was upsetting me, but because I wasn't sure. I knew Mama Dee, and if I opened up and told her anything negative about Savannah, she'd never let it go, even if I did decide to marry her. Now she had me wishing I would have been a fly on the wall when she talked to Savannah, because never in a million years would my mama say she'd want me to marry Tasha's ass.

"Mama, you know I'll talk to you about everything when I can talk to you about everything. It's like you said, I got to learn to jump one hurdle at a time." I flashed my inmate informational wristband at her like it was an expensive watch.

"Well, Dre, if you like it, baby, then I love it. If she's the one you want . . ." She took a deep breath, and then said, "You have my full blessing. But know I'll be praying and praying hard. My intuition ain't never led me wrong. The way that girl talks to folks, she ain't long for this world, or she got some good security protecting her." Underneath her breath, she said, "Security like my Captain Save-the-World son."

Mama Dee must have taken my silence as me getting upset because her reaction was the one she always gave when we disagreed. She always put her thoughts and better judgment to the side to agree with mine. That didn't mean she wouldn't tell me, "I told you so," later on, if I were wrong. It meant she wanted me to know she respected me as a grown man with the right to make my own decisions, even if she felt I was making the wrong ones.

"Thank you, Mama," was all I managed to say because it was time to wrap up our visit. Before she left, she told me to call her later to talk to my son. She said she had put money on her phone and "on that girl's," meaning Savannah's, too. We exchanged the words, I love you, then headed in our separate ways with a promise that she'd return next week.

After dinner, I walked past the payphones and stretched out on my bunk. I'd call my son tomorrow after they got out of church. Calling Savannah could wait. I knew everything I needed to know about her status from my mama. Savannah was down to stick around, and that's all I really wanted to know. Her introduction to Mama Dee didn't go as I would have liked it to, but they both sounded willing to give each other a try.

Let me take that back. They were both willing to give each other a try for me. That alone said enough. I'd call Savannah after I went to court Tuesday morning. I needed the next few days to figure out how I would drop the bad news on her.

Sunday flew by, and so did Monday, and I still didn't know how to tell her yet. On the ride to court, I reminded myself that it didn't matter how much time the judge gave me because Savannah wasn't going to like what I'd have to say anyway. Whether he sentenced me to serve two weeks or two years, the facts wouldn't change, because once I was released, I'd still be on probation. That meant no more Seattle, Washington. How would I explain this shit to Savannah? I couldn't just say, "Hey, baby, I got another four years of probation to serve, and I can't leave Tennessee, so quit your job, pack up your shit, sell the house, and come start all over here with me, and when I'm done paying what they say I owe society, we can move wherever you like."

In a perfect world with a tamed and submissive chick, that might work, but it wasn't going to be that easy with Savannah. She would put up a fight. She'd want me to try my best to get my case transferred to Washington, and that's something I wasn't willing to do. Why drag my fuckups from the past into my new future? I knew my decision not to have my case transferred meant losing time with Sade, but I wasn't ready to snatch her up from the Jeffersons after they'd built that bond with her anyway. I was sure they'd been standing on eggshells ever since they found out the truth about Savannah and my past. They'd gotten the chance to know me and to see the man that I was. I was sure they knew I'd prefer to have Sade full time and give them the part-time parenting role, but they knew my heart wouldn't allow me just to snatch her away. I'd never told them I'd be willing to take them to court to get my child. I just went along with their program. Savannah caused all this, and I had no knowledge of any of it. I had every right to pursue getting my daughter, but I didn't want the Jeffersons to have to deal with that heartache, nor for Sade to keep being passed around like a doll.

I planned to stay here in Tennessee until my time was served and I was completely off of papers. Then I'd get the fuck out of Dodge and move on to bigger and better things. Maybe I would pack my mama and Andre Jr. up and move them to Washington to spend time with Sade and the Jeffersons before I got off of probation. You never know. But for now, I had to worry about my current state. Sade would have to visit me as much as possible, and I'd request permission to visit her as well. This all made sense to me, but it wouldn't to Savannah. All she would be looking at was her own losses. Guess in that aspect we are alike, both selfish, and we both want what's best for us. The only difference was I had to think about what was best for Sade, Andre Jr., my mama, and the Jeffersons. In the end, one of us would break down and see it the other's way, or else we'd go our separate ways. Those were the only options I could see at this point. Either Savannah would pack up and move to Tennessee, or we were through. I was hoping that with all the energy she'd been exhausting toward our relationship, the end result would fall in my favor.

When I made it to court, my lawyer was in the hallway waiting on me.

"How are you feeling this morning, Andre?"

"Like I'm ready to get this shit over with. Is my mama here?"

"You know your mama is here. I think she was the first person seated in the courtroom. Knowing her, she might have slept here," Mitch said with a chuckle.

He was the only lawyer I've ever used, and that was because he was the only lawyer I've ever trusted. We went to high school together but never hung out. He was one of those dudes I always spoke to because he was the star of the basketball team and I, the star of the football team. Our love for opposite sports kept us away from each other, but our drive to give our all on our individual playing fields is what made it mandatory to show each other mad love and respect whenever we were in each other's sight.

It was funny that we both ended up taking the cop exam together, but Mitch didn't stay for his test results. One of those questions did something to him, and two years later, I found out that the question is what sent him back to school to finish his degree in criminal law. A few years after that word spread that he was a criminal defense lawyer, a damn good one at that, I hired him the first time I could use him. He remained a phone call away after that and always answered on the first ring, no matter what the hour was.

"Yeah, knowing her, she did sleep here."

"Ready to recap our conversation? I know we talked on the phone the day before and went over the particulars, but I think we should go over them again now that the shit isn't being recorded."

"Shit, I want what every man headed to jail wants that values his time . . . to get sentenced to the least amount of time possible in jail and to serve the rest of it on probation in the streets."

"I hear you," which were the exact words he used on the phone. Mitch was a shark, not in a bad way. Well, not to me anyway. He didn't want me to have to serve any more time, and he even wanted me to be released with fewer restrictions on my probation, so I could use the freedom to get custody of my kids. Needless to say, when it was all said and done, I walked out of the courtroom feeling great, and Mitch left feeling like the case was lost. Even my bunkie could tell I was in good spirits when I returned.

"Looks like court went well for you. You don't look like you're ready to kill a nigga anymore." He laughed and then continued to look at some pictures he had just received. I was good, and that's why I decided to talk to him finally.

"Yeah, it went damn good. Your girl sent you some pictures?"

He jumped off his bunk and handed them to me. They were pictures of a beautiful bright-skinned girl that looked about seven or eight months pregnant. "Yeah, that's my baby mama. She's nine months pregnant with my son. It's my first seed."

"She looks like she's ready to push."

"Yeah, she's dropping him any day now. She's been having pain and shit for about a week."

Emotions ran heavy on his face. I didn't have to ask him what was wrong. I knew. He would be locked up and miss the birth of his son. That's a fucked-up feeling.

"Aye, this shit is going to sound impossible to do, but don't let it get to you. It's only going to make this time in here harder. Go to the library, look up first memories. Right now, the shit feels like it's about you and your memories of being there for everything from the time he comes out, but it isn't. Your girl will save you all the memories she can. She understands what you're going through."

"Shit, that ain't what it feels like, and that's not how my girl is taking it. Every chance she gets, she reminds me how her parents are going to have to be there when she goes in labor and how they will help her get up with my junior in the middle of the night and how they have to do my job for me. Really, I wish none of their asses was going to be there to steal my memories. I don't want anybody doing my job, but I don't want her stressed out from doing it alone."

"Understood, but do you think your son is going to remember who was in the room when he got his first whiff of air in his lungs or who woke up with him in the middle of the night to change his wet diaper? Hell no. I'm in the same boat as you locked up, so I'm the best motherfucka to tell you. He will be too young to make memories, but by the time you serve your time and get out, he will start to build them, and he will be able to say you never left his side if you get your shit together after this fuckup."

"But what about my memories?"

"Easiest way for me to say it is, fuck your memories. You sacrificed those when you played with chance and copped this charge. You have to look at it like what it is. . . . The loss of your freedom to be there to make memories with him is a part of your punishment and keep pushing. Instead of stressing over what you can and can't do, you should be plotting your next moves as a free man."

"I feel you. Do you have kids?"

"Yeah, I have two and peep this shit." I told him about my kids and the shit Savannah pulled with Sade while I was in jail. I wasn't a talker, but I felt his pain.

"What the fuck? She gave your seed away before you touched down?"

"Yep, and when I read that letter, I was sure she was lying to fuck with my head. You know how women do when they get mad at you for some shit and see you vulnerable. I laughed the shit off, but after reading it a few more times, I had my boy look into for me, and he said he found her with no baby in sight. I got out and went on a manhunt for mine."

"So, is shorty still breathing?" he asked, crossing his arms in front of his chest as if my story were going to send him to handle Savannah for me.

"Funny you asked that question, but I understand why. I'll just say this. Shorty is about to be my wife, but I got my revenge where it hurt her the most. Fucked up as it may sound, that shit felt good." I finished with a laugh that must have been contagious because he joined in.

"And the baby? Did you get your daughter back?"

"Yeah, but that shit is complicated too. I have full access to her, but I have to go through the people who adopted her for it. That's why being in here again isn't helping shit, but it's my punishment for the decisions that I made. Every day I have to think about another man raising my daughter, and my daughter calling another nigga daddy when she has me ready to step up to my responsibilities. I'm right here when I need to be right there, you feel me?"

"Yeah, I feel you."

He told me what he had done to get in here and how he had a court-appointed attorney handling his case. I gave him some advice and told him to get at my lawyer. Tez was a cool young guy. He just needed some guidance and to learn the difference between friends and foes.

When I was done chopping it up with him, I decided to make that call to Savannah. As soon as we were done with our greetings and she had explained the incident with Memphis answering the phone, I went straight into my spiel.

"Look, baby, I don't know how you're going to take this, but you're going to have to move back to Nashville. When I get out, I can't leave the state until I'm off of probation, and that's not for another four years." Savannah had gotten so silent I thought she had hung up. "Baby, are you there?" I asked.

"Yes, I'm here, Dre. My daddy said something like that might happen, so I knew you might say that, but, damn, Dre, back to Nashville?" I was thankful that her dad had prewarned her of possible outcomes. It made it easier to talk to her about it. "Why can't you ask them to transfer your case to Washington? You can tell them it will help you get a new start."

"I don't know enough about Washington to say transferring my case there would work in my favor."

"You have time to look in to it."

"Yeah, I do, and you have time to adjust to moving back to Nashville."

We went back and forth for a little about being transferred there. I told her why I didn't want that, and she told me why I should want it. Her main issue was that she didn't want to quit her job, and I understood that, but I couldn't think of another way to get around her not having to. Then she shocked me.

"How much time did the judge give you?"

I didn't know why I felt the need to lie to her, but it was out of my mouth before I could take it back. "Nine months to a year, depending on my behavior. Why?"

Savannah didn't hold back and showed me I wasn't the only person with time to think and plan shit out.

"Well, what do you think about this? We keep this house in Washington and rent it out so we can return when you're off of probation. I move back to Atlanta and keep my position at William and Williamson's while you serve your time. I'll drive back and forth to Nashville to visit you while you're in jail every weekend. That will give me time to try to set up a work-from-home deal with my company and only have to drive back and forth from Nashville to Atlanta for mandatory meetings. Once you get out, I'll have a place already set up for us in Nashville while you serve your probation, and when you're done, we take Andre Jr. back to Washington with us so we can be a real family with Sade. Then I can go back to the office there. What do you think about that?"

I wanted to say no, but I couldn't think of one good reason why I should object. I had to smile at the fact that Savannah didn't want to sit around and live off of my money. She wasn't like Tasha when it came to that, and her independence was a turn-on. I liked how she said she'd visit me every weekend while I was in jail, and I loved the part about us taking my son back to Washington with us to be a family with Sade. My only real objection was . . . Who would protect Savannah from harm while she was in Atlanta?

Part Two

Savannah

Chapter Five

Did You Really Think I'd Be Quiet?

Jail had Dre tripping hard. What would make him think I'd be willing to give up all that I went to school for and worked hard to achieve to sit up under his mama while he served time? That wasn't about to happen. I'm glad he agreed to my move back to Atlanta because the way I saw it, we only had two options. Either he'd agree to me keeping my job and moving back to Atlanta, or we'd have to call it quits. It wouldn't be easy to walk away from the $175,000 I invested into us to get rid of Trisha or all the love I had for him, but there was no way I'd be an ex-drug dealer's housewife. The title Trap Queen didn't look good coming before or after my name.

I felt like Dre was trying to be slick. He tried to feed me a fast line about quitting my job and moving to Nashville being my only option. How could he see me moving to Nashville as the only option? I think his true intentions were to have his ghetto-ass, Bible-thumping mama babysit me while he did his time. Once again, that shit wasn't going to happen. After talking to her on the phone the few times I did, I couldn't believe she was kin to him. Besides being a street pharmacist and the use of bad grammar or hood talk every now and then, Dre had a class about him that I couldn't see him getting from her.

From our very first conversation, I knew Mama Dee, as he told me to call her, and I weren't going to get along.

She was too outspoken and ran her mouth about things she had no business being involved in.

"So, Georgia, where did you and my son meet?"

This would make the fifth time I would have to correct her on my name. "It's Savannah, and did he not tell you that already? We met years ago in Nashville."

"Uh-huh, so y'all met years ago, is that right, Augusta? But how long have y'all been together?"

"You probably didn't hear me all the other times I said it with you being up in age and born and raised in the South, but my name is *Savannah,* and we've been together for about the same length of time. We never called it dating or being together. We aren't old, nor do we believe in that traditional stuff you Southerners do. We met, and a few years later, we got engaged."

"You mean you don't believe in the traditional stuff because I raised my son to have morals and to stand by his beliefs and traditions. Do you have a job, Atlanta? Or what did you do for a living before my son had to start providing for you?"

"Let me stop you right there because your son doesn't have to provide for me. I have a career. I provide for myself. I guess there are a few traditions I do believe in, like if a man thinks he's going to call me his woman and wants me to act as such, then he needs to handle all my needs. Whether or not I can handle them shouldn't be a concern to a real man, and seeing I'm only a wedding day away from being your son's wife, he has bills he needs to pay, and my name is Savannah."

"Sounds to me like you don't know what it is you believe in, Marietta. You say one thing, and then you say another. How did you get my son to agree to marry you when you sound like you don't know what you really believe in when it comes to life?"

I couldn't see her face, but I could tell she turned her nose up at me like I wasn't good enough for her baby boy. Did she think I wasn't good enough for Dre? Bitch, please. It was *me* that had to lower my standards to be with him. If she couldn't tell that by our telephone conversations, she was dumber than I thought she was. That's why I didn't bother answering her. If she had questions, she needed to ask her son about them.

"I guess you don't have anything left to say then, do you, Leery?"

"It's Savannah, and, no, I don't. Not until you put on your hearing aid or talk to your son."

I never pictured Dre as being a mama's boy, but the more I talked to her, the more visible it became. She started throwing around hood ethics mixed with what she thought was Southern hospitality. I took it all as insults. Dre should have given her a brief summary of me before asking me to contact her, and she would have known better than to offer me to join in her hood lifestyle. If he had told her a little bit more about me, it would have saved her feelings from being hurt. Come to think about it, Dre couldn't have told her anything about me at all. After all these years and a baby later, the gangster mama's boy had kept me a secret. Now I know why . . . because he didn't want her to look bad. Look at her and the little she had compared to me. I wouldn't have wanted him to hurt her feelings with rants and raves over the professional intellect of his fiancée either.

"Well, Alpharetta, I have to get off this phone and go attend to my grandson. You have my number. Call me when you need to. I'll go ahead and still get the extra bedroom together if you decide to change your mind and not waste all that necessary money that could be spent on my granddaughter on a hotel room."

I hung up before I had to cuss her out over my name. I still can't believe she asked me to stay with her in a house across the street from the projects. Who did I look like being caught on South Ninth and Shelby Avenue? There's a reason why they call that side of Nashville, "The Bottoms." I'd been over there before when I was in college at TSU with a friend to pick up some weed, and I will never step foot over there again. We hadn't been in those projects but five minutes, and I witnessed a fight followed by gunshots. That's definitely *not* the place for me, and I wasn't going to sugarcoat that to spare her feelings.

She didn't sugarcoat me either, calling me "another floozy" and questioning if I knew how to cook, clean, and mother a child. Why should I have to sugarcoat my words and give her more respect than she was willing to give me? We both were grown, and I don't give a damn whose mother she was. Respect ran on a two-way street, with traffic moving on both sides. Then when she was done with all the shit she talked, she tried to apologize and offered to cook me dinner at her house. What part of *I'm never coming to your house* wasn't she understanding? Of course, I turned her down in a nice way and told her we could have lunch by whatever hotel I stayed in downtown. She started her shit talking all over again about the type of woman her son needed. Fuck what she thought her baby needed because my man felt differently.

Some people just have no class about them, and I'd have to accept that my soon-to-be mother-in-law was one of those classless people. The only part that confused me was if she really had all of Dre's money, why didn't she ask her baby boy for some of it to move someplace else? I'd come visit then. I can't grasp why she wouldn't want more for herself and her grandson. She raised Dre in the projects, and now she thought she'd upgraded by raising her grandson across the street from the projects. Andre Jr. would definitely be moving back with us when we left Tennessee. I couldn't allow history to repeat itself with my stepson. Her small-minded ass would not hold another black man back from having and getting more, not if I had a say-so.

I'd never doubted that Dre had money before. He was paying the bills and buying everything else that we needed after I got out of the hospital. But knowing he banked with "Hood Mamas-R-Us" confirmed that I wasn't about to quit my job to depend on him. I'm used to being my own provider and having a security blanket of knowing I can provide for myself. Keeping my job kept me secure, and I couldn't wait to get back into my old office in two weeks—no hood day care for me.

At the announcement of my return, Mr. Williams, who was a founding partner of my firm, was excited to hear I was coming back. I wish I could say the same for the other two partners. Mr. Williamson, who was the other founding partner, was concerned about me abandoning our Washington location with the lack of leadership.

"Are you saying that you don't approve of my return or that you won't approve of it?"

"I'll approve it, but I don't approve of it. You transferred to Washington to manage your own office, which has run successfully under your leadership. I don't believe it will continue to produce the numbers we have seen without you."

"If the numbers drop, I'll be on the first flight back to Seattle," I assured him. "The success of all of our locations is and will always be my number one priority."

"Glad to hear it. Now, hurry back. A few things were neglected in your absence. I can't wait to have you back."

The newest partner, Stephanie, my ex-secretary, ex-lover, and ex-friend, was downright in disagreement about my return. She tried stating facts, lies, and getting the West Coast clients involved to force the partners to reject my return, but it didn't work. It was my fault that she felt the need to attack me, and it was also my fault that she had the power to have her voice heard by my partners.

I was feeling horrible about everything I had done in the past once my supposed mother cleaned out my account. It made me reflect on why she had done it and how Karma played a nasty role in it. Guilt weighed in heavy, and with Dre back in jail, that guilt made me recommend that we make Stephanie a partner. After all the fucked-up shit I put her through and did to her over the years, I felt like it was a small step at apologizing. That ho didn't even send me an email thanking me for upgrading her, but I deserved it. She was shining like the star she was in her new position. With the apology I extended rejected, I found comfort in knowing it would piss her off that I was coming back to dim that shine. Stephanie wasn't a factor, and I loved proving that to her.

Mr. Williams's overly flirtatious ass had no problem with telling me what Stephanie had to say about my return. He quoted her as saying, "Why do we keep allowing Savannah to control the progression of this company? We, as professionals, should not have to shift our business's structure around her personal issues, and furthermore, her work ethics should be in question after the California incident. We all think highly of Savannah, but for the last five years, her soap opera of a personal life has leaked in and infested our company. May I remind you that it was all of my legwork as her assistant that got us the contract with Strax Industries in the first place, because, once again, Savannah had personal issues to deal with that were more pressing than this company's growth. When will we force her to keep her personal life as just that: personal?"

He said Stephanie's words held no weight with him, but Mr. Williamson had eaten every word she fed him. It didn't surprise me in the least that she'd try to prevent my return. It seemed Stephanie had forgotten that she had crossed me first by trying to steal my man and my identity. I can credit a lot of the success I've had with the company to her assisting me, but she needed to remember who got her as far as she is now. I will devote every second that I'm back reminding her and showing her who's the bigger asset to the company. Now, we were equally yoked within the company, neither having more power than the other because our company threw out that seniority policy years ago. If she kept the bullshit going after my return, I'd be plotting on getting her fired next. I hope she hadn't forgotten who she was playing with.

Before leaving Washington, I parked Dre's vehicle at my father's house to be shipped to us at a later date. As for my Cadillac, back to the dealership it went. Mr. Jacobs had no problem with buying it back from me. All I had to do was mention my crazy fiancé that had previously visited him, and he was cutting me a check for it.

"I normally don't buy vehicles back at the price I sold them, but I understand your unique situation and thank you for keeping it in such great condition. By the way, how is your fiancé doing? Hope all is well between the two of you and that he is fully aware of your visit here today. I wouldn't want him to feel disrespected."

"He's fully aware." Which I said in truth, but the bitch he was displaying bugged the hell out me. We had sex once before, and I couldn't stomach knowing that I fucked a chump. I had to mess with him. "He actually told me if you didn't buy it back at the price that I paid—or more—that he would come and negotiate a price that you'd both agree on. He seemed anxious to see you again.

I'm sure he won't be disappointed that you gave me this check, although he did tell me to request cash."

"Cash? You didn't ask for cash. If you can wait for a few minutes, I can give you the money. I'll just need to—"

"Don't trouble yourself. This check is fine," I interrupted.

"No trouble at all." He almost ran out of his office and returned ten minutes later with a large package-sized envelope.

"This is all of it, and please make sure you tell your fiancé I said hello."

"I sure will."

After that visit, I went home and packed up our clothing to be shipped to the one-bedroom suite at the Residence Inn I'd be staying in. I didn't have time to find an apartment in Atlanta before moving. My partners wanted me back in the office within two weeks of my announcing to return. I placed all our furniture in storage with plans on having a mover drive it down to me once I was settled. The last thing I had to do was place a "for rent" sign in the yard outside the house and place an ad in the paper with the Jeffersons' contact information. I had asked them to be the landlords for us and to keep us updated on any issues they came across with managing the property.

I spent Thanksgiving with the family and went Black Friday shopping the next day for all of Sade's Christmas gifts, which I left with my daddy, then off to the airport I went early Saturday morning.

I didn't realize I had missed Atlanta until I felt myself getting excited as the taxi drove past downtown's skyline on Interstate 75. I couldn't wait to have breakfast at Gladys Knight's Chicken and Waffles and get some shopping in at Atlantic Station. Atlanta felt more like returning home than when I had moved back to California. That's because I had nothing but bad memories in California, and returning only left me with more bad memories to add to the list. They say, "Home is where the heart is," and my heart was here in Atlanta. This was my first love, and you *never* forget your first love.

I was filled with warmth and happiness . . . until I checked into the hotel. When I gave the front desk attendant my name, her face lit up like a candle at a match's touch. She stepped back into the staff's office and returned with more than likely every staff member that was on duty. Then she reached under the desk and handed me a welcome home basket with an unsealed card. With a grin the width of her ugly black face, she said, "Ms. James, this arrived for you earlier today."

Even though there wasn't a signature on the outside envelope of the card, I already knew who the sender was by its contents. The basket was filled with condoms, a whip, a two-headed extralarge dildo, and an all-black leather outfit in my size with a rhinestone matching paddle. Under the outfit was a dental dam, oils for heating, edible panties, spray-on body candy, a silver bullet, a box of suckers shaped like dicks and breasts, two pornos—one of them being a lesbian flick and an extralarge tube of anal lube. The card inside read, "*Welcome home, Savannah. Let's see how many people and their lives you can manage to fuck this time.*"

How embarrassing. If Stephanie really wanted to go to war with me, I'd accept this as the first attack. I thanked the staff, who were all smiling and grinning, and asked if they enjoyed the show. One by one, they returned to the office, and the front desk agent handed me my room key, but not before she reminded me, "There is no prostitution of any kind allowed in our hotel. Please keep in mind some small children live here and keep your visiting guests to a minimum."

I need to find an apartment ASAP, I thought.

By sunrise, I was dressed and heading out the door. The clothing that I shipped hadn't arrived yet, but I had carried enough clothing with me to last until they did. Unsure if the staff from the night before was still on duty in the lobby, I bypassed the office and decided against calling a taxi by cutting through the parking lot and jumping on the train. I hadn't ridden Atlanta's public transportation before, but I knew I had made an early start, and getting around on public transportation would allow time for businesses to open.

The first stop on my agenda was getting a nice cup of coffee in me and a Southern-style soul food breakfast. I asked a few people on the train for some recommendations by upcoming stops and was referred to a place called K&K Soul Food. No one told me that it was in the hood, but it didn't matter now, because after I transferred from the train to the bus, I was there.

The food was just what I needed to start my day. It wasn't the best cup of coffee, but who cared about coffee when the food tasted as good as theirs did? My eggs were scrambled hard with cheese, my chicken was smothered in the best-tasting brown gravy I'd had in years, and my potatoes were seasoned so perfectly that at first bite, I pushed the ketchup bottle away. I'd definitely be back, but not for breakfast. I wanted to sample their lunch and dinner menu next. I overheard some people talking about the oxtails and mac 'n cheese they served here while I ate. Now I had two more reasons to come back. I was too full to walk back to the bus stop. My first adventure on public transportation for the day was over. I called a taxi to pick me up. It was now 9:00 a.m., and I was sure there was a car dealership open somewhere in Gwinnett. I told the driver my destination while answering the ringing of my phone.

"Good morning, Dre."

My greeting was followed by a recording informing me that I had a collect call from "Dre." A prerecording of him saying his name played, then it was followed by, "An inmate in the Davidson County Hill Correctional Center . . ."

The recording, which I had grown to memorize, advised me to press "1" if I wanted to accept the call. Dre had told me he could hear me before I accepted the call, but I couldn't hear him until I pressed "1." The urge to tease him came over me.

"I don't know if I want to press '1,' operator. My fiancé has been up for the past three hours and only decided now that he wants to talk to me. Maybe I should wait three hours before I accept his call too. . . ."

I stayed silent for a minute. Then the recording played again from the beginning. I immediately hit "1" on my touch screen before it gave me the option to press it again.

"Girl, you better stop playing with me," he chuckled a little in his morning voice. He must have gone back to sleep after he ate breakfast this morning because I'm sure this wasn't his first time waking up today.

"Ugh, Dre, listen to you. You must've just woken up. You sound horrible."

He confirmed my suspicion while he tried to clear his throat to make himself sound slightly better.

"Yeah, baby, we ate around 5:30 this morning, and then I worked out. I would have called you earlier, but the phones were tied up, so I lay back down and ended up falling back asleep. How was your flight?" I went to open my mouth to answer, but before I could, he was already on to his next question. "What's all that noise in the background? Sounds like you're in a car or something. Who you got taking you around early this morning? It's only eight o'clock. How long have you been up?"

I really disliked this jail version of Dre. He was so quick to think the worst of me and drown me with questions.

He knew I hadn't been through this jail stuff with a man before, and now I see why I've never been willing to. Every time he called, he wanted every little detail of my day. This was getting old and irritating fast.

"Damn, Dre, don't I need to get a car and an apartment? I'm in a fucking taxi leaving from eating breakfast by myself. I'm on my way to the dealership to buy me a car. I used MARTA to get around this morning, so I got an early start. Do you want to know what I'm going to do after I get the fucking car too, or what color panties I put on after I got out of the shower?"

"Hell yeah, I want to know. Especially the part about the panties."

He laughed, making a joking out of it like he wasn't serious about knowing my next move, but I knew he was. He treated me like I'd cheated on him before. Even though I had, he didn't know it. The most he had ever caught me doing was I once came home smelling like cologne. I gave him a lie that covered up my slipup, and he never brought it back up. As far as my creeping was concerned, Dre had no proof of me doing any of it.

"Dre, if you're going to twenty-one question me every time we talk, maybe we should put off conversing until we're face-to-face. I don't like feeling like I'm under interrogation because you're sitting behind bars stressed."

"Interrogation? Only those suspected of committing or witnessing a crime get interrogated. Are you feeling guilty about something because I questioned you to make sure your ass is safe? Don't forget that there are motherfuckas that don't want you breathing out there!" he roared back at me.

"Bye, Dre."

I hung up the phone, turned my ringer volume to silent, and made sure to drop it at the bottom of my purse. I wasn't about to argue with him every time we talked.

He needed to realize me answering my phone wasn't mandatory. I did it because I loved and missed him. He being in jail allowed us to talk more and really get to know each other, and I can't lie, I fell in love with him all over again, but his jailhouse instantaneous menstrual cycles were getting on my last nerve. He always used that "protecting me" line to cover up his spying, like the tracking system he had placed on my car. When I confronted him about that, he said the same thing. . . . "I did it so I could know where you were just in case you got caught up somewhere."

I knew he'd be mad when he called back and only got my voicemail, but he'd have to get over it.

It took going to three different dealerships to find what I wanted at the price I needed it to be, but I got my all-black Charger. I missed my old one, and since the only reason I gave it up in the first place was to hide from Dre, I felt it was only right that I got another. I was on a tight budget now, and the 2009 version of it was in my price range. The new car smell had me feeling good and made me forget about Dre's overly protective self. I was driving around in no particular direction, breaking my car in like I didn't have business to handle. When I finally snapped out of my daze, I was a few blocks away from Atlantic Station.

"Time for some shopping."

I heard myself say those words out loud. Good thing my car windows were tinted, or the passenger in the car next to mine would have thought I was taking to myself. Looking past the car next to me, I saw a "Now Renting" sign on The Metropolis at The District. I knew these to be luxury apartment homes, and I hurriedly signaled and got over. Business had to come first, and finding a place was next on the list. I put in my application, paid the deposit to hold the unit I wanted if approved, and now it was time to shop. Seeing that it was Sunday, I wasn't expecting to hear anything back from The Metropolis until Monday or Tuesday.

I went crazy in this new boutique that had just opened in Atlantic Station. Everything I saw I wanted to take home with me, which was fine because the prices were reasonable, and I needed new work clothes. After hitting up 80 percent of the stores, I rested in a chair outside the ice-cream parlor with a double scoop of butter pecan ice cream. This was another thing I loved about Georgia. No matter what time of year it was, it was never too cold for a scoop of ice cream. Here it was, the first week of December, and there still wasn't a need for me to wear a jacket.

"Look who the cat dragged out."

The wrong use of the cliché with that heavy accent meant it could only be one person standing behind me: my old Jamaican fling, Amir.

"I wasn't sure if that was you at first, den my eyes got a good look at that booty and knew it was you," he laughed.

"Then you need to tell your disrespectful-ass eyes to stop looking at something you will never get to have again. Excuse me."

Grabbing my bags and leaving my half-eaten cup of ice cream on the table, I pushed my way past him. His ass was stupid to think I had forgotten how badly he talked to me at our last encounter. When I made it to the escalator that would take me to the underground parking garage, I glanced back in his direction. He was standing in the same spot I left him in, cuffing his dick through his jeans and watching my departure. I had to laugh and shake my head at him because I knew he didn't have any drawers on.

Why did Amir have to be so damn sexy? He had this famous Jamaican singer-songwriter face, accept he had greyish green eyes that threw it all off and was slightly younger than the handsome man's face that was pictured everywhere reggae music could be heard. With a body build similar to a light heavyweight mixed martial arts fighter, lying in those arms felt like protection. He had light skin to where he almost looked Hispanic and actually spoke more Spanish than he did English. Amir made all those rumors about big muscles equaling a little dick pure fabrication. He was working with a banana boat, aka a donkey dick—or so I liked to call it because when he whipped it out, he surely acted an ass. I got to enjoy his Caribbean loving for slightly over six months, and it would have been longer if it weren't for his smart-ass mouth. Before fooling around with him, I knew nothing of Jamaicans, and I'm not saying I can judge them all from my interaction with one, but I learned they had no shame about speaking their minds. From what I could see, Jamaican men had strong beliefs and lived by them. I hope that living in America where everyone ran wild and free wouldn't change him or what he stood for because, in a strange way, I liked it. The only real problem I had with his beliefs was I wasn't ready to be submissive and follow them.

I wasn't surprised that I ran into him. What shocked me was after all this time away from him, he *still* turned me on, and I knew why. Amir had turned me on to the pleasures of limitless sex—not in quantity but in freedom. Sex with him had no restrictions, and anything edible could be used to bring pleasure. He showed me the ecstasy of getting my salad tossed and the joys and painful pleasures of anal sex. He was a master of exotic pleasure, and even though his sex wasn't as emotionally fulfilling as Dre's, he was a close second place.

There you go fucking up again, I thought to myself, feeling the moisture in between my legs consume my panties. It had only been seven weeks since Dre had laid me down, but to the beast in between my legs, it felt like years. The beast always wanted to be fed, but this time, she'd have to starve, because the only person who would ever feed her again was locked away in jail.

I dug my keys out of my purse and pulled out my cell phone too. As I unlocked the trunk to throw my bags in, I looked at my phone's screen. I had nine missed calls from Dre. I turned the ringer back up so I wouldn't dare miss another one of his calls. I needed to hear his voice to get me back focused on what it was that I now wanted out of life: him.

The hungry beast between my legs and lust had me broke and miserable. Allowing myself to be fed by someone other than Dre had taught me a very important lesson. It didn't just clear out my bank account. I learned that sex with whomever I wanted wasn't better than the love of a good man. There wasn't a need for me to cheat on him. The only reason I did it was because he tried to cut me off of it. That was like telling a heroin addict to stop using cold turkey. It wouldn't work for them, and it wasn't going to work for me. I'd need to be tapered down, but in Dre's eyes, tapering wouldn't be as effective as cutting me off completely. If he only knew his method didn't work and sent me to get it elsewhere. . . . Otherwise, he'd never attempt to teach me that way again.

With thoughts of sex filling my mind, Stephanie's welcome home basket wasn't looking like such a bad idea. There was a porno I could watch, a silver bullet and a dildo I could use, but when I made it back to my hotel, I decided against it. I wouldn't give her the pleasure of knowing that she knew me well enough to know that I'd actually use the gift. Instead, I put on my black stretch pants and a blue, oversized T-shirt and went to work out in the on-site fitness center.

I was in the room alone with full control of the TV and remote. I turned on CNN, then hopped on the exercise bike. While I was getting my fill of current events, it dawned on me that I never called my daddy to let him know that I made it to Atlanta.

"Hey, Daddy, sorry I didn't call you sooner, but I made it here, and I'm safe."

"I know you made it, baby." He exhaled the smoke from his lungs, then said, "Dre had his mother call me earlier with him on the line. He said something was wrong with your phone."

Dre knew the only thing that was wrong with my phone was I wasn't answering it for him. "My phone is fine, Daddy. It's Dre that's the problem. He wants to call me day and night just to start an argument about nothing. I can't keep arguing with him, so I turned my ringer off."

My daddy was wrestling with something in the background. I could hear the sound of plastic being crumpled, and then it stopped. A lighter was stroked, then he inhaled deeply.

"Daddy, didn't you just smoke a cigarette? You know how I hate you smoking them things, and now you want to start chain-smoking. You need to quit, Daddy, I'm—" I stopped talking because my brain had finally caught up with my mouth. Something was wrong. The only time I've known my daddy to spark up a cigarette back-to-back was when something was bothering him. "Daddy, what's wrong? And don't you say nothing."

"Savannah, Savannah, Savannah." He said my name three times in between exhaling and chuckling, then said, "You think you know your daddy, don't you?"

"I *do* know my daddy, and if you're chain-smoking, then something's wrong. Come on with it, Daddy, I don't need the suspense."

He coughed like his lungs were going to give out on him at any second. He always owned a smoker's cough, but it sounded like it was full of phlegm, and I was right because I heard him spit next.

"I'm just tired, baby. I've lived my whole life trying to do what I thought was best for everybody but myself, and now I sit back and look at everything that has happened in it, and the only thing I can be proud of is that I never committed suicide during it all—"

"Daddy!" I yelled into the phone. I had never heard him talk like this, and I wasn't sure if I wanted to.

"No, Savannah, it's the truth. It's been one heartache after another. No matter how hard I tried to make my mama happy after my father went to prison, I never saw her smile again. Then I made sure to love your mother with everything in me, but I could never keep her satisfied. Either she complained that I was giving her too much, or it just wasn't enough. Then she left me but gave me a piece of her that I could always hold to, you and Memphis. And with all the protecting and sacrifices I made to keep you and your brother from being anything like your mother, I failed again."

He took another puff of his cigarette and inhaled it deeply. There was no way that my father just sat around, and depression attacked him out of nowhere. Something had to have triggered it. "Where is all of this coming from, Daddy? Something had to have happened."

"Your mother is what happened," he replied. "She took the time out of her busy life with her new rich husband to write me a letter. She wanted to tell me how much of a disappointment I was to her and the rest of the world. She told me falling in love with me almost ruined her life. In her eyes, I was and will always be nothing but a homicidal, alcoholic loser with not enough strength in me to be a real man."

He smoked some more of his cigarette, then continued to recite what he had been told.

"Your mama said I was solely to blame for my mama's depression and said she died from the disappointment of knowing she'd given birth to three worthless sons that were no better than their murderous father." He began laughing hysterically. "Peaches said she knew I would never remarry because I'd be weak enough to sit around still in love with her, waiting for her to come back. It's funny that she knew me that well. That woman knew me too well because she was right. Boy, was she right. I couldn't even sleep with another woman without feeling like I betrayed her. Isn't that funny, Savannah? I thought *I* was betraying *her*." He hit his cigarette again, coughed, and then took a drink of what I prayed was water, but by how hard he swallowed, I knew it had to have been something stronger.

"Daddy, are you drinking . . . liquor?"

"Thirty-three years, baby, it was thirty-three years off the bottle." He shook his glass around so I could hear the swishing of liquid in his cup. Then he took another deep swallow. "And I ran back to it in less than ten minutes because it was the only place I could remember finding comfort."

"No, Daddy." The heat from the tears falling out of my eyes was the only sign of me crying. I didn't want to sadden our conversation any more with him hearing the crying in my voice.

"Yep, leave it to Mrs. Perfect Trisha. I'm to blame for Memphis being as behind as he is. You know, when it comes to his smarts and all. I'm also to blame for the pitiful way you turned out."

"She's to blame. *She* left *us,* Daddy," I interrupted. "She walked out on us because being a ho and her love for money came first. Don't let her blame you for us and the way we turned out. Memphis is gullible, not slow, and that's because he puts his faith in people, and I'm . . ." I took a deep breath because I had just realized the truth. "I'm my mother's child. You raised the hell out of us, but no matter what you taught me, her DNA seems to have shined through. I've been around her, Daddy, and I've seen her in action. My way of thinking is fucked-up, just like hers."

I couldn't hold it any longer. I broke down crying like I had never cried before. I had snot seeping from my nose, and I was shaking uncontrollably.

"Now, you stop all that crying, Savannah. Don't let me pull you into my mood and watch your mouth. We've talked about respect. I needed to hear what she had to say, and I know she was being evil, but a lot of it was the truth." He took another swallow of his liquor, but I didn't hear him inhale a cigarette.

I gathered myself long enough to speak to him. "Daddy, pack up a bag. I want you here with me for the holidays."

"No, no, baby. I don't need you trying to comfort me or protect me from myself. I'll be fine. Larry is on his way here to keep me company and watch the game. I was just enjoying my last few glasses of my old friend, Paul Masson. He's empty, and now I'm full."

He was drunk, and I never wanted to hear him drunk again. I don't know how bad of an alcoholic he was before my birth, but he was grown, and I couldn't tell him not to drink. He really didn't need to. I'd try to call Mr. Jefferson before he made it to his house. I wanted him to keep an eye on my daddy for me, and I needed to thank him. I was truly thankful for him for being in all of our lives because he didn't have to. He was my daughter's foster parent. That didn't require him to deal with the rest of us. But Larry Jefferson and my daddy had built a real bond. At first notice, it was weird to me due to all the circumstances around the way they were put in each other's lives. Now, I'm thankful for my daddy having him as a friend. Besides my uncle Johnny, I didn't know of my father hanging out with anyone else, not even his other brother, Uncle Steve.

"Are you sure, Daddy? You're more than welcome to stay here with me, or I'll come home if you need me to until Dre gets released. He didn't like the idea of me coming back this way anyway. . . ."

There was no time for me to get my father's answer because the reason why Dre didn't want me in Atlanta alone immediately flashed across the television. It was news footage of a funeral that had taken place the day before, and the caption at the bottom of the screen said: *"Mourners came to grieve the tragic death of college basketball star, Anthony Wallace . . ."*

I stopped pedaling, dropped my phone, and dashed to the TV to turn up the volume. I was only able to catch the ending of the report, but I heard the reporter say, *"After months of being in a vegetative state, Wallace's family discontinued the player's life support earlier this week. His teammates speak out about their sadness over his tragic death tonight at ten."*

There was an enlarged picture of Big Ant smiling on the screen. Then they showed a huddle of mourners wearing his jersey on his old college campus, and the last shot on the screen sent my heartbeat into overtime. Hugging Ant's mama, face to the camera and dressed from head to toe in all black, was his baby mama, Melinda. My heart and mind started racing. When did she get out of jail, and why hadn't Will called to tell me? Will was supposed to be my best friend. He couldn't have still been mad at me for not wanting to hear him tell me that Dre and I had no future together. He was wrong for overstepping his boundaries and not being happy for his best friend. A real friend understands that it's okay not to see eye to eye all the time and that there will be times when we piss each other off. But when those times occur, a friend will still have your back, because that's what real friends do. If Will were aware that Melinda had been released and he didn't tell me, then he wasn't a friend of mine. I ran back near the bike and picked up my phone.

"Daddy, I'm going to call and check on you a little later. No more drinking. I love you."

He barely was able to say it back before I hung up the phone. I scrolled through my phone's contact list until I reached the contact stored as "Best Friend" and hit send. The phone rang twice, and then a message played saying I had been forwarded to voicemail. I tried to call back twice more but received the same message as before. Will couldn't be that coldhearted that he wouldn't tell me I was in potential danger. He couldn't have known Melinda was out, and I wouldn't let myself believe that he did. It was seven o'clock eastern standard time, which made it six o'clock Dre's time. He'd call me before he went to sleep . . . or would he?

Chapter Six

Be Careful of What You Ask For

I waited all week for Dre to call, but he never did. To say he was supposedly concerned about my safety and protection, you'd think he'd call just to hear my voice, then hang up. That wasn't the case. He wanted to make a point by not calling, teach me a lesson, so to speak, and he did. I was wrong to hang up in his face. I shouldn't have done it, and even after I did, his next call would have been answered. This, I knew, but I wouldn't apologize for doing what I felt was right at the time. Instead, I wouldn't make the same mistake twice.

I made it to Nashville Friday night and checked into a hotel near the airport. Memories of my days and nights spent here during and after college flooded my mind. Surprisingly, to say the least, meeting Dre here was my fondest memory. He had something special about him that was so tangible I could feel it the first day we met. Never in a lifetime would I have thought I was meeting my husband when I bought that sack of weed from him. It was a situation that happened daily between those who sell and the others who consume. How ironic that I found love while in search for my next high. Life is funny that way sometimes. I wouldn't question it, because it was Kismet that brought us together.

The next morning I was up with the birds, getting as fly as I could for my visit with Dre. The jail had a dress code, but I made sure to be the sexiest woman in there while still following it. I put on a white, fitted, long-sleeved T-shirt and wrapped a leopard print scarf around my neck. I made sure to leave one tail of the scarf in the front to fall in between my breasts. I put on the darkest blue and tightest jeans that I owned and gave them a dressier look by applying a leopard print belt that matched perfectly with my scarf. I threw on my all-black, no-heel, knee-high boots, grabbed my leopard print bag, and threw on a black blazer that stopped at my belt loops, so all of my round ass was in view. It was colder in Nashville than it was in Atlanta, and my outfit went perfectly with the weather. After polishing my nails black, adding gold earrings, bangles, and an extralarge gold fashion ring, I only had one complaint about my look, and that was my hair. My weave had been up for over three months. It was time for a touch-up, but Dre wouldn't notice. I braided all eighteen inches of the hair up the night before, sprayed it with setting lotion, then blow-dried it so now I looked like a curly-haired Indian.

Once I was all signed in and waiting on Dre to come out, I applied some clear lip gloss to give him something to stare at while we talked. As the inmates came pouring out for their visit, each one made sure to do a double take at me, and I made sure to greet all of their horny asses with a smile. I understood that they hadn't seen anything pretty in a while, and I didn't mind being their eye candy and possibly the woman they stroked their dicks to that night.

Dre was the last to enter the room, looking like a hairy beast. His dreads needed twisting, and his face and neck needed to be shaved and trimmed. I didn't stare, nor would I comment on his appearance, because I'd seen him looking that way before when he wasn't behind bars. It was that time he was going through his man thing and refusing to keep up his hygiene back in Washington.

"Stand up and turn around," he said.

What a strange request, I thought, but I stood up and did it.

"Naw, step back some and turn around slower. Let a nigga look at you."

"Well, hello to you too, Dre. You could have spoken first," I said as I took a few steps back and turned slowly as he requested. While Dre stared at what I'm sure he felt was his, so did every other inmate on his side of the visiting row.

"Damn, baby, you're bad as fuck. Come sit back down 'for I have to kill me a nigga in here. That body is back looking right. I like the extra meat you've put on."

Before I could get in the seat good, Dre was already switching the mood and talking shit. He pointed his finger at me until it pressed against the glass, then said, "Ay, don't you ever fucking hang up on me again. I don't give a fuck what I'm saying to you or how it makes you feel. You sit there and listen. I ain't one of them sucka-ass niggas you used to dealing with, Savannah. I ain't gon' keep reminding yo' ass of that either. Better make that shit the first and the last time you do it, or you ain't gotta worry about a nigga calling you at all. I wasn't gon' accept your visit over that shit, but I knew you needed to see my face to feel what I needed to say to you. You mines. You better start acting like it."

"Okay, Dre, you don't have to talk to me like I'm dumb. I know I'm yours, daddy. I understand that, but that still don't make it right that you didn't call me the rest of the week. I thought you said you questioned me because you were trying to protect me, but where was my protection that week while I sat in my hotel room, scared to leave?"

Dre had a look of confusion on his face. Instead of wasting time, allowing him to guess what I was talking about, I ran down what I had seen on CNN and how Will was refusing to answer and not returning any of my calls.

"She must have just gotten released, baby. Calm down. Nobody knows you're back in Atlanta right now, or where you are in Atlanta. What the fuck you do to Will? You have to stop burning all of your bridges with good people. Damn! Did you at least get you a car and yourself a place?"

"Yes, I got approved for it two days before Christmas but am still staying at the hotel until I sign my lease and get my keys, and I bought me another Charger. I don't know what the fuck Will's problem is. The last time I spoke to him, he was fucked in the head over his man cheating on him and was full of negativity. I like how you just assume *I* did something to fuck up our friendship. Why couldn't it have been him?"

"Because I know you. That's why I assumed *you* fucked it up."

I rolled my eyes and curled my lip up at Dre in disgust before I started back up. "*Whatever*. And what makes you so sure that no one knows I'm back in Atlanta? Who's to say Keisha didn't tell her where I work, and she didn't call there looking for me? What if the receptionist told her I worked out of the Washington location and gave her the number there? All it would take is the receptionist in Washington to tell her I just moved back to the Atlanta office but wouldn't be there for another two weeks. All it would take is for your best friend Stephanie to be mad at me and tell her where I was staying."

He stared at me for a second like he wanted to say something, and then shook his head in disbelief. "You did all that fucked-up shit to them people in California, including Stephanie, and your ass is scary as fuck. Look at you, about to shit on yourself in them tight-ass jeans. You're really scared, huh, baby? But you're allowing fear to get you too paranoid. Baby . . . Baby, look at me."

I wasn't about to shit in my jeans. *He* was making me feel like shit. I didn't want to look at him in his eyes. My feelings were hurt. I hated when his words affected me like this, but I knew I had to keep pretending to be strong, so I forced my eyes to meet his.

"I know me being in jail ain't making your paranoia any better, but you gotta trust me. I'm not about to let shit happen to you. Do you hear me? I'ma have my niggas get with you after we set something up so you can be and feel safe. As a matter of fact, since you're already down here, I'ma have them get up with you tonight. Answer every 615 number that calls your phone, okay, baby?"

I agreed, and then the subject changed again. Somehow, Dre turned it into a conversation about his mama and son. He called himself giving me background on them both, but it was a little too late for that. I had my first opinion about his mother, and nothing he could say would change it.

"Y'all have to work this shit out, Savannah. This whole situation with me getting married is new to Mama, and the fact we already have a baby that she didn't know anything about—"

"You decided not to tell her that she had a granddaughter," I retorted. "And having a mother-in-law that won't even call me by my name because she thinks the shit is cute to disrespect me is new to me too."

"How do I tell my mama that I have a baby in foster care because her mama was mad at me for getting back locked up and gave her way?" he snapped.

"Is that why you think I gave Sade away?"

"Hell yeah, that's what I think. You haven't told me anything else."

"And you never asked me either."

"I shouldn't have to. That's some shit you should have felt the need to explain to me. I'm the nigga that knocked you up."

It never occurred to me that I hadn't given Dre an explanation for my actions with Sade. I always felt like the letter I sent him while I was pregnant was good enough. He deserved the truth like he said.

"You being locked up at the time didn't have anything to do with it. When you left that note about the police raiding my place looking for you, I got sick and had a few sick episodes after that but didn't look into them. I thought I was just stressed and overworked. I finally made it to the doctor, and she told me I was pregnant and too far along to get an abortion."

"Shit, abortion should have never been an option."

"You're a liar. It should have been my first option, and it was. You left me to spend family day with your girl and son, did you forget that?"

"Sundays are family day. No, I didn't forget that, but I don't ever recall telling you that she was my girl. That's my baby mama, and we were under the same roof raising my son, that's all."

"That's your truth—it wasn't mine. Anyway, I never wanted kids. They weren't in the plans I had for my life, and finding out that it was too late to do something about it left me with no choice but to give her away."

"You had another choice. You could have reached out to me and told me what was up. I should have been the first person you offered her up to. That's *my* blood in her veins," he yelled, and I yelled back.

"Yes, the blood of a criminal who can't seem to stay out of jail for long. Don't you see where you're at now? Locked up for doing right because doing right violates the agreement you have over your head with the probation system and the state of Tennessee. You're in debt to these motherfuckas for breaking their rules, so you couldn't raise a child, and to be honest, I felt like giving her away would be better than you or I failing to raise her.

She'd have a chance to break both of the crazy cycles we were spinning around in."

Dre had been shaking his head through my words. He didn't agree with anything I was saying.

"That wasn't a decision you could make on your own. I went half with you on her, and you threw her away without seeing if I had any options to fix the situation."

"Well, I'm glad I did because it made you track me and her down. If the shit hadn't played out like this, we wouldn't be together or engaged."

"You are the plus in this situation, Savannah."

"A plus? What is *that* supposed to mean?"

"It means that I wasn't tracking you down. I was after my baby. I had to find you to retrace your moves to lead me to her. Being engaged to you is the plus. I was only in it for finding Sade."

I drowned his voice out of my head with thoughts of who Dre would send to protect me and if they really could. Like usual, Dre said something that caught my full attention.

"What time do you want me to tell my mama y'all going to dinner tonight? You might as well eat at a restaurant by Opry Mills Mall since your hotel is by the airport. That's the halfway point between y'all."

"Who said I was having dinner with your mama tonight? Don't be volunteering me." I didn't mean to say it in a nasty way, but that's how in came out.

"*You* said it. Didn't you tell her y'all would have lunch or dinner when you came to town? I told her you'd be here to visit and for her not to come today. She cleared her schedule so that y'all could meet. It's lunch now, so y'all will have to have dinner. I'll call her and let her know to get with you about it. You ain't got shit to say back but okay. What you thought you was gon' do tonight? Cruise around downtown by yourself?"

"No, Dre, you know my extrascary ass wasn't going to go cruising around anywhere by myself."

I'm so glad he couldn't read my mind; otherwise, he'd be cussing me out over my thoughts of meeting, let alone eating with his mama. I hadn't made plans for the night, but going downtown and walking around Second and Broadway would have been nice. I hadn't seen it since the floods washed it away and it was rebuilt. Like most cities, downtown is where the tourists hung out, and that's exactly what I am now. It was time that I changed the subject.

"So, will you be serving all of your time at this facility? Getting here to visit you was easy. I know my way around Antioch, especially Harding Place."

"Naw, that's what I needed to talk to you about. I'll be getting moved soon to a place in Whiteville, Tennessee, which is about two hours from Nashville. You don't have to visit me there, but you need to keep money on your phone until I get me a cell phone in there. I also want to see some letters and pictures coming in from you."

I was glad to hear that because commuting wasn't how I wanted to spend all my weekends. I would do it if I had to, although I'd dread it. We finished our last ten minutes of the visit with talks of "how good I looked" and with him saying how he couldn't wait until he could do more than look at me through the glass.

"What do you plan on doing to me once the glass isn't there?" I asked seductively. Sex was my favorite subject and had been since I mastered the art as a junior in college. The action was one of my favorite pastimes, but the excitement I got from talking about it came close to trumping it. Wait, I'm lying. There's *nothing* better than dick.

"You're evil for that one, baby. Why are you trying to send me back to my bunk with my dick hard?"

"I'm not trying to send you anywhere besides in between my legs. I thought you would have known that by now."

"I do baby, but I can't get in that pussy right now, and my hand don't fuck my dick like you."

"Nothing or nobody will fuck and suck your dick like me. Don't you *ever* forget it."

I stood up and turned to the side slowly so that he could get a good look at my ass, and then I rubbed on it at the same pace. To my surprise, Dre stood up and grabbed his dick through his pants and gave that big ole thing a shake.

"You ain't never lied. That nasty little mouth of yours will have me in here plotting my escape. You can throw that neck on the dick way better than you throw that pussy on it with yo' lazy ass."

Leaving Dre behind to do time left me sad, but I knew he'd be calling me soon. I stopped by a grocery store on my way back to the hotel and grabbed myself a gallon of ice cream. I was hungry and hadn't eaten a thing all day, but I knew Dre was making dinner plans for me. I could wait until then. I kicked off my boots and curled up on the bed with my ice cream and watched whatever movie was on TLC. Suddenly, my hotel room's phone rang and woke me up.

"Hello?"

There was nothing but silence on the other end of the phone. There wasn't a background sound or any masked breathing. That paranoia Dre had confronted me about was ready to kick in. Then there was a clicking sound, and the front desk operator spoke up.

"I apologize, Ms. James. We seem to be having issues with our telephone lines today. There is a gentleman here waiting for you in the lobby. He said his name was Ryan, and you should be expecting him. He said he was sent at the request of an Andre Burns."

Dre said he would be having someone contact me, but he never said there would be a face-to-face visit. If I recall right, he said phone and even mentioned Nashville's area code. Paranoia wanted me to decline the visit, but the thought of not accepting Dre's security made me accept. I threw on my boots and walked into the lobby. I didn't have to check with the front desk to be directed to my visitor. His face was familiar to me. Standing in front of me dressed like a businessman, minus a tie and briefcase, was the same white boy that handed me the letter from Dre years ago in Atlanta. He was good-looking, like *GQ* magazine-style, when he wasn't dressed like a hip-hop dancer.

"Nice to see you again, Savannah."

He approached me with his hand extended for a shake. I grabbed it and shook it as if I just closed on a business deal with him.

"I don't know if I can say the same. The last time I saw you, you surprised me with a letter that sent me into labor."

He blushed as a sign of embarrassment. The redness in his cheeks made his ocean-blue eyes stand out even more on his summer-tanned face. His lips were thin, but he had a Brad Pitt/Johnny Depp sex appeal about himself. It was the middle-length haircut that grouped him with the famous actors. His looks really couldn't be compared to theirs because he was the closest human-to-visual perfection I'd ever laid eyes on.

"I apologize for that. I was doing a favor for my friend, as I am now. Dre asked me to come and meet with you. If you're okay with it, maybe we can talk over dinner? He said protection and safety needed to be the topic of our conversation. Does that ring a bell?"

Yes, it rang a bell. I started to ask about the dinner arrangements Dre was making for me with his mother, but Ryan informed me they had been canceled since this dinner meeting with him was more important.

"I don't know if you've had the, um, pleasure of meeting his mama yet, but please know that I'm speaking in love and in truth when I say, hands down, I'm the better dinner date."

"After talking to her on the phone and getting cursed out without her using a word of profanity, I won't question that. Give me a minute or two to get myself together."

"That's Mama D for you, and I'll give you ten."

I excused myself to return to my room to get my purse. First, I freshened up a little, then returned to the lobby so we could head out to dinner. I waited to see if Ryan would ask where I'd like to eat, but that question was never asked. When I looked up, we were pulling into an Italian restaurant called Maggiano's on West End, and he had us seated alone on an outside balcony. Once our orders were placed and our waiter brought out our wine, it was time to get down to business.

"Dre has kept me up-to-date with the events that have occurred since my delivery to you, so there's no need to relive what happened in California. What I want to know is what type of person Melinda is. Give me some background information on her."

I went back to Melinda's and my childhood relationship up to the last day I talked to her as an adult. I gave him facts first, and then gave him my opinion on what I thought she was capable of now.

"I don't know them anymore. As children, they wouldn't have harmed a fly, but after being shot by Keisha, the most timid in their crew, I think Melinda would be capable of more. She was the—"

He held up his finger to silence me at the waiter's return with our food. He reminded me of Dre with how he took authority and controlled the conversation. Other than a difference in race, the only difference between the two was that Ryan had more of a police style about himself. I could see why he and Dre were so close, though. It was hard to believe that I previously thought of him as a hip-hop dancer.

"I apologize. Please continue."

"Melinda was the one that had the most promising future and lost the most. Big Ant was on his way to play basketball professionally. I'm not sure if they were still in a relationship, but he making it would have changed their child's life. Out of all the people who could come after me, I'd fear her retaliation the most."

"Well, Savannah, tell me what type of protection you would feel most comfortable with having, and I'll tell you what Dre and I have come up with for you."

Only five hours had lapsed since my visit with Dre, and he managed to come up with a plan with his friend already. I didn't know what they were capable of, but I gave out my ideal anyway.

"In a dream world, I'd want to have an armed guard with me 24/7 that would transport me to and from work. I'd want the guard to live with me in my two-bedroom apartment like celebrities have their security." I had to laugh out loud at myself before I continued. "I know I'm asking for the Secret Service's protection, huh? But honestly, I'd be content with learning how to shoot a gun and obtaining a gun license until Dre is released."

"How about a combination of them both?" he said in between eating the stuffed mushrooms he had ordered. "Dre and I were thinking that maybe I should go back to Atlanta with you tomorrow until I return to work after the holidays. You will need to learn how to shoot and a few other self-defense moves. I know Dre would feel a lot better knowing you learned that stuff from me, just like he had done. After I've returned to work, Dre said he could have his other friend, Mike, stay with you during the week, and I'd be here in Nashville when you come to visit before Dre is moved. After that, we'd set up for me to visit on my days off. How does that sound?"

"It sounds expensive and like it would potentially cause problems between you and your wife. I couldn't ask you to stay with me for three weeks. That would be asking too much. Maybe you can teach me the self-defense stuff and how to shoot a gun. I'll just have to tread carefully."

He nodded his head while I talked and continued to enjoy his meal while I nibbled on mine. I was starving and wanted to pig out on my Parmesan chicken, but first impressions were everything.

"First off, you wouldn't be asking me to. Dre would, and he paid me way before you ever got in the picture. Even if he hadn't, that's what friends are for. Dre is my boy, and he loves you. He said you're going to be his wife, and I know you had his child, my beautiful, intelligent niece, Sade." He looked at me and smiled. "It's not a problem for me at all. If you'd prefer me not to be under the same roof as you, I can get a hotel room where you're staying, and when you get moved into your place, I can check into a hotel closer to you."

How could I say no to that? I told him that would be fine and that I'd feel a lot better with him under my roof. There was a weight lifted off my shoulders, and now I was able to dig into my plate.

"You're a blessing, Ryan. I truly appreciate this."

"That's nice to hear from a mouth filled with food, but I have to remind you that I'm doing this for Dre, and next in line would be Sade. I don't want you to see this as personal protection. I'll be working a job, and my only employer is Dre. When I piss you the fuck off, take it up with him."

"Wow!"

"Wow would be a great place to start. It will turn to hell later."

After finishing our meals, we headed back to my hotel. Ryan confirmed a noontime departure to Atlanta for the next day, and I got out of his car.

As I walked away, he rolled down his window and said, "Oh yeah, Savannah, I'm not married, nor do I have kids. Y'all women are too much for me to handle, and after keeping up with you all these years, I'm scared to date in fear I'd end up with a woman who mirrored you."

He drove off, laughing, and I was left thinking that maybe Ryan was gay. That would account for his cuteness and why he wouldn't see me as the best catch Dre ever caught while fishing.

Dre didn't call me that night. He waited until first thing Sunday morning. I told him I had agreed to Ryan coming back with me and our departure time, but he already knew it. He wasn't calling me for an update. He was calling me to tell me what I needed to do.

"Look, Ryan is my nigga for a reason. He's not gon' take your shit, Savannah, so try not to run him off. He can teach you a whole lot of shit, but you have to be willing to learn. He taught me the majority of what I know, but he doesn't have the patience for bullshit like me. Whatever he says goes, and that's final. If he lays out a plan, I expect you to execute it. None of that back talk, Savannah's-way shit you like to pull. He will be with you until January the sixth—that's three weeks. You need to make the most of the time. After that, I'm going to have my boy, Mike, the one you met at the gas station, stay with you for a while—"

"Mike?" I interrupted. "The fool with the gold teeth in his mouth? Didn't you say he messed up your deal, money, or something like that? You feel safe with someone with a dollar sign on their tooth protecting me?"

"Hell yeah, I feel safe with him protecting you. He's been ten toes down for me since kindergarten. That shit with the money was a setup that I knew about weeks before it happened. He couldn't stop that from happening, and from what I found out, he pushed shit to the limit trying to. And what the fuck does him having gold in his mouth have to do with your protection anyway?"

I should have responded to his question, but I knew he would have a negative response. He promised to call me back after dinner and wished me a safe journey home.

Ryan and I made it to Atlanta around four o'clock in the afternoon in our separate vehicles. When we made it up to my room, my boxes had arrived, and so did the office supplies I ordered. The welcome home basket that Stephanie had given me was sitting on the coffee table, and I saw Ryan lift an eyebrow to it.

"From another one of my enemies, but this is one I can handle."

"What's the name of the gift giver?" he asked, pulling out his Blackberry and retrieving a saved note.

"Stephanie."

"Stephanie Teasdale, coworker, ex-secretary, ex-friend, and ex—" he said looking from his phone to Savannah's face.

"Ex what?"

"Ex-lover, which makes this gift make sense," he said, quickly putting his phone away.

"Ex-lover? Is that what Dre told you?"

"Of course not," he said, pulling out his phone and flying through the files he had saved on it. When he found what he was looking for, he held his phone in front of me. "This is where I got that information."

Ryan had a transcript of Stephanie's and my text messages from what had to have been eight or nine years ago. Besides the sexual content of our messages, Stephanie had sent me a picture of her clit ring attached to her clit with a message that read, My clit can't wait for you to lick it tomorrow, baby. She misses your freaky ass. We love you.

Before I could respond, Ryan said, "I don't think Dre knows the severity of your relationship with her. In our talks, he references her as your best friend, but if he ever asks, I'll tell him. I'll also send him everything I have on the two of you, and if your memory serves you correct, this picture is rated PG compared to the others and the videos. I've seen and read more about you than I'd like to share with anyone, which is another reason why I'm doing this for Dre and Dre alone. You're a handful."

"Let me move my welcome home gift out of your way," was all I managed to say.

I don't know why I hadn't thrown it out, but instead, moved it into my bedroom and set it on the nightstand. Through yells, I explained that the sofa let out into a bed and gave him directions to the book with all the features the hotel offered. I was too embarrassed for a face-to-face.

He gave me an hour's worth of space, and after he had walked around the facility, he was ready for us to grab something to eat. We ate in silence at a Chinese buffet not too far away from the hotel. Then I started to get myself mentally ready for my first day of work. Dre had called that night, but not for me and not on my phone. He called Ryan and had him pass a message to me.

"Dre said he'd give you a call tomorrow when he's sure you're off and asked me to tell you that he loves you."

It somewhat upset me that I couldn't hear his voice, nor did he ask to hear mines, but I had shit to do to prepare for the next day. After laying all my stuff out for work, I went to the gym, showered, and went to bed.

By the time my scheduled wake-up call from the hotel rang the phone in the morning, I was dressed and ready.

Ryan was up, bed put away, and doing push-ups on the living-room floor. I told him good morning and to have a nice day as I headed out the door.

"Where do you think you're going?"

I almost didn't hear him and wasn't sure if he had said anything or if my ears had turned his heavy breathing into words.

"Excuse me?"

He stopped his workout and stood up. "You're excused. Where do you think you're going? You're leaving two hours before your shift starts to get somewhere less than twenty minutes away, and you're trying to go there alone. Sit down another twenty minutes while I shower. Then I'll take you to grab some breakfast to go and drop you off at work. I'll be waiting in the parking lot for you when you get off at four o'clock."

"No, I'll take myself, and I'm leaving now so I can grab breakfast and start working on my office before I get into my accounts. This is my normal routine."

"Right," he snapped back at me, "this is your normal routine, and that's why we're switching it up. Come on and have a seat. I'll be ready in twenty minutes or less."

I wanted to protest, but I kept hearing Dre's words about executing Ryan's plans. I slammed the door closed to show my dislike for being told what to do and then sat on the couch and turned on the news until he was ready to go.

"Is this the sample of the 'wow' that will turn into hell you spoke to me about?"

"No, but if you think this is, I feel bad for you. It *will* get worse from here."

All week I dealt with Ryan's shit. He made out a whole routine for us, and none of it included anything that I wanted to do. Monday was my last day of freedom, and if I had known that, I would have squeezed in more me time. As for Tuesday through Thursday, my schedule, which he posted on my mirror, went like this:

6:00 a.m.—breakfast
7:00 a.m.—drop off (work)
4:00 p.m.—pick up (work)
4:30 p.m.—arrive at the gun range
5:30 p.m.—leave the gun range
6:15 p.m.—arrive at the gym (self-defense course)
7:30 p.m.—leave the gym
8:00 p.m.—back home

Friday's schedule was identical, except after we left the gun range, we hit the road to Nashville so I could visit Dre. Ryan only left my side when I went to work and from 7:00 p.m. to 7:30 p.m. at the gym because I was in a thirty-minute woman-only workout group. I was surprised that he allowed me to walk to the car by myself afterward while he waited. He had become my full-time shadow, and there was nothing I could say to get away from him. He wouldn't let me go to the fitness center at our hotel alone, nor would he let me grab dinner by myself. He was overdoing his job, and what made matters worse was that he wouldn't talk to me besides mandatory interactions, like questions on what I wanted to eat or directing me during one of our self-defense lessons. Every time I tried to sit down and have small talk with him, he reminded me of what I could be doing with the time instead.

"There're people in jail you don't have updates on because of your shaky relationship with your best friend. I don't have to walk you down memory lane. As a matter of fact, you could be watching those self-defense videos instead of trying to get to know me better. We aren't friends, nor do I want us to be."

I complained about his overprotection and dry attitude to Dre during visiting, but nothing would be done. He agreed with what Ryan was doing like I knew he would.

"Listen to what you're bitching about, baby. He's there to protect you. What did you expect?"

"I didn't expect this. Y'all are best friends or brothers like y'all call it, and he refuses to talk to me about anything but protection, and if he does ask me anything, it's more like a homicide detective during an interrogation."

"That's how he is. It took hours of being under him for training before he warmed up to me. The nigga had me thinking he didn't like me for months. I know it can be irritating, but I promise you, he's going to keep you safe. Just do what he says."

"I *am* doing what he says, but what about being comfortable?"

"You're finding reasons to whine. Why aren't you comfortable?"

"I'm not whining. And how can anyone be comfortable under the same roof with someone who won't take a minute to help you get to know them?"

"The armed guards in the bearskin hats outside of the Buckingham Palace don't say shit to anyone, because talking doesn't have shit to do with protecting the queen. They don't sit around, laughing and joking with her. If she doesn't ask them shit, they don't say shit."

"Well," I said slowly feeling pissed at Dre's defense of the stranger he hired to protect me, "I hope the duchess brings her California swag to the Royal Family and switch that up when she moves in that bitch."

Dre laughed, and it took him a little longer than what I liked to regain his composure to respond to me.

"Baby, Buckingham Palace is the queen's house, and honestly, she doesn't even live there really. She has a handful of places to go to."

"You can laugh all you want. I don't care where the queen lives. The guards still follow her, and they still stand outside her palace, regardless of whether she's there. If she likes them silent, that's her choice. As *your* queen, I want my armed guards interacting with me, or there will be a permanent changing of the guard in Atlanta."

When visiting hour was over, I was put back on schedule, and there still wasn't any chitchat between us. We hit the road back to Atlanta the same day and made it there around five o'clock. I thought we would head back to the hotel, but that wasn't a part of Ryan's plans. He took me to the Metropolis to sign my lease and get my keys before the office closed at six thirty. I was tired and wanted to rest, and after I voiced it several times, Ryan gave in and drove us to the hotel.

I must have been exhausted because I don't remember falling asleep. It was 11:00 p.m. before I woke up, and I was hungry. I knew Ryan wasn't going to let me grab something to eat, so I yelled from my room if he minded going for me. He didn't answer. I asked again and again, but he still didn't answer. I walked into the living room, assuming he was asleep, but Ryan was gone. There wasn't a note left just in case I woke up or anything. He hadn't left me by myself in almost a week, and it frightened me a little, but it also gave me the opportunity to go out by myself without my shadow. I threw on my shoes, jumped in my car, and drove off.

There were plenty of fast-food restaurants near my hotel, but I didn't want a turnaround trip, nor did I want anything fast. I needed freedom and wanted to be around other people without being monitored.

My hotel was located downtown on Peachtree, which was already one of Atlanta's event-filled areas, especially on Saturday nights. All I had to do was drive down the street and eye the outside of establishments to see where I would fall in. I ended up getting valet parking at a restaurant/dancing club called Scout. From what I could tell by looking at the packed balcony, it was definitely where I needed to be. The last call for the kitchen was at 11:45 p.m. I wouldn't waste time because I was hungry and ready to eat.

As I ate and sipped on my wine, so many men approached me that you would have thought I was the only woman in the house. I'd never had to reject so many offers to dance and attempts at flirtatious conversations in one night. It had my self-esteem on high and made me decide to stay and receive a couple of those free drinks I was being offered. The night was young, and I was sure Ryan was already pissed off that I had left, but what could he do about it now? It's not like he could call and tell Dre on me. Even if he had a way to track my location, I doubt he was big and bad enough to put me across his lap and whip me.

One free drink turned into two, and then the drinks turned into a dance, and the next thing you know, I was in full clubgoer mode. I was tipsy and had danced from one end of the club to the other. The hip-hop the DJ was spinning was great, but when he switched the music to reggae, my hips were in heaven. I closed my eyes and let the music take over me. My arms were extended above my head and winding to the beats. I felt someone approach me from behind, place their hands on my hips, and grind with me, and that was perfectly fine with me. I needed a dance partner and hoped they could feel how deeply the music was moving me, and apparently, he did.

"What the fuck!"

The words came out of my mouth as I felt a hardened penis rub against my butt. I knew grinding the way we were would cause some heat between us, but this motherfucka behind me was overstepping his boundaries. As he got harder, he pulled my thighs in to him so that he could rest his hardness on me. Then he began rubbing himself up and down on me like he was attempting ejaculation. I hate to admit it, but it felt so good to have a hard dick touch me that I delayed getting away from it. I wanted to guess how long it was, how hard the head could get, and if it belonged to a man who knew how to control his nut until there was no doubt that he had pleasured my pussy. I creamed on myself and out of embarrassment, I tried to loosen his grasp, but he tightened his grip on my thighs and started rubbing it faster against me. I had to dig my nails into his hands to get him to release me. When I turned around to face the perpetrator, I found myself making eye contact with Amir.

"He misses you, Savannah, and how you were grinding on him says that you miss him too. I know that shake. I've felt it around my dick many times. You wet those panties, didn't you?"

"Fuck you, Amir!"

"Yes, please, you come home with me and fuck Amir."

"In your dreams."

He stood there with a perverted smile on his face as I turned on my heels to walk away. I made it down the stairs in the club and out the exit before he caught up to me.

"Savannah!" he yelled. "Please, wait, please. Hear me out."

I made my way to the valet parking booth and requested my car. By the time I was done, Amir was back standing in my face.

"What, Amir? What the fuck is it?"

"I'm sorry, Savannah. I really am. I'm sorry 'bout every ting. What I said to you years back was disrespectful, and I was upset, but I didn't mean it. I had feelings for you that I thought we shared, but I was wrong. Please forgive me. I don't like how you are treating me. You were my baby."

"I forgive you, now, leave me alone. It was only sex, Amir, nothing more. I was never your baby."

As the word "sex" came out of my mouth, the beast in between my legs awakened. All the drinks I had must have kicked in. Instantly, I could feel all of Amir inside of me. I'd never forget the rhythm his dick pulsated to. It was as Caribbean as he was. I let him play his bongo drums on my cheeks as his guiro slid in and out of my ass. It was my first dance to his reggae funk, and I enjoyed it. I never thought I would, but the pleasure of the pain he caused made me crave it. Dre had tried to dig through my rumble, but as quickly as his shovel entered me, he was pulling it back out. The two seconds that he gave me triggered cravings, and with my dance instructor in my face, the urge to pull down my panties and bend over to show off my dancing shoes had taken over me. Where was the valet with my car?

"Then let me sex you. I know how to give you what you want and give your body what it needs. I don't believe that you don't miss me pleasing you." He took a step closer to me. "I don't believe you don't miss my tongue touching you places fingers won't reach. You remember my touch, don't you? Do you remember what my tongue and lips feel like on your skin?" I turned my head, and he walked around to stand in front of me and said, "Do you remember how my dick throbs inside of you?"

For a second there, his words had me frozen, and not only could I remember his touch, but I could also feel it. Thank heaven that the sight of my car coming up the ramp snapped me out of it so that I could move out of his voodoo's reach. As I walked away to switch positions in the driver seat with the valet, Amir yelled out, "Think about it. And when you do, I'll be at my family's restaurant ready for you. Sex only."

Chapter Seven

Full-body Protection

It was my last full week under Ryan's protection, and I prayed it went by fast. He had been acting like a bitch ever since the night I left for food while he moved my boxes into my new place. How was I supposed to know that he left to get me settled in? There wasn't a note saying where he had gone or when I should expect him back. Those facts were the exact ones I used for disappearing that night for food, and they were what I used to convince him not to tell Dre on me. Although I looked upon it as a battle won, it was more of a loss the way Ryan tightened his security on me. He didn't let me attend my women's workout class for three days in order to cram in some more training—or so he claimed. But I knew a punishment when someone placed me on one. From that day forth, he made me spend every sixty seconds of a minute with him besides my eight-hour work shift.

I was glad to be back at work, not just because it freed me from Ryan's prison, but because I really loved my job, and I was good at what I did. The only part that felt weird about returning to the home office was that I'd been back at work for almost two weeks and hadn't seen Stephanie once. We had a company meeting my first week back, but it was a telephone conference. I was starting to think the conference call was arranged so that we wouldn't have to see each other by Stephanie's request. I had seen the other two partners because they came to my office to say hello and to welcome me back. I didn't expect that from Stephanie. We are no longer friends and judging by the welcome gift she left for me, we never would be again. I guess there wasn't a real reason for us to see each other anymore. Our offices were on two separate floors, and there was no reason for me to go downstairs or for her to come up. Maybe it was best that we didn't see each other because with all the tension between us, it felt like we were in constant competition anyway. I would report my progress on my accounts in the evening and carbon copy all the partners on my email. In the mornings, she would do the same, so we always knew who was making the most progress, and without a doubt, it was me.

I hadn't known Stephanie's real whereabouts until Christmas Eve when Mr. Williamson emailed us to wish us all a pleasant week off for the holidays. He concluded his email by saying, Glad to see Savannah James and Stephanie Teasdale have gotten settled in our Atlanta and California offices. The numbers you both have put up this last week are record-breaking. I hope your drive for the growth of our company continues in the approaching year. Happy Holidays.

The little bitch couldn't take the heat, so she moved away from the furnace. That was the best thing for her to do because there was no way I'd let her be in my presence in peace. It didn't matter that we weren't in the same office. I'd still find a way to get under her skin for that basket she sent me. Now that I knew where she was, it was my turn to put together and send a gift. Instead of a basket, I sent her a box. I took the last hour of my shift and went through a hand full of my pictures with my short hairdo and printed them off. When I made it to the house, I went through my clothing and found the outfits from the pictures. When I had five pictures and outfits together, I boxed and wrote a cute note to go with it.

Hey, Little Savannah,

You're doing such an excellent job at mimicking me as a partner and trying to live my life that I couldn't help but to contribute to your mission. Here are a few of my favorite outfits and pictures to show you how to wear them properly. I hope they bring you as much joy as they brought me. Oh, and if you need any help with getting adjusted to my life in California, I'm a phone call away. I hope becoming me finally brings worth to your meaningless life.

—Savannah, The Original

It was now Saturday, January the 5th, my last full day with Ryan and my last visit with Dre. He would be moved to Whiteville, Tennessee, this week, and we would go to phone calls and letters only as our method of contact. We made the most of our last visit with each other by not arguing once and expressing our love and lust for each other.

"My first meal as a free man is my pussy. I want you to lie back, spread them legs, and open that pussy up. You come in this bitch looking like dessert every visit, and I can't wait to eat your ass up. Better start getting your hydration up, beautiful. I'm draining your ass for days."

"Is that right?" was all I could manage to say. He didn't know how much I hated talking about sex and not getting any, but it seemed to make him happy, so I didn't complain.

"Yeah, that's right, and I am coming with the steel. That first nut I get off, I ain't gon' lie to you. It's gon' come quick, so I'll let you swallow that one, but after that, I'm nutting all in my pussy. You need to be saving those vacation days you get at work. If not, when I'm done, they're gonna have to put you on sick leave."

I laughed, and when we said our last face-to-face goodbyes, he reminded me that I would be going with Ryan to pick up Mike tonight and that I needed to drive safely back to Atlanta because he was sure Mike would be riding with me dirty.

When I made it back to my car, Ryan had parked his car and was sitting on the passenger side of mine with a wrapped gift.

"For you, my dear. Happy early birthday," he said with a smile.

My birthday wasn't for another three weeks, but there was no way I'd be rejecting his gift. I tore into the paper until I reached the metal box. There was a key taped to it, which I used to unlock it. Inside of the case was a brand-new 9 mm Glock 19 pistol, an extra clip, and a box of bullets. I only knew the name of the gun because it was identical to the one I had practiced with at the range.

"Aww, my very own gun. Thanks, Ryan."

He took the gun out of the case and turned it to the side so I could read what was engraved on the slide of the gun. In cursive writing, it read, *"Savannah's Bitch."*

I reached across the seat and planted a kiss on his cheek. I didn't mean anything by it. The kiss was a friendly gesture. But he looked at me as if I'd crossed into enemy territory.

"Calm down, Ryan. That was a grandmother-to-her-grandchild kiss. If I didn't try to cross the line with you in three weeks of living together, you don't have to worry about me trying to now."

A crooked, boyish smile appeared on his face as he tried to play it cool. "So, where does the birthday girl want to go eat and celebrate getting the hell away from me? I won't make it back to check on you until February, so we'll have to celebrate it now."

Did I make it that obvious that I was ready for him to leave and get the hell away from me? I looked at him and laughed to stop myself from confirming that he was right. I drove us to B. B. King's restaurant downtown, and we enjoyed our last meal together there. Ryan's phone was ringing, and besides phone calls from Dre, it was the first time I'd heard it, especially that ringtone. A classic by the group called The Dramatics blared out of the back of his phone. The song was about backstabbers.

"Hello?" His voiced changed from relaxed to somewhat angered as he greeted the caller. The fluctuation of his voice and the ringtone made me want to eavesdrop more. "She's right here with me. I told you she'd be ready around five or six . . . What? Hell naw, y'all need to be almost there by then. Look, if you can't handle—" Ryan didn't finish his sentence because the person on the other end of the phone had ended the call before he could. Ryan looked at me while he put his phone back in the holder he had connected to his belt. "That was Mike. Have you ever met him?"

"We met briefly on the same day I met Dre. I don't remember anything about him besides those bright gold teeth and the dollar sign he had engraved on one of them."

I laughed, and so did Ryan.

"Mike is, well . . . He's a mixture of a hard head and Dre's past." He stopped talking like his words had satisfied my curiosity about the type of person Mike was. When he saw that they hadn't, he started back talking. "I don't like discussing other people because I believe you should make your own opinion about them with your first impression. You don't need to enter a new relationship biased from what I told you."

"Fuck that, tell me. If he's going to be living under my roof for months, I need to know all I can about him. I'm still going to have my own opinion about him. Whether my opinion agrees with yours is what will be questioned."

Ryan looked me in my eyes as if he was trying to make sure that I really wanted to know. Then he called the waiter over and ordered himself a beer.

"Since when does Drill Sergeant Ryan drink beer? In three weeks, all I've seen you drink is water and fruit juices."

He blushed a little as the waiter returned with his long neck. He took a deep swallow, eyeing me out of the corner of his eye, and said, "I was on duty these last three weeks. When I'm not working, I'm drinking, and . . ." He leaned over the table, closer to me. "I might just roll up and take one to the head when I make it home tonight."

Now, *I* was in disbelief. I'd wanted to smoke all this time, but thought I was in the presence of some Goody Two-shoes cop that would arrest me for possession if he saw me with a sack. I should have known he smoked weed if he was as close to Dre as they both had said. When Ryan saw the initial shock of his last words had worn off my face, he picked up where he had left off with telling me about Mike.

"To be blunt with you, Savannah, I don't trust dude. I don't doubt he can and will protect you at all. It's all the other shit about him I don't like. He's not real about his. He called himself making a career out of selling drugs, but he's a small-timer, and it's in his head that he's one of the biggies in the game. He rides around flossing and fronting like he's the man, but if it weren't for Dre keeping him on his feet and out of shit, he'd probably be dead or in jail somewhere with all the lying he does. From what I know, he and Dre have been down since elementary, and Dre's been saving his ass since then too.

Dre looks at him as his friend because of the number of years he's known him, not the quality of the friendship. Dre says he's a friend, but I think he's a foe."

"Well, damn, is that what you've gathered from him? You think he'll smile in Dre's face and stab him in the back at the same time, huh?"

Ryan kept drinking his beer, but he was nodding his head at the same time.

"Do you think I'll be safe?" I asked because I wanted to know the truth, and it didn't seem like he'd hesitate to give it to me straight.

"Like I said, you'll be safe without a doubt, especially if he wants the pay Dre promised him for protecting you. All I'm going to say is sleep with your bedroom door locked and don't get friendly with him. He's a snake, regardless of whether Dre sees it."

We left the conversation about Mike at that. Then Ryan ordered another beer. The live band had B. B. King's dance floor packed as people danced to the sound of the blues blaring through the speakers. Ryan saw me watching the dancers and moving to the beat, so he grabbed my hand and walked me over to the floor.

"Come on, Savannah, I promised Dre I'd show you a good time."

We danced to three songs consecutively, then grabbed our belongings and headed out the door. I did have a nice time with Ryan, and he was actually a cool guy when he wasn't being an asshole to protect me. I wondered what I should expect from Mike. Ryan said he was sure I'd be safe in Mike's protection, especially if he wanted the money Dre promised him. That made me wonder just how much Dre would spend on protecting his woman.

As Ryan opened the door of my car for me, I asked, "How much is Dre paying y'all for protecting me?"

I didn't think Ryan would answer the question by the way he looked at me, but he did.

"Me? Nothing. That's my boy, and, hell, I didn't want to spend the holidays alone. But as for Mike, he's paying him too much."

"What's too much to pay for someone to protect your wife?"

"There's not a price that's too much to pay when it comes to protecting someone you love. That's not what I meant by that."

"Okay, then help me to understand how you meant it," I said, giggling to keep the mood we were having from changing.

"Mike is in debt to Dre, and the number is too great to even describe in money. The problem with that is, Mike knows he's in debt, and Dre refuses to open his eyes to see it. Broken loyalty can cost people millions, but in the life we live, the only way to pay that type of debt is with your life."

We drove fifteen minutes to a small city next to Nashville called Madison and pulled into an apartment complex. Ryan sent a text, then got out of the car. About five minutes later, Mike came walking out with four large duffle bags, and I popped my trunk. I couldn't hear the conversation that was going on between the two because I had my music on. I didn't want to make it obvious that I was trying to listen in by turning it down, but something was wrong. By the body language between the two, it looked more like an argument than a conversation. When they finished almost ten minutes later, Ryan sat back in the front passenger seat, and Mike hopped in the back, ready to spark up a conversation.

"What's up, Savannah? You ready for this little adventure we going on 'til my boy gets out?" Then out of nowhere, he screamed, "Free my nigga, Dre!" He started laughing like he was tickled by his own words.

I looked at Ryan, then glanced over my shoulder to get a good look at Mike. I couldn't see him that well because it was the end of the sunset, but from what I could tell, he was high. He had a weed high, and there was a good chance that he was drunk as well. His eyes were bloodshot red and low to where they almost looked closed. Even though it wasn't cold in Nashville, Mike had on an ankle-length black leather jacket, a button-up brown and cream shirt that I bet was long-sleeved, a pair of brown corduroy pants, and short-laced, untied, chocolate-brown boots. Sweat beads were popping up all over his forehead, an indication that he was hot, but yet, he didn't take the jacket off.

"Hey, Mike," was all I mustered up to say.

"It's Mike's birthday today, Savannah, and as you can see, he started celebrating it already." Ryan was pissed off and not trying to hide it, but I understood why. By the same token, I couldn't allow myself to be mad at Mike for being under the influence. It was his birthday, and I'm sure babysitting his best friend's fiancée wasn't the way he wanted to spend it.

"Dirty thirty in this bitch, Savannah, and we partying in the 'A' tonight. You gon' shake it with me, right?" Mike started dancing around in the backseat to give his definition of "shaking it" to me. It was funny, to say the least.

I looked at Ryan before answering and thought I should say what best suited him while he was in the car with us. "I might have a drink with you at the apartment in honor of your birthday. My thirty-plus-one is in three weeks."

We made to the jailhouse parking lot to retrieve Ryan's car, and he nudged me to get out with him. When we made it out of earshot of Mike, he said, "Here's my number. Call or text me anytime you need me, and I'm on my way. I know it's that fool's birthday, but don't let him do a lot of partying and drinking tonight. He's supposed to be protecting you. He's a paid employee of y'alls, not a visiting friend. Make sure he doesn't forget that. I'll be checking in on you." He leaned in and gave me a peck on my cheek. "You be careful and keep going to the range daily. Make sure you get Savannah's Bitch registered to you Monday, even if you have to take a few hours off work. Get it done!"

The ride to Atlanta was eventful, to say the least. We weren't on the interstate more than ten minutes before Mike was taking a swig out of the bottle of vodka he had hidden in his jacket pocket. When he saw me watching him, he held the bottle in front of me. "You want a swallow?"

At my decline, he started running his mouth about everything. He started with talks of his favorite liquors to places he'd fucked while he was drunk and even started naming the women he fucked while drunk. This went on for about an hour into the ride before he scared the shit out of me by begging me to pull over on the interstate.

"Savannah, pull over quick. I gotta pee, and a nigga can't hold it no more. Pull over."

He didn't have to ask again, because there was no way I was going to sit back and let him spray his urine around my new car. After he made that initial request, it seemed like the bathroom breaks came every thirty minutes that followed. This made an already long ride home even longer. We needed gas, so I pulled over at a truck stop about an hour away from our destination and filled up. There was a Cajun chicken fast-food restaurant conjoined to it that I had eaten at before, and I decided to grab something to eat while we were there.

"Are you hungry, Mike?" I asked as he pumped my gas, expecting him to say no because he was drinking.

"Hell yeah, I'm hungry. I'll take a few pieces of chicken. Do you mind if I hit this blunt a few times in your car before I come in?"

"Hell yeah, I mind," I snapped at him. "You can go over there and smoke while I grab us both a box to go. What sides and drink do you want?"

I pointed him to an open field I had referenced behind the truck stop, took his order, and walked back into the gas station. Dre had warned me that Mike would be riding dirty, but how dirty was he? I had assumed dirty meant an unlicensed gun, but I guess dirty meant drugs too. I got our food to go so I could hurry up and get him back to the apartment with all his illegal paraphernalia. Mike ate everything in his box, including scraping up the crumbs from his biscuit. Then he went straight to sleep. I had to listen to him snoring loudly the rest of the ride home. I don't know how Dre thought this was going to work if this is how Mike acted all the time.

I was tempted to leave him asleep in my car when we made it to my apartment. If it weren't for not knowing what he had in those bags in my trunk, I wouldn't have gotten him up. When we made it inside, I pointed him to the guest room while I went to use the bathroom in my bedroom. I kicked off my heels, rubbed my feet for a little bit, and threw on my house slippers before heading back to the living room. In less than five minutes, he had emptied the contents of two of the four bags he had brought with him across the living-room floor, had left the toilet seat up in the hallway bathroom, and was in the guest room playing rap music on his phone while he ironed a pair of jeans on my carpeted, although bare, floor.

"What the fuck do you think you're doing? We're not in a fraternity, and this ain't no dorm room. If you don't clean that shit up in my living room, put the toilet seat down after making sure you flushed, and get a towel or ask for my ironing board to put under them jeans, I'm dropping your ass off at the Greyhound station. I don't give a fuck if it's your birthday or that I need your protection. You ain't coming in here, fucking my shit up."

He turned his music down and eyed me for a second. I don't know what he was thinking, but I knew what I was. The thought of having to use my brand-new Glock came to mind. He walked past me, headed to the hallway bathroom, and said, "My nigga Dre said you could be a bitch about dumb shit."

Seconds later, I heard the toilet flush and watched him start picking up his shit in the living room. I wasn't going to babysit him as he cleaned up until he continued to talk shit.

"It's my motherfucking birthday, and I want to go out tonight. It's already ten o'clock with your slow-driving ass. You don't even have furniture in this bitch, yet, and you acting like a nigga fucked your shit up. Keep talking shit, and I'm gon' leave yo' ass here while I go party tonight by myself."

Who did this drunken motherfucka think he was talking to? Angels must have been on his side because my cell phone started ringing before I could curse his ass out. It was Dre.

"Dre, you need to talk to your boy before I put his ass out tonight."

"What? What happened, baby?"

I told Dre what he did and said and included the bitch he had already managed to call me.

"Put that nigga on the phone."

Dre was hot, and I'm sure Mike was about to hear it. I handed him the phone and stood back. I wanted to hear what the bitch had to say now.

"Hello," he yelled into the phone. "My nigga, Dre. Huh? Naw. Man, it's my birthday, and little David and the rest of them niggas had brought me some drank and shit before we left . . ."

He got quiet for a while, then started laughing and shaking his head. "That's what I thought when I saw them niggas too. Ha-ha. Yep . . . Yep, but we straight up in here. Yo' gal got mad at me for fucking up her living room with all this nice-ass invisible furniture she got in it. I'm cleaning my shit up now, my nigga. You got you a handful you're about to marry, but she seems like she's cool. Her ass might be detoxing from that military shit your boy Ryan be on." He fell silent and then broke out in laughter. "Yeah, I won't fuck up all this expensive shit she has in here. Okay, okay . . . be easy."

Mike handed me back the phone and continued cleaning up his mess. I was pissed because their phone conversation sounded more like happy times than Dre checking his boy for disrespecting me.

"What!" I yelled into the phone at the sound of Dre saying my name.

"Ay, don't be saying 'what' to me like that. That nigga Mike is drunk. He ain't really like that. Let him enjoy his day, and tomorrow, you'll see how he really is. Stop getting mad and tripping. Where do you plan on taking him tonight?"

I didn't plan on taking his ass nowhere but the Greyhound station. It would be like Dre to want me to babysit his drunken-ass best friend. It's going to pain me to do it, but as his wife, I guess I have to.

"I didn't know I had to take him out until now. I don't know where we'll end up going, but I promise you it won't be nowhere far because he's fucked up, Dre. If we get out here, and he acts a fool, I'm leaving him."

There was a click, and then the phone hung up. I looked at the time on my phone. It read eleven o'clock. Dre's phones got cut off at ten, and he was an hour behind me.

"Be ready to go in thirty minutes, or we ain't going nowhere," I said, rolling my eyes at him before I headed to my room.

Thirty minutes later, he was sitting like an Indian on my living-room floor drinking out of his vodka bottle with a blunt full of weed behind both of his ears. I walked over to him, snatched one of his blunts, and smelled.

"Is this weed only?"

He looked at me like I were crazy, then said, "Hell yeah, that's weed only. That's my bitch Kesha in that blunt you holding. I don't smoke bullshit."

"I'll be the judge of that. Give me a lighter."

"Aw shit, I forgot you blew trees. That's how I met your thick ass, and I fucked around and sent you to Dre. That nigga owe me for that one. You could have been my girl."

He dug around in his pants pockets, then handed me his lighter. I fired it up and inhaled. It was Kesha, all right. I hit the blunt twice more, then handed it to him. We smoked the whole thing in silence, then left. I hadn't smoked since the night I had smoked with Dre over two months ago, and I was high. Saying I was high was candy-coating the truth. The truth was that I was floating on clouds. I decided that a club full of loud music and people was too much to deal with. I needed something more private. I needed somewhere I could sit down, have a drink or two, and relax. That's how we ended up in the VIP lounge at the strip club.

I still don't recall how I ended up in the men's bathroom, gap-legged on the sink rubbing my pussy all over Mike's face like a washrag while he licked my clit and stuck his tongue in and out of my hole or how we made it back to my apartment to fuck on the kitchen counter. What I did remember was he worked that dick good, and he was, hands down, the owner of the biggest dick I had ever encountered.

"You fucked up. This could have been your pussy," I whispered in his ear as we switched positions on the countertop to allow me to sit on it.

"It can still be my pussy. Fuck you mean? Don't it feel like your dick?"

"It feels like my dick right now."

"It can be your dick until that nigga gets out, and the way he lives his life, every time he goes back in that bitch."

"Sounds good."

"It is good. You feel that dick in you?"

I started grinding on it until I could feel him in my guts and then slid up to the head of it slowly before dropping down to repeat the action. After the fifth go-around, I jumped off of it, flipped my body, and sat my pussy in his mouth like Dre had mentioned earlier that day as I sucked my fluids off of him.

"Hell yeah, suck all of this dick like it's yours while I suck on this phat-ass pussy. Yeah, you my bitch now, and you gon' do what the fuck I tell you to do. Bust on my tongue, bitch."

His voice made me want to get nastier with him than I had ever been with anybody. It was rougher and heavier accented than Dre's, so when he said anything to me, my body shook. I wanted to show him why Dre had chosen me and make him jealous of what his best friend had for the rest of his life. Mike was fucking my high down, and whenever I noticed it, I grabbed my glass, took a swig, and made him light up another blunt. Those sober moments let the guilt of what I was doing come in, but it was already too late to stop. I let my high boost back up and then vowed after fucking him until my thighs and everything between them went numb that I'd never do it again.

I slept in all day Sunday, trying to avoid him and the awkwardness that would follow. Around five o'clock that evening, I heard him leave from the front door. I dashed to the kitchen and grabbed enough food to make it through the night before he made it back. I heard him come back at around eight o'clock. I wondered where he had gone but wasn't curious enough to find out. Around ten o'clock, I heard Mike knock on my bedroom door, but I pretended to be asleep.

"Hey, I went and grabbed you something to eat from the little spot down the street. It's in the microwave whenever you feel like getting up. I . . . um . . . came up with a little plan for the week too that I'd like to go over with you, and Dre called. He told me to tell you he . . ." Mike went silent like he was thinking of how to say it, "He told me to tell you he loved you, and he'd call you tomorrow or whatever."

He knocked on my door again about an hour later, but I still didn't respond. I held my breath until I heard him walk back to his room and close his door.

The next day I was dressed and left the house so silently that I'm sure when Mike woke up, he thought I was still there, asleep. Around lunchtime, I got a text from Ryan saying that Dre had been moved and that it might be a few days before I heard from him. That was fine with me. It gave more time to rub off the guilt of fucking his best friend. I sent a text back to thank him for the update on Dre.

Ryan had said that he didn't trust Mike and thought of him as a backstabber. All of a sudden, I felt the need to know why. I dialed Ryan's number because texting wasn't sufficient.

"Hey, Ryan, I'm sorry to bug you, but there was something that you said to me the other day that's been bothering me, and I need to know why you feel that way."

"What's up?" he asked puzzled.

"Your ringtone said the story, but then you confirmed it. I need to know why you think Mike is more of a foe than a friend."

"Man," he grunted, "I just do. It's more of an intuition than fact."

"You're lying, Ryan. I can hear it in your voice. I won't repeat it to Mike or Dre. I really want to know who I have living with me."

"Is something wrong, Savannah?"

There was a lot wrong already, but I wouldn't tell that to Ryan. I'd never tell anyone about what happened between Mike and me.

"No, I'm fine, I just need to know, Ryan. I don't get the same comfortable vibe that I got from you, and maybe if I knew more, I'd know how to treat this situation."

"Savannah, I really can't give details because I don't have all the facts. I wouldn't want my assumptions leaking out and fucking up my friendship with Dre."

"Fuck, Dre," I yelled out, but I had no clue where the anger came from. "Dre isn't here to protect me from him, and neither are you. I need to know your thoughts. I understand they aren't facts." I hit my desk with the pinky side of my closed fist, trying to release the frustration that was building. Ryan needed to tell me. "Please, tell me what your assumption is, or I'm going to decline any further protection from anyone. If it's my time to go, so be it."

I didn't mean a word of what I said. I wasn't just going to accept my possible death as an option. But I needed Ryan to feel where I was coming from.

"Okay, but this goes no further than this phone conversation. If it comes out, I'll deny it, and I *will* retaliate."

Ryan began telling me a story about Dre and his baby mama having issues a few years back. To make a long story short, Dre had asked Ryan to keep an eye on her while he was gone, but Mike had already beat him to the punch.

"So, you think Mike and her had been creeping, is that what you're saying?"

"It was too sloppy to be called creeping, but you get my gist. I never brought it up to Dre, but he started catching on, all on his own. He confronted Mike, who lied and denied it completely. I should have spoken up then, but Dre had taken the little shit he uncovered on his own hard. Even if he had proof of them fucking off behind his back, Dre loved Mike too much to believe it, and I loved my brother too much to force him to choose between Mike and me on who to believe about it."

Ryan still didn't give proof that Mike had slept with her, but he originally said he didn't have facts. There was still something in his voice that made me feel like he was holding back from me. "How do you know Mike wasn't telling Dre the truth?" I asked.

"I just do. But I have to go, Savannah, I'm at work."

He didn't say good bye. He just hung up. Something wasn't right about his story and left me feeling more lost than before I had asked my question. I made up my mind that I wouldn't be going straight home after work, but that I would continue to keep the schedule Ryan had me on with an extra hour or so at the gym. I wasn't sure of how long I'd be able to duck and dodge Mike, but I would try to keep it up as long as possible.

My plan to get away from him was cut short because Mike was waiting by my car, smoking a Black and Mild when I got off work. He didn't let me hit the unlock button on my doors before he started up.

"Look, Savannah, I know what we did the other–"

"Can you wait until we get in the car, please? Damn."

I didn't care that there wasn't anyone around us. There was a place for everything. If we were going to talk about our dirty deed, then we needed to discuss it in private. He waited until we were out of the parking lot and down the street before he continued.

"Like I was saying, I know what we did the other night was wrong, but hiding from me isn't gon' make the shit no better. I got a job to do, and I promised Dre I'd protect you. How do you think he'd feel if I failed him?"

"How would he feel if you failed him?" I repeated his question in case he didn't think before asking it. He nodded his head at me, so I corrected him. "You have *already* failed him—I mean, we have. How do you think Dre would feel about his closest friend in the world fucking his fiancée while he was paying him to protect her? Have you asked yourself *that?*"

Mike turned his head and looked out the passenger-side window. "Why would I think about it? He'll never know because my dick doesn't talk, and nor does your pussy. You wasn't planning on telling him, were you?"

"Of course not. Are you crazy? Dre would kill us both. I just wasn't sure if you felt obligated to. I mean, y'all are best friends and probably have some kind of pact against letting women come in between the two of you."

Mike still wasn't looking in my direction, but I was looking in his. He shook his head.

"Naw, I don't feel obligated to tell him shit. We're both grown, and we both wanted it, so it happened. You started talking about how you ain't had no dick, and I wanted some birthday pussy. When you grabbed my dick in the club, I assumed we were going to get down like a business arrangement or some shit. Even the way you said the shit sounded like some 'scratch my back and I'll scratch yours' shit. I just didn't think the pussy would be that good. I know what y'all got, and I won't step on my nigga's toes, but I enjoyed the hell out of fucking you. What I look like snitching on myself about the best pussy and head I've ever gotten to the owner of it, and who's to say it won't happen again?"

"*I* say it won't happen again."

"Why? I didn't mean to say it like that, but why wouldn't we do it again if we both enjoyed it?"

"Because it won't, and it can't. It doesn't matter if we enjoyed it."

"And why is that? I'm only asking, not disagreeing with you."

"Whatever. You just want to hear me say the shit. Okay, you win. We can't fuck again because if I do fuck you again, I'm leaving Dre to be your girl. That was some amazing shit, Mike, and nobody has ever done my body like that. However, I love Dre, and I can't let lust cause me to walk away from him."

"Yeah, I understand, and that's my nigga. Our friendship means everything to me. If he loves you like he said to me on the phone, that nigga might put you before our friendship." He turned and faced me with sincerity in his sexy-ass voice and said, "And you're right. That nigga is crazy. He would kill us both."

Chapter Eight

Stuck behind Enemy Lines

I wish I could go back in time and kick my own ass for sleeping with Mike last month. Although I have to admit I felt safe around the sober version of him, the inebriated one was something scary. Mike was fine as long as he only smoked weed. He stayed professional and kept his distance besides our mandatory outings to work, the range, and the gym. He even allowed me to go on mini "me outings," although he never let me out of his sight. He gave me space, and no one would know we'd arrived together unless they watched as we departed.

Mike drunk was a horse of a different color. He became a Gemini with his personality divided in two. This only happened when he had liquor in his system. He went from this quiet, all-business protector to this loud and obnoxious sex-crazed jerk. Whenever he had one too many, which one drink seemed to be too many, he wanted to bring up his birthday night. He'd tell me how sweet I tasted and how good I felt wrapped around him. Some nights, he'd pull his dick out and make it wave at me. Usually, I'd be able to get away from him by locking myself in my room, but that didn't work for me tonight. He picked the lock on my door as I slept, and I was awakened by him tugging on my panties, trying to get them off of me.

"Let me eat it, baby. Daddy misses you on his tongue."

I was half-asleep, but I knew this fool whose head was underneath my covers was *not* daddy.

"Move, Mike. I told you we weren't doing that ever again. This is your best friend's pussy, remember him? His name is Dre."

Even with mentioning Dre, Mike didn't let go of my panties. I could feel them ripping away from the pressure of rubbing against my hips.

"That's the same shit Tasha said until this dick put her ass to sleep. Stop acting like you don't want it. Y'all hoes dream about being fucked by friends. I'm just trying to grant your wish."

There went the truth behind Ryan's assumption, and so went my panties. "I'm not Tasha. That's his baby mama. I'm his *wife*."

"That's not Dre's son or his baby mama," he screamed at me like those words made him upset, "and you ain't his wife yet, bitch!"

He got more aggressive in his attack and locked his hands around my throat. I couldn't breathe. I tried to get out of the grip he had on my neck, but I couldn't.

"You don't have to be scared, pretty bitch. I'm not going to rape you. I just want you to suck this dick and give up the pussy willingly. Can you do that?" he asked, tightening his grip with his left hand as he freed his hardened dick with the right. Using the tight hold he had on my neck to control my movements, he brought my face to his midsection, and then without using his hand, made his dick touch my bottom lip. I had a decision to make, which was to pass out and potentially get raped or suck his dick and be raped consensually.

Thanks to Ryan's self-defense lessons, I didn't have to choose either. I kicked my legs around wildly, which caught him by surprise, and he released his grip. As he stumbled back, my wild kick landed dead in the center of his face. He staggered backward away from my bed, and I was able to get up. Before he could regain his footing and take another step my way, I reached under my mattress and pointed my gun at him. He didn't hesitate to step back.

"Listen to me, Mike, and listen well. You need to go and pack you an overnight bag and find somewhere to sleep this shit off. You've seen me at the shooting range, and you know that at this distance, I can turn your drunken ass into a slice of Swiss cheese. There will be no more drinking of any kind the rest of your stay here, or you will deal with me and Savannah's Bitch or Dre about Andre Jr. and the shit you pulled here tonight. You understand?"

It was the first time in a month that I really got to look at him. When he had his mouth closed, he was more average-looking than I had noticed. There wasn't anything about him that stuck out or demanded your attention. He had the normal dark brown eyes that looked black, an average-sized nose, and medium-sized lips that didn't look kissable from all of the weed residue stored on them. His haircut was low with a line, and his style of dress was more uniformed than flashy. Even his height said average as he stood in front of me at five foot ten. What I did notice about him, looking past the fear he had on his face, were tracks of weakness. He looked unhappy and displeased with himself. That might have been why he acted out like he did. You see it more commonly in small children when they consistently get in trouble in search of attention. It was rare to see it in adults, but it happens.

I don't know if it was my words or the fact that I had a loaded gun pointed at him, but Mike did exactly as I had said. He skipped packing a bag and headed straight out the front door. Still holding my Glock, I went to chain and lock the door behind him. He didn't have a key to get in, so I wasn't worried about him returning, but there was no way I'd be just lying around here after that. I needed to talk to somebody or do something to get my mind off what had just happened. I couldn't call Ryan and tell him about what happened because, unlike Mike, he felt like he had an obligation to Dre. If I told Ryan, he'd be sure to make Dre aware of it. My supposed best friend Will wasn't talking to me for whatever reason that helped him to sleep better at night, and my other friend Sandy had been keeping her distance from me ever since she heard about what I did to those people in California. I had Stephanie to thank for telling her that, and for the first time in years, I didn't have Stephanie to run to either. Not knowing what else to do with myself, I dressed and went to the gym. It stayed open 24 hours, and I could work on some of the self-defense moves Ryan had taught me since I didn't use them when I was under attack.

For two o'clock in the morning, the gym was somewhat full. I managed to find an empty yoga room to stretch and work on my self-defense moves. I had worked up a sweat, but I still didn't feel confident that I'd use any of the moves I had been practicing if I were attacked again. Then an arm encircled my neck. Without thinking, I stepped to the side, elbowed my attacker in the gut, and then flipped him while twisting his arm as he landed on his back. When I went to put my foot into his neck, that's when I realized it was Amir I was putting the hurting on.

"Don't kill me, Savannah," he screamed in horror.

At the sight of him curled up on the floor with his eyes closed, anticipating my next hit, I didn't know if I should laugh or feel bad. I reached my hand out to help him up.

"Don't run up on me like that, Amir. I could have killed you."

The words felt good coming out of my mouth. Scary-ass Savannah James now had the power to hurt somebody.

"I'm *sorry*. I wanted to surprise you. When did you turn into Wonder Woman?"

We both laughed as he made it to his feet.

"I'm not Wonder Woman. I'm just learning to protect myself from people like you who like to run up on people when they're not paying attention." I pretended to punch him in his stomach, and he acted as if he were hurt.

"I'm going to my car to smoke after that beat down," he said, walking ahead of me. "I'll see you around, Savannah."

"Hey," I yelled after him. "Are you sharing?"

He nodded his head, and I followed him out of the gym. We smoked and talked for about an hour before he invited me back to his house for an early breakfast. Food never made it to my mouth, but he managed to eat me, that is. It was my fault because I initiated it by rubbing on his dick until it rose on the ride to his house. I was stressed, and the weed wasn't enough relief for me. I needed to relax the best way I knew how, and that was by having sex with him or Dre. Dre wasn't an option right now, and if he hadn't been in jail, I wouldn't be stressing. I needed instant gratification, and a workout in bed with Amir always worked. Once I got him standing at attention, I reminded him of the rules.

"Sex *only*, right, Amir?"

I could feel his pulse speed up through the throbbing in his jeans.

"No, *great* sex only, baby," he corrected.

We were tongue-tied and touching every part of each other's bodies before we made it into his driveway. I didn't want to kill the mood with obvious questions, but I noticed Amir had moved out of his apartment and into a new house.

The only question I managed to ask was, "Do you still have a roommate?"

He shook his head as we pulled into his two-car garage. I walked across the front of his car to meet him at the garage's entrance to the house, but we never made it to the door. He ate his breakfast right there on the hood of his all-black Benz. The heat from the engine had the hood hot, but the noninsulated garage's cold air made it nice and warm. When the pleasure ended from his mouth, he put on a rubber and pleasured me with his rock hardness. I was fully naked, and he had stripped down to nothing but his tube socks and gym shoes as he joined me on the hood of his car. When the metal became too much for his knees, he carried me in the house and laid me on his king-sized bed. I woke up around ten o'clock in the morning to the aroma of cooked food.

"For you, my love," he said as he handed me a tray of food.

There was a plate-length omelet with chicken, mushrooms, onions, bell pepper, tomatoes, and cheese stuffed into it. Next to it was a slice of cantaloupe, three strawberries, and a handful of grapes. He had even made me a glass of freshly squeezed orange juice and added a slice of the orange on the side of the glass for presentation. I was impressed, but only a little. Amir was a chef at his family's restaurant. He prepared meals like this daily. After I was settled with my food and eating, he sat at the foot of the bed and began massaging my feet while I ate.

"When did you move here?" I asked in between bites to break the silence.

"Almost a year ago. When I took over the restaurant for my parents, I thought it was time to get settled here."

I was impressed, to say the least, as he took me on a tour of his three-bedroom, two-and-a-half-bath house. Amir had upgraded a lot in the last five years and even had framed articles from the newspaper about the success of his restaurant. I showered and dressed. Then he drove me back to the gym so I could get my car. I promised if I freed up later, I'd give him a call so I could return.

It was Sunday around noon, and there wasn't much to do, so I went and sat by the fountain at Centennial Park. It was a nice day out, a little chilly, but still nice. It was the perfect day just to sit, clear my mind, and enjoy the scenery. There was a couple, hand in hand, sitting on the bench across from mine. They were staring into each other's eyes deeply. I could tell they were in love because they wore their feelings on their faces. Even if they tried, they wouldn't have been able to hide their love for each other. I had never shared a moment like that or those deep feelings with anyone but Dre. They must've thought I was crazy by the way I stared at them, but if they could've read my mind, they would have understood.

Mentally, I had turned the man's face into Dre's and envisioned myself as the woman. We were sitting there, enjoying each other, confessing our love and planning out our future together. The more that I stared at the couple, the stronger the cravings became of getting my happily ever after with Dre. It was time to be honest with myself and admit that the only thing that was stopping me from having what the couple in front of me had . . . was me. It wasn't Dre being in jail, nor was it the way I was raised. It was the decisions I allowed myself to make. I hadn't learned shit from Mama taking my money and Dre away from me. I kept fucking up, and this time, I really needed to right my wrongs without being forced to. I wouldn't tell Dre that I had slept with Mike or Amir. I'd clean up my mess without a confession like I did with Royce. It was going to be hard to go another four months without dick, but I had Stephanie's basket, and I would have to learn how to satisfy myself. I was proficient with a gun now, so Mike's ass could go back to Nashville, and I had left Amir with an understanding that it was just sex this time. I could cut him off like I had before.

The thoughts going through my mind had lifted my spirits, and I was ready for the new start my mama told me I was paying for. I walked up to the couple and thanked them without giving a reason. Then I pulled out my cell phone.

"Hello, is this Mama Dee?"

I called Dre's mama and had a civil conversation with her that lasted an hour. I made arrangements to come to her house for dinner Saturday night so that I could meet her face-to-face. She was thrilled, and we ended up laughing as we said our goodbyes. My next phone call was to Ryan. I told him I'd be driving to Nashville this weekend to spend some time with Dre's mother. I said we needed to talk face-to-face Sunday. I decided that I would tell him what happened between Mike and me. I wouldn't tell him about us having sex but the person Mike became once he drank. He agreed to meet me, and I moved on to my next call.

In Washington, it was nine o'clock in the morning, and I was sure everyone was getting ready to go to the eleven o'clock service, but I needed to hear my family's voices. I spoke with Sade first, then Mr. Jefferson for an update on my father.

"Your daddy is holding up fine. He hasn't had a thing to drink since that day, and he even has a lady friend he's been hanging out with from the church. Now, don't go telling Mrs. Jefferson on me, but she's a good-looking woman. Nice and round, and she always smells like candy. So far, she's keeping your daddy smiling, and that's just what he needs."

I was happy to hear it and told him to send my daddy and Memphis my love. I'd call them when I thought they were out of church. I had one more call to make, and I knew I would get his voicemail, but that's exactly what I wanted.

"Hey, Will, it's me, Savannah. I've been trying hard to figure out what it is that I've done to you that would make you not return my calls and stop protecting me, but I've figured it out. I've been one-sided in our friendship, wanting you to give your all into it and not returning the same. I should have been there for you when you told me you and Alvin had broken up. Instead, I wanted you to be there for me as I continued to fuck up. I apologize for mistreating our friendship. I love you, and I'm here for you whenever you forgive me. Please call me when you do. Bye."

Leaving Will that message had me choked up, but it felt good to apologize to him, regardless of whether he'd accept it. If I could just hear Dre's voice, my day would be complete.

Amir called my phone the rest of the day, and I sent him to voicemail every time. When I made it home, I lay across my living-room couch and watched gospel on BET. I wasn't religious, but I knew I needed to build a relationship with the Lord. My future husband went to church twice a week, and so did the rest of our family. I wouldn't continue to be an outsider to the Lord or miss out on blessings.

Around ten o'clock that night, Mike came knocking on the door. I let him in, and he was ready to talk, but I turned down the conversation invitation by going to bed.

My week was going great. Dre had called me from his cell phone on Monday. He told me how much he loved me, missed me, and was proud of me for trying to get to know his mother. He gave me his cell phone number but told me to send a text; then he would call me back, just in case the guards were around. Tuesday was an even better day because one of the deals I had been working on for the past month went through, and the partners gave me companywide recognition. I knew it was eating

Stephanie's ass up. Every time I reread the email, I tried to picture her reaction to it. Besides Amir calling my phone all day and night, my week couldn't have gotten any better. Then along came Wednesday. I woke up to a private number calling my phone. I normally don't answer blocked numbers, but I wasn't sure if it was Dre.

"Hello?" I said in my morning voice.

"Is this Savannah?" a woman's voice asked.

"Yes, this is Savannah. . . . Hello, hello?"

The caller hung up but called back a few hours later, while I was at work.

"Hello?" I repeated the greeting from earlier.

"Watch your back, bitch. I'm coming for you."

Before I could say anything else, the caller hung up but continued to call me all day. After being hung up on twice, I stopped answering the calls. I was going to tell Mike about the calls when I got off of work, but I decided to wait until Sunday and tell Ryan instead. I focused back on work. Then lobby security notified me that I had a visitor at the front desk fifteen minutes before the end of my shift. It was Amir, holding what must have been three or four dozen roses.

"Amir, what are you doing here? I'm working." I tried to whisper it because the security guards were staring dead at us, trying to listen in on our conversation.

"Why haven't you returned any of my calls? I call day and night, and you don't answer. Are you mad at me?"

"No, Amir, I'm not mad at you, but remember what we talked about. . . ." I leaned my face closer to his ear. "It was sex only. If and when I want more, *I'll* call *you*. Never come to my job again. Do you understand me?"

"Yes, I understand you, Savannah, but I need sex too. I want to sex you and cook for you. Let me massage you and make the tension go away, baby—"

"No." I had said it louder than I meant to, which caused the security to listen in even harder.

"Amir, you need to leave. I will call you when I get a chance. Bye."

I was ready to walk away when he asked, "Can you please take the flowers I brought you, at least? They're for you."

I grabbed the flowers and headed back to my office. It didn't surprise me to look back and see Amir still standing there watching me walk off. I sat at my desk for another ten minutes to give him some time to leave. After I was sure he was gone, I grabbed my flowers and headed out the door to meet Mike in the parking lot. As we swapped seats, and I waited for him to get in the passenger side, Amir was parked directly behind us, watching the entire time. I drove off without giving him any extra attention.

Amir blew up my phone from the time I pulled out of the parking lot at work to the time I made it home. I had to set his calls to go straight to voicemail. When I walked into the house, I threw the roses on the kitchen counter and went to use the restroom. Mike's voice greeted me as I walked out of my bedroom.

"To Savannah, the only woman I've ever loved, and the only woman I will ever love. You own my heart and my dick. They are both yours forever. I love you baby. Amir."

Mike was holding the card that came in the flowers in one hand and tossing the flowers in the trash with the other.

"Does Dre know about your 'one true love, Amir'? You think I'm gon' sit here and let you play my boy?"

"Mike, you have no idea what you're talking about. I'm not playing 'your boy.' This is an old stalker from way before Dre and I met. Apparently, he's starting back up."

Mike held the card in front of his face like he was reading it again because he felt he missed something. Then he looked at me and said, "Bitch, please."

He walked past me and went into the guest room, closing the door behind him. I wondered if he would tell Dre, or if I should beat him to the punch and tell Dre myself.

The phone calls from Amir and the blocked number poured in all day Thursday, and so did the rain. It seemed as the rain came down harder, the worse the bullshit got. I checked my voicemail because the indicator light kept blinking, which meant my mailbox was full. Thirteen out of the fifteen messages were from Amir. He sounded like a lunatic with all his confessions of love, future plans, including children, and threats to kill my boyfriend, which I guess he was assuming was Mike. I wouldn't correct him or stop him from getting Mike if that's what he really wanted. That would be getting rid of two headaches at the price of one. The other two messages were from the woman with the blocked number. I was sure it was Melinda calling and threatening me, but Stephanie could have put somebody up to do it on her behalf. One of the messages was just her laughing, but the other was more informative.

"Why aren't you answering my phone calls, Savannah? I want to play with you. Don't you like playing games with people? I'm coming to Atlanta for you, Savannah, and we will play a game that I think you're going to love because you play it a lot. It's called 'Revenge,' bitch, and I'm coming to get mine, so watch your back. Don't you wish Dre were there to protect you?"

How did she know Dre wasn't here to protect me? I didn't tell my job I was moving back because he went to jail, so Stephanie couldn't have known. That worried me, because if it were Melinda, how would she have known of Dre, period? It wasn't public information that I was dating or engaged. This shit was stressing me out. I needed a break from all the bullshit, and I couldn't wait for Friday so I could drop Mike's ass off in Nashville and spend some time with my in-laws. I couldn't get the thought of meeting Dre's mother out of my mind. I decided to finish up my work today and take Friday off to get my hair and nails done before meeting her. It would also put me under Ryan's protection so that I could feel safe.

I looked up salons in Nashville and made a three o'clock appointment for a full sew-in at one with high ratings. Afterward, I set up my auto response on my office phone and email, letting those who tried to make contact with me know I'd be out of the office until Monday. Then I headed out the door to meet Mike. My car wasn't parked in the parking lot, nor was he anywhere to be found. I waited thirty minutes and called his phone over twenty times, but it went straight to voicemail. After another thirty minutes passed, so I called a cab to get home.

When I walked in, my house was a mess. Empty Chinese food cartons covered my coffee table in the living room, pizza boxes and empty vodka bottles covered my kitchen counter, and the whole house smelled of weed and Black and Mild smoke. I charged into the guest room, but Mike wasn't there. All of his belongings were still in the house, but he was physically missing. I looked out of his room and noticed the bathroom light was on from the space at the bottom of the door, but before I could make it in there, my bedroom caught my attention. I could hear the sound of my headboard hitting the wall repeatedly and soft moans. As I approached the door, it was cracked enough to where I could peek in. Not only was Mike in *my* room, but he was also stark naked lying across my bed with a white bitch straddled across his face and another one riding his dick as he used his phone to record it. If he hadn't been lying on top of it, I would have gone for my gun and cleared my house out, but instead, I went back to the living-room closet and grabbed one of my old crutches.

Then I kicked the door open in the room and started swinging and screaming, "Get the fuck out! Get your nasty asses out of my fucking house!"

My crutch had connected with the side of the girl's face that had been riding Mike's dick. She fell over like a domino while the other jumped off his face and grabbed her clothes, begging not to receive the same fate. As the women scattered to get dressed and exit my house, I noticed Mike didn't make a move. He didn't even attempt to cover his naked body. He grabbed his half-smoked blunt out of the ashtray he had sitting on my nightstand, lit it up, and smoked it like he was a king. When I heard my front door slam behind Mike's sluts, I started in on him.

"Who the fuck do you think you are, motherfucker? You bring two unknown hoes in my house and have the nerve to fuck them in *my* bed. Get your nasty ass up!"

He just looked at me like I hadn't said a word and continued to smoke. I cocked the crutch back to get in the position to swing, so he'd know I meant business. That seemed to get some of his attention. He at least spoke up.

"They were twins," he smiled, then continued, "and I'm already up. Don't you see how hard my dick is? I had a little talk with your friend Amir today, man to man, and he told me about you. Why don't you give me a sample of that throat? From what Amir said, you don't gag, and I think I'm going to need it if you don't want me telling Dre how you got dog-fucked last weekend on Amir's car."

He put the blunt back in the ashtray, closed his eyes, put his right hand behind his head, and held his dick out with the left. I took a deep breath, pulled all my strength together, and swung the crutch as hard as I could, making sure to not only hit his dick but to connect with his balls too. I repeated the swing until I had connected with every part of his body I could reach as he ran for protection.

"Bitch, I'm gon' kill you!" he yelled out in pain as he held his dick, which was now covered in blood. He grabbed his T-shirt off the floor, wrapped it around his dick, and then charged at me. Thanks again to Ryan's training, in two quick moves, I had him lying on his back with a possible injury to his spine. As he lay there screaming in agony, I made it to the side of the mattress that stored my gun again and aimed it at him.

"Get out. Get the fuck out of my house now, Mike. I don't give a fuck about you being hurt or naked. You need to go. You can tell Dre about me and Amir. I don't think he'll give a fuck, especially after I tell him he will have to get a DNA test for his son and how you raped me."

"Ain't nobody rape you, ho. You gave it up."

"It's your word against mine, *bitch!*" I spat at him. "And after he finds out you've been lying to him for all these years by fucking his baby mama, I'm sure he will believe me over you."

I took a few steps nearer to him, and he scooted backward on his naked ass into the hallway as I continued.

"Mike, I'll give you two options. You can keep your mouth shut about the little shit between Amir and me, and I'll do the same with the shit between you and Tasha. I'll let you get your shit and get dressed, and you can leave here in a taxi to the Greyhound station and head back to Nashville like you left because we both feel I'm now capable of protecting myself. Or there's Option Two. I can call Dre before your naked ass makes it to the elevators and tell him how you stuck your dick in me trying to rape me and how I had to fight you off. I can tell him how you bragged about fucking Tasha and that his son really is yours. Then I can call the police and have them come out and take a report and hint that they need to check the contents of those other two bags that you thought I didn't know were full of weed. Yes, I know everything. And you thought you were slick trying to sell them while I was at work. There's a lot about the night we fucked that I try to block out of my mind, but I'd never forget you opening the wrong bag in search of your condoms and seeing just how dirty you really were. I watched those bags get lighter and lighter every week. So, which option is it?"

He held his index finger up to indicate he was choosing Option One. I wasn't dumb, so I left him in the hall and removed his bags out of the room, minus the two guns he had brought with him. I'd drive them back to Nashville myself and have Ryan give them to him. He wasn't going to shoot and kill me. Next, I went to my linen closet and threw him a washcloth. I told him to freshen up before the cab arrived. When he was dressed and ready to go, I locked the door behind him and started cleaning my apartment. When the sheets were in the dryer, I packed my bags for Nashville, showered, then hit the road around eight o'clock that night. If Mike returned, he'd have no idea of my location.

I slept in until my hair appointment, and when it was over, I went to the nail shop and had my nails, eyebrows, and lashes done all in one place. I wasn't tired, but I assumed Mike was back in town by now, and I didn't want to make the mistake of running into him. I went back to my hotel and hung out by the bar until I was ready to go to bed. It dawned on me as I ordered room service the next morning that I hadn't heard from Dre since early in the week, so I sent him a text. The message came back, saying, Undeliverable.

Not understanding why it couldn't be delivered, I sent a text to Ryan, who immediately called instead of texting back. "Why didn't you tell me you were on your way down here? Did Mike at least ride here with you?"

"Umm, Mike is what I need to talk to you about. I know I said Sunday, but if—"

"Where are you? I'm on my way."

He didn't let me finish my sentence, but I guess he heard it in my voice. Less than an hour later, he was knocking at my hotel room's door.

I didn't tell Ryan everything that happened from the time Mike moved in. I only told him enough. I made sure to leave out the part where we had sex and Mike's confession of being Andre Jr.'s dad. I wasn't sure if or when Dre should have to hear it. Dre has been Junior's father for the last seven years. I can't imagine what knowing that information would do to him, but I told Ryan everything else.

"This is exactly the reason I didn't want him near you."

"You knew he was into raping women?"

"No, I knew he couldn't be trusted, and that part I did voice to Dre many times. I didn't care how big or small the task Dre was putting him on. I didn't trust what he'd do while he was on it. Is there anything else I need to know?"

I fought with my better judgment for a few seconds, and when I shook my head to give my nonverbal no, my mouth said, "Yes, you're right not to trust him. When he was trying to convince me why I should sleep with him, he confessed to sleeping with Tasha and . . ."

"And what, Savannah?"

I couldn't get the rest of the words out of my mouth. They didn't have shit to do with me, but thinking of being the person who held the information that would break Dre's heart was a title and job I didn't want.

"Savannah, I need you to tell me *everything*. Do you trust me?"

"Yes, I trust you . . . to a point, but you're Dre's boy."

"What are you saying?" he questioned like he didn't understand what I was talking about.

"I'm saying, you knew Mike wasn't to be trusted around me for all those months, and I know you voiced that to Dre because you don't seem like the type to bite your tongue. Yet, he still sent him to protect me supposedly, and if it weren't for the self-defense training you put me through, I could have been raped . . . or even dead. Dre's confidence in the wrong person could have cost me my life. How am I supposed to feel about anyone else he invites into my situation?"

"You're right to feel how you feel, and he is my boy, but more like my brother than a friend. I know you are scared and don't know who you can trust, but I need you to trust me. If I don't know the truth about anything else, I do know he loves you and wants you protected, even from him and his spurts of anger. As his brother, I'm promising right now to keep you safe and protected from everything and everybody. Do you hear me?"

"Yes, I hear you but—"

"No buts. I need you to believe that as long as I know you have my brother's heart, I'm going to keep you protected. That protection includes protection from him and his bad decisions. You should have never been left alone with Mike."

The truth of his words was in his eyes. They were filled with concern, hurt, anger, and slight fear. I believed him.

"Ryan, Andre Jr. is Mike's son, and the way he said it to me sounds like Tasha knows it. He let it come out of his mouth like he didn't care about Dre at all."

"Damn, I already knew he fucked that ho, Tasha. I caught those two leaving motels a few times and watched him pull up to Dre's place and not leave to almost sunrise, adjusting his clothes. He has to die for this shit. Seven years of letting my brother believe that's his son and almost raping you, I have to let Dre know what's been going on." Ryan jumped out of the chair he was sitting in and pulled out his cell phone.

I had to stop him.

"No, Ryan. Please don't. I need this to stay between you and me for now. You have your reasons for not telling Dre about Mike and Tasha, and I have mine. Please don't call him. That's a face-to-face conversation to have when he's free. And I think they caught him with his cell phone because I tried to text him the other day, and it wouldn't go through."

"He changed his number. Are you sure you don't want Dre to know about this? Because I think it's time he knows that Mike ain't his friend."

My mind didn't accept anything that came out of Ryan's mouth once I heard him say Dre had changed his number. Why didn't he call and tell me it changed, but he made sure to update Ryan?

"Savannah, is there anything else I should know?"

As he spoke, he searched my face as if I had hidden stories I hadn't shared with him on it. I thought about his question, then pulled out my phone and played him the threatening voice messages I'd been getting.

"That's it. I'm coming back to Atlanta with you. Stay here while I make my arrangements at work. Then I'll be back to get you for dinner with Mama Dee." Ryan left the room before I could protest.

When we made it to Mama Dee's, I knew my week had gone from bad to worse because we were given entrance to her house by none other than Tasha, Dre's ghetto-ass baby mama, or at least that's her claim to fame. From our first encounter, I knew the bitch and I would be exchanging words before we would make it to dessert. I hoped I wouldn't have to beat this ho's ass in my mother-in-law's house.

Part Three

Dre

Chapter Nine

Tired of All the Games

I don't know what the fuck was up with my mama lately, but she was tripping. First, she gave my baby mama Tasha my cell phone number. She knew Tasha had snitched on me once. Why she thought she wouldn't do it again, I don't know.

Tasha had called my phone three times from three different numbers in less than ten minutes, and she found a way to leave me five voice messages. I was in the meal hall eating and couldn't answer. When I called back, some stuttering nigga answered the phone, then handed it to her.

"Why you ain't been answering my calls when I call from my cell phone, Dre?"

"Cuz I'm in jail and don't have your cell phone number. How was I supposed to know it was you?" Tasha always asked dumb-ass questions, and when I threw a question back at her, she never had an answer worth listening to.

"Uh-huh. I saw Mama Dee at the football game Saturday, and she told me you were getting married. Why I gotta be the last to know that my baby daddy is getting married? I thought your lying ass said marriage wasn't for you. Why are you always lying to me, Dre?"

I didn't understand the purpose of this conversation. She had given up custody of my son to my mama, and she had moved on with her life. She was pregnant by some weak-ass nigga that sold CDs and DVDs that he illegally burned in front of the liquor store. I went to school with the nigga. He was a ho then, and he was a ho now. If she were supposedly happy, why did I have to give her an update? Instead of hanging up on her and having her blow my phone up all night, I answered her question the best I could.

"I don't know why I didn't tell you, Tasha. Yes, I'm getting married, and I guess she changed my mind on marriage."

"Who is this bitch, Dre? I don't want none of your hoes around my son. I'll cut that bitch, and you know I will. And how you gon' marry somebody when you still in love with me, nigga? You're just going around saying that shit because you mad you found out I was pregnant. You don't gotta be jealous. If you wanted a bitch back, that's all you had to say."

This is exactly why I thought Tasha's ass was crazy. How do I getting married to somebody else mean that I wanted her back? If I wanted her back, wouldn't proposing to her be the way I should show it? This stupid shit was getting on my nerves.

"What's up, Tasha? Why are you calling me with all this bullshit? We don't have shit to talk about. My mama has Andre Jr., and we both have moved on. I ain't got time for this dumb shit."

"If I was that other bitch, you would," she yelled into the phone.

For the first time in a long time, I had to agree with her.

"Yep, you right." I hung up the phone, then called Sprint and changed my number.

I was pissed at my mama for giving her my number, so I didn't call her for a few days, and when I did, she told me of the second mistake she made. She slipped and told Tasha she was meeting Savannah for the first time when

Tasha came to visit Junior. She said Tasha had found a reason to linger over there all day and that's when she and Savannah met, and they had it out—badly.

"I don't know which one of them started it, Dre. I could hear them cussing each other out from the kitchen. Tasha was in her bitch-this-and-bitch-that mode, and Savannah was yelling them right back, which really shocked me, but all I know is when I walked back in the dining room from getting the rolls out of the oven, food and dishes were being thrown across the room. Ryan was able to get Savannah and leave, so I don't know if she was hurt, but Tasha had to get stitches in her cheek from Savannah tossing a steak knife at her. Did I tell you I'm starting to like that Savannah more and more, baby?"

"What do you mean you don't know if Savannah was hurt or not? You didn't call and check on her? And where was my son when all of this was happening?"

She started rambling about Ryan, saying he'd handle it and giving one excuse after another on why she hadn't checked on Savannah.

"She's so uppity, and I don't know how to come at her, Dre. I mean, I'm warming up to her, but she's kinda too bourgeois with the proper etiquette stuff and all. Well, until you make her mad, which seems kinda easy to do because she had Tasha soaking in gravy. Savannah really doesn't seem like your—"

"Mama Dee," I said, cutting her rambling off, "where was my son at when his mama and my fiancée started fighting?"

"He was at the table when it first started, but Ryan scooped him up and took him to his room before the fight broke out. By the time Ryan had him situated and came back, he had to help me break it up. I mean, all my good dishes and glasses are all broken up."

I told my mama I had to talk to her later because I needed to call Ryan and then check on Savannah. I called Ryan, and his phone went straight to voicemail. That wasn't like him not to answer, so I called him again. The phone rang several times, but he didn't answer. He called me back an hour later.

"What's up, Dre? I was at the range with Savannah and didn't hear my phone ringing."

What the fuck was he doing at the range with Savannah on a Wednesday? He never mentioned he was going back down to Georgia to check on her when we talked Friday. Something wasn't adding up.

"You didn't hear your phone ringing? The first time I called, it went to voicemail, like you sent me to voicemail." I knew I sounded like I was accusing him, but if he were innocent, he wouldn't respond like he was guilty.

"My service fades in and out here. What's up? I know you counting down now. What you got left in there, about two weeks?"

"One week and six days, but you supposed to keep that on the low. I don't want Savannah knowing I'm getting out. I thought I told you that. What are you doing in Atlanta anyway? Mike is supposed to be watching her until I get out."

"Mike, you know how he be doing his thing and stuff. Busy working and not working." He mumbled around in search of words. The only thing he managed to say clearly was, "Savannah isn't around me at the moment. I mean, we both are at the gun range, but you know how they separate the shooters, so we won't accidentally shoot each other."

Ryan has never had a problem with talking. I didn't know what was going on, but I was going to get to the bottom of it.

"Aye, Ryan, let me call you right back. My bunkie need to call his lawyer before he leaves for the day."

I hung up the phone and called Savannah. She was cussing me out before I could get a word out.

"So, now you want to remember you're engaged. You changed your fucking number, didn't give it to me, then call me over a week later like the shit is okay. Did you hear about your ghetto, blue-hair-having-ass baby mama pouring brown gravy all over me at your mama's house? Ryan wouldn't let me get to that bitch, but I'm sure my steak knife did. Why would your mama invite her over while I was there? That was messy as fuck of your mama. Just when I tried to give her project ass a chance, she pulls some shit like that on me, and I know she did the shit on purpose because she hasn't tried to call me yet. I'm done trying to get to know your mama's sorry—"

"Aye, don't say shit else about Mama, Savannah! Watch your motherfucking mouth when it comes to that one right there." I knew she was mad, and she had every reason to be, but I couldn't sit back and let her go in on my mama. That was still my mama.

"Oh, I forgot, you's a mama's boy. A big country, project-descending mama's boy," she snapped back at me, mad as hell.

"I don't have nothing to do with being a mama's boy. It's about respect."

"Why are you always getting on me about respect, Dre, when nobody you have around me or want me to meet is showing me none?"

"What do you mean by nobody around you? Where the fuck is Mike, and why is Ryan there with you?" I didn't know what else to say to get her to change the subject, but that seemed to work.

"Mike had to . . . Well, Mike went back to Nashville because he felt I was able to protect myself now. Ryan came back because he . . . He wanted to teach me some other self-defense stuff that he didn't have time to show me before he left. I thought you would prefer me being around Ryan because he trained you. I just want to be trained by the best, that's all."

She was lying, and I could hear it in her voice. She went from mad to nerves too fast, and although I do think she is a little bipolar, her mood shifted too quickly. If this bitch was fucking Ryan, I'd kill them both. Instead of letting her know what I really thought, I pretended to believe the story and go along with it.

"Aw, is that right? So, Ryan is teaching you some new stuff? Sounds good to me. Are you okay, though? You didn't get hurt or anything at my mama's house, did you?"

I really didn't give a fuck at that moment if she was hurt or not. Something didn't feel right, but I didn't know what it was yet. I stayed on the phone with her for another five minutes listening to her side of what had happened between her and Tasha.

"I'm okay, but that girl is crazy. Why would your mama let her be there when we were meeting for the first time? It should have been about getting to know me and letting me spend time with your son alone."

"You're right, baby, and I'm going to call and check my mama on that."

When I couldn't take any more of her whining, I told her I had promised my bunkie I'd let him call his family tonight, but that I'd call her back tomorrow.

If I wanted to know the truth, I knew where I'd have to get it. I called Mike, but he didn't answer. I'd expected him not to. He didn't know my number, and with the little bit of drugs he pushed, he wasn't answering numbers he wasn't familiar with, so I left him a message. It took a whole week for him to call me back. At first, he seemed uninterested in talking to me. Then I asked why he had left Savannah alone in Atlanta.

"Man, homie, all I'm going to say is that bitch ain't the right one for you, and that's coming to you from my heart. I know you were going to pay me but keep your money. I couldn't babysit that ho. She didn't deserve the protection."

That wasn't like Mike to turn down money. I offered him $50,000 to protect Savannah until I touched down. That's more than he has ever seen at one time in his life. He was going to have to tell me what was really up.

"Come on, Mike. You of all people know me better than that. We've been down for too long for you to be biting your tongue. Tell me what I need to know about my bitch."

"Man . . ." he held the ending sound of the word so long that it turned into a hum. "Your girl is a ho. I found out she was fucking some Jamaican nigga down there named Amir. Dude said they had been off and on for some years. She would dip off before I'd make it to her job to pick her up after work, and she'd stay gone overnight. After a while, she stopped hiding the shit and even came home with roses the nigga brought her. I couldn't sit there and let that bitch play you like that, my nigga, so I packed my shit and jumped on the Greyhound to Nashville. I promised the bitch I wouldn't tell you shit, but you know you my boy, and I can't hide shit from you."

Something about Mike's words sounded practiced, but this was my best friend, and he wouldn't lie to me.

"It went down like that?"

"Look, I got the nigga telephone number. Why don't you call and talk to him so when you confront that ho, you ain't gotta mention me at all? I don't owe her ass shit, but she's a cutthroat bitch, and she knows I push a little weight. I ain't trying to go to jail because she's mad at you."

"Damn," was all I could say. I wrote down dude's number so I could call him next, but I had to ask one more question before I hung up the phone with Mike.

"Do you think something is going on between Ryan and Savannah?"

There was no hesitation in his answer, and he seemed positive that what he was saying was true.

"If they ain't fucked yet, they're about to. That bitch has him brainwashed and wrapped around her finger. I told you I ain't never trusted the nigga."

The shit was finally making sense to me. My mama said Ryan was quick to snatch Savannah up and leave, saying he had her. When I called Ryan, he was mumbling and shit about why he was back in Atlanta with Savannah, and when I asked her about it, she lied and came up with some self-defense training shit. If she really had been playing me again, I'd kill her and Ryan's nonloyal ass too.

I was mad that I had put all my trust in him and had given him my release date. I couldn't pop up on them, because he'd be expecting me. I've known Mike for years, but I trusted Ryan more than I had ever trusted Mike, and look how he let me down. If he hadn't already lain down with Savannah, he was close to it, and I still had a week and six days to go. The thought of losing a good friend over a bitch had me feeling like my world was closing in, and I needed to talk to the only true friend I had. Mama Dee.

"Mama, have you ever gave somebody your all over and over again, just to watch them shit on you every single time?"

"Andre, you're talking to your mother. What's going on, baby?"

"It's been a lot, more than any man should have to take or put up with just to love a woman."

"I hear you talking, son, but you still haven't said a word."

I needed to hear the truth, even if I had to hear her say I told you so. I started from the beginning and told her everything about Savannah and me, including the shit she pulled in California and the shit I pulled with her mother in Washington. My mama didn't open her mouth until I was done.

"Boy, you must really love this girl even to allow her to do half of that to you. You didn't even take that much from Tasha, and y'all had years under your belts. Not only has she done everything and everyone around her dirty, but she also did it to her own flesh and blood, *my* flesh and blood. O Heavenly Father, protect my grand-baby." She started reciting protection scriptures before she started back talking to me. "I told you, the Lord always opens my eyes when it comes to people like that. You should have told me this a long time ago, and I would have never opened my house to the devil's helper. I would have told you to cut this off a long time ago, Andre. This ain't healthy. You don't need a woman like that in your life. You need to do your time, get out, and worry about these babies you've brought into this world with these heathens. God will never put more on you than you can bear, Andre, and you know that. You know the Word, I made sure of it. If it doesn't fit right in your soul, baby, you have to let it go. You have to let it go."

I knew my mama was right, but even her words didn't do anything to coat the anger I was feeling. I kept thinking about all the time and energy I had wasted on Savannah and all the betrayal and games she gave in return. I loved that girl with everything in me, but my love meant shit to her, and she proved it over and over again. I didn't understand what she felt like she was gaining by constantly playing with me. It would be easier for her just to say commitment was too much, and she'd rather us go our separate ways than to keep doing the same shit over again. My daddy used to tell me when I was younger that a person would only do to you what you allowed them to, and I've allowed her to do way too much. I couldn't be a victim on Savannah's list of destruction any more. It was time somebody taught her a lesson she'd never forget, and I felt the need to be the teacher.

I started thanking my mama for her words of wisdom so I could end our phone call, but she wasn't done asking questions.

"Do you think this letter that came in the mail for you had something to do with Savannah? You said she plays a lot of games."

"What letter, Mama?" I had no clue what she was talking about.

"You got a letter the other day, and, yes, I opened it because it came from the courts. It's a paternity establishment action. The state of California is petitioning Tennessee to establish paternity under their laws. You have to get genetic testing or something like that. I asked one of the doctors that I work with what all of it meant and he said a DNA test was needed to prove you were the father of a baby born or being born in California, and the mother is seeking child support. Don't tell me you got another baby on the way, Andre!"

"Hell no, Mama, I didn't touch anybody while I was in California. I was too busy hunting Savannah down to see my daughter. Does it give a woman's name or anything in the letter?"

She put me on hold as she retrieved the letter. When she got back on the phone, she read it to me, but all it said was, *"The State of California vs. Andre Burns."*

I felt like Mama and had to ask myself what the hell was Savannah trying to pull now? If she had filed while she was in California, how did she expect to get child support for a child she gave up custody of? I had a way to get to the bottom of it all—that's *if* he'd answer his phone. I told my mama I'd call her back later, then called the Los

Angeles County Sheriff's Department to speak to Will. He seemed shocked that I had called him and even more shocked that it wasn't about Savannah.

"Can you look into that for me, please? I hate to call you only when I need something, but you're the go-to man and my Cali connect."

We both laughed, and then he asked me how Savannah was doing. I wanted to tell him the truth, but I knew he was her friend.

"She's fine. Hanging in there like she always does. When was the last time the two of y'all spoke?"

"We haven't, and I don't think I plan to speak to her ever again. She must have been high the other day, and it temporally fixed her brain because she called me like three or more times in a row, but I wasn't in the mood and forwarded her to voice. I almost choked on my diet soda when I heard Savannah's evil ass on my answering machine apologize for everything she's done and admitting to being a bad friend. It even sounded like she was crying a little, but I couldn't tell if she was acting or if it were the real thing. I meant to call her back to see if I could tell if the apology was sincere, but there is just too much drama around her all the time. I'm tired of her using me to help her sort out her wrongdoings against people, and to be honest, I'm scared if I piss her off, I'll end up in jail, unemployed, or laid up somewhere battling AIDS."

"I can't blame you, and I can't be mad at you. I didn't want to say it at first, but Savannah ain't changed. Same bullshit, just a different day." I was trying to show him that I understood where he was coming from, and then he threw me off.

"I thought you were calling to tell me Melinda and Stephanie had started working together and had gotten Savannah. I was about to feel guilty for not picking up a phone and warning her." He laughed, but when he didn't hear me join in, he hurried up and started shooting off questions. "Wait, you *did* know that Melinda got released from jail, right? I sent you a letter in Washington from our victim program. Don't tell me you never got it?"

"I didn't get a letter, and if Savannah did, she didn't mention it. I found out ole girl was out because the funeral made the news, but what does Stephanie have to do with it?"

I didn't know if Savannah had gotten the letter or not. Knowing her, she probably didn't even forward the mail to Atlanta. I didn't understand where Stephanie fell into this.

"Stephanie came out for Big Ant's funeral and sat with me. She didn't tell y'all?"

"Why would she tell us?"

"Um, because she's Savannah's best friend?"

"No, she *was* her best friend, if that's what you want to call their relationship."

Will did not know about Stephanie and Savannah's falling out, and it was strange that Stephanie didn't let Will know.

"You said y'all spent time at the funeral together, and I thought y'all only knew each other because of Savannah introducing the two of you. Wouldn't her name have come up between y'all?"

"Yeah, she brought up Savannah, but not negatively. Hell, I was the one talking shit about her, and Stephanie just sat there listening. The only thing that was strange to me was that Stephanie begged me to introduce her to Melinda so she could give her condolences. About a month later, I saw the two together having lunch at a Mexican restaurant not too far from my courthouse on Olvera Street here in L.A. I could see it in both of their eyes that they had been out there eating and plotting.

I tried to think positively and said Savannah might have had a change of heart and had Stephanie do the apologizing for her or maybe Stephanie was feeling guilty about her part in everything, but the way them hoes was huddled up, I threw my shades on and kept it pushing. When I got back to my office, I looked into Stephanie and saw she had new utility services in her name. I didn't know she moved back to Cali, nor did she mention it at the funeral."

I didn't know she had moved back to California either. Shit was getting weirder by the minute. Will was a sheriff, but he wasn't a trained investigator, and surely not one trained by the Bureau of Investigation. I needed Ryan to help me figure this shit out. Ryan didn't know that I had talked to Mike or what he had told me, so I could still use him to do some work for me until I confronted his ass.

"Yeah, that shit right there sounds suspect. Keep an eye on that if you can for me too, and I'll be in touch. Call me back on this number if you find out anything about that paternity shit," I asked, and that's when he gave me something else to think about.

"I will, but this shit is getting a lot stranger. You *do* know that Stephanie is about eight or nine months pregnant by that married firefighter, right? Or so that's what she told me when I was rubbing on her stomach. Maybe she filed the petition on you to fuck with Savannah's head. If you are a part of the reason she and Savannah fell off, it sounds like an attempt to get some revenge. I just hope her dumb ass remembers who she is playing with. Savannah has dedicated her entire adult life to doing whatever she wants and hurting whoever she wants."

I wouldn't have given it a second thought, but there was no way Stephanie's baby was really mines. It did make sense for her to file the paperwork, though, to fuck with Savannah. I'd get the test done as soon as I was released just to nip that bullshit in the bud. After all the shit Savannah had put that girl through, that was a good way to get her back. I just hate that she had involved me.

I called Ryan and told him what Will had told me about Melinda and Stephanie, and in return, he told me about the telephone calls Savannah had been getting. Talking to him about Savannah's protection had me feeling torn. I hadn't called the Amir guy yet to get confirmation that she had cheated, nor had I talked to Ryan about crossing lines with her, but here I was again, ready to play toy soldier for her. Half of me was saying fuck her and let Melinda give her what she deserved. And the other half of me was saying protect your wife. That torn feeling had me the same way with Ryan. I wanted to work with him to get the issue resolved, but the other half of me wanted to question him and find out what the fuck was really going on between him and Savannah.

"Savannah's accuracy is unbelievable for a first-time shooter. The only person I've ever known to handle a gun they've never used before is you. Although her attitude hasn't completely evolved, I do see small progress in different areas. When I told her your number had changed, I was expecting to hear her cuss both of us out. Instead, she said she would await your call and took her anger out at the range. Her emotions don't affect the accuracy of her shot. I know someone else like that."

As I kept talking to Ryan, I couldn't feel a negative vibe from him, and that made me feel like something wasn't right again. I felt like I was still on the phone with my boy—the nigga that helped me stash over a million dollars, the nigga who drove way to Atlanta to spy on Savannah for me, the same nigga I had watching Tasha for me, and the same cat that not once—but twice—broke the bureau's confidentiality to inform me that I was going to jail. Savannah's pussy was good, but not good enough to break a bond that strong. Giving some more thought to it, Ryan was too devoted to his job to marry the woman he'd been seeing since ninth grade. He wouldn't even allow her to use the title that they were dating because he didn't want to let her down when he had to put work first. What was there about Savannah that would make him change his ways? The answer to that was . . . nothing. He knew everything about her, including her holike ways, and he had even tried to convince me that I could do better. It was time for me to start thinking like the investigator I was trained to be. I needed to stop acting like a paranoid inmate and ask what questions I needed to ask to get to the bottom of this.

"Ryan, we'll come back to this in a minute. I need to talk to you about some real shit, and I don't need you lying to me to protect anybody. If we both wouldn't have broken the oath we were sworn in by, I'd ask you to swear." He cleared his throat to prepare for his time to talk or answer questions, then waited on me to talk. "What's going on between you and Savannah? I asked why you returned to Atlanta, and you gave me a run-around conversation, never answering my question."

"That's because I didn't want to lie to you. I never have, and I never will. Nothing is going on between Savannah and me. I'm here because I'm doing a favor for a friend. I've returned because that's what real friends do. We step up to the plate when we know other people can't handle the job or have already failed at the job."

His answer was professional yet personal, and I respected him for taking my question seriously. "So you felt I made a wrong decision by hiring Mike to protect Savannah, or did you feel you could just do a better job?"

"I knew you made the wrong decision when you hired Mike, and we both know I could do a better job."

I wanted to laugh at his answer but didn't want to break the professionalism in our conversation.

"With knowing Mike wasn't sufficient enough to protect Savannah, you allowed him to take watch for a little over thirty days. What I need to know is, why the change of heart? What was the breaking point for your return?"

I know Mike told me he packed up and left her alone, but I needed to make sure that her being alone was the only reason for his return. It seemed like Ryan was waiting for me to ask that question because his answer was 100 percent personal.

"I can hear the severity in your voice, but I have to speak candidly. That bitch-ass nigga tried to rape her. That's why I came back. I wanted to tell you, but Savannah was in fear you'd kill him. She didn't know it, but I gave her ass a lie detector test by pulse. I pretended to hold her hand in comfort while she told me the story. She passed with flying colors. The nigga had tried to get her twice while he was drunk. The last time, she busted his dick open with some crutches, stole his guns, and put his ass out. I guess all the training I've been giving her is working. I followed up on her claim and was informed he was a patient in a nearby hospital and was being treated for an almost severed penis."

I could hear Ryan holding back a laugh from the time he said Savannah had busted his meat open. I was glad he did because he had just told me some heartbreaking shit that had me ready to kill a nigga. My best friend since school days had tried to rape my fiancée while I was paying him to protect her. Look at the danger I had put her in. Maybe hate for me sending him to protect her caused her to fuck that other nigga. No, I wasn't going to help give her an excuse for what she had done, but on the same token, look at who I got that information from. It was the same nigga who tried to fuck her and had lied to me about it when I asked for the truth. My mind started running around in circles, going over the same thoughts twice.

"Do you know anything about a cat named Amir?"

Ryan repeated the name a few times, then went quiet for a minute. "Naw, that name doesn't ring a bell. If I'm not mistaken, when you had me monitor around the birth of your daughter, I believe that name came up. Why, what's up?"

"When I called Mike to find out why he left, he told me he found out Savannah had been fucking some Jamaican guy in Atlanta named Amir. Can you look into it for me? I don't know how much weight it holds, but he gave me dude's telephone number." I gave Ryan the number.

"No problem, I'll look into it first thing in the morning. Something about the name and the fact he's Jamaican does sound familiar."

I debated it as he spoke but felt Ryan should know what brought along the line of questioning.

"Mike played me, Ryan. He told me he thought you and Savannah had or was about to start fucking. He said she had you wrapped around her finger. I couldn't have my boy trying to fuck my fiancée or whatever she is to me. That's why I had to ask you what was up. My bad for doubting you."

"What do you mean, whatever she is to you? If you no longer see her as your fiancée, why am I here? Don't let that time get to you."

"It ain't the time. It's the case." I had to laugh at my own words. "She's become a case, and when it come to our relationship, there's no respect. You're there until I make a definitive decision. I just can't keep dealing with all the secrets and lies."

I guess it was time for confessions and apologies because Ryan went next.

"Naw, Dre, it's not your bad for doubting me. It's my bad for not telling you everything."

"There's more?"

"Yeah, a different case I've been working for years. I didn't know how to tell you that Mike's been off and on fucking Tasha for years. When you told me you suspected it, I thought you knew what I knew, but then I realized you didn't and never corrected you for letting it go. When you had me keep an eye on her, she was meeting him at motels like once a week. That didn't mean they were fucking, but then the nigga got cocky one day I caught him coming out and rubbed his shit and put it in my face. I don't know her scent, but that's who he went into the motel with. He said it was a random ho he had in the room, but I knew the truth. He told Savannah he was fucking her too to get her to agree to fuck him. Savannah didn't tell me he told her this at first, and I could tell when she did, that there's more she's hiding when it comes to Mike. He might have confessed to Savannah some other shit he's done to you behind your back. My bad, Dre."

I didn't know what to say, but the truth was always best. "When I get out of this bitch, I'm going to kill him."

Chapter Ten

The Line between Love and Hate just Got Thinner

It was two days before they'd open up the gates and let me out. Where was all the happiness and excitement I was supposed to be feeling? I felt cheated because instead of coming home to crawl in some pussy, I had to get out and clean up bullshit. Will hadn't heard shit about the case yet, which made me think Stephanie had generated the letter herself. It didn't matter either way it went, because I called Mrs. Jefferson and had her get with the lab I had my DNA test on Sade at. She had them forward that information to California a week ago, so if the shit were real, I should be receiving a Maury letter soon.

"When it comes to baby no-name, Andre . . . You are not *the father."*

Ryan had confirmed there really was an Amir at the number Mike had given me, but he still didn't know if Savannah had been intimate with him recently. As he suspected, it was the dude from her past, and he found proof they had a bad falling out before my daughter was born. When Ryan followed up on Melinda for me, he found out she had been released on house arrest. He had tracked her bracelet back to her home address, which meant she was where she was supposed to be. Phone records indicated multiple calls between her and Stephanie, and some involved the other two women Savannah had revenge on. Seeing jail calls were recorded, even though they swear they aren't, he said he would try to get records that provide there was a plot against Savannah in the works.

I spoke to Savannah briefly whenever I called to talk to Ryan. The torn feeling hadn't gone away, but I felt like shit that I had set her up for danger with Mike, so I kept the peace. She didn't know that I knew about the incident because I told Ryan I wouldn't say anything to her about it, and I'd just handle it without her knowing I had.

I hadn't slept since Ryan told me what Mike had done. Night after night, I dreamed of confronting him, then killing my best friend of over twenty years. Then I'd wake up in cold sweats with the urge to vomit. I still don't know what I could have done that would make Mike sleep with both of the women he knew I loved. I was tired of asking myself questions I didn't have the answers to. I said I would wait until I was released, but fuck it, I needed to know. I dialed his number.

"My nigga, Dre." Mike had greeted me with the same greeting as far back as I could remember. I can't believe his words held no weight.

"What's up?" I tried not to sound dry, but I wasn't in the mood to fake. "Mike, is there something you need to tell me, my nigga? I'm hearing some foul-ass shit about you, and you know I'm not the nigga to be giving out passes."

Mike had to be in front of somebody, or after all of these years, the nigga had finally got some heart, because he went in on me. "Aye, nigga, don't be calling my phone with that bullshit. I don't give a fuck about you or no passes. If you got something you want to ask me, then ask me. I don't have time to listen to you pour your ho-ass feelings out. I'm trying to get this money."

"Damn, it's like that? So, I guess you did try to rape my bitch, and that shit I'm hearing about you fucking Tasha must be true too."

"Mane, get yo' soft ass off my line with all that, ho. Those flips wanted this dick. You acting like a ho over some pussy that ain't even yours. Yeah, nigga, I fucked that bitch Tasha a few times, and she swallowed this dick up like a pro. So, now you want to beef with yo' boy since knee high over some hoes? Then fuck it. It is what it is. Yo' bitch Savannah wanted this dick too. She can scream rape if she wants to, but I know what it really was. That bitch got you brainwashed, but I got something for her ass for that little trip to the hospital. You got another four months in that bitch. I doubt they let you come to her funeral. It's gon' be closed casket anyways. I'm offing that ho before Sunday. I'll see you when you touch down, my nigga."

Mike laughed, then hung up the phone. A threat from him was a confirmed promise. He wasn't much of a drug dealer, but he had a few bodies under his belt. It was Thursday now, and I'd be released late Friday night or early Saturday morning. If he was on his way to Atlanta, I couldn't wait to meet him there. He bragged about his body count, but real killers knew better. We kept our shit on hush. Fuck a teardrop. That's like snitching on yourself. I called Ryan and told him what happened and the threat that was made. He was ready for Mike to pop up and prayed he had the pleasure of handling it before me.

"You shouldn't have to be the one to pull the trigger. Too much history. Plus, I want the body under *my* belt."

It was time for him to pick up Savannah from work, so he said he'd call me back, but he assured me he was ready for anything.

I called Mama Dee to kill time until my boy called me back, and the drama never seemed to stop.

"Why is Tasha calling my phone telling me she's going to court to get her son back and fuck you and me? That little bitch has crossed the line with me one too many times, Andre. I've prayed for the Lord to keep me from getting her, but God must be busy and missed my plea because when I see that heffa, it's gon' take all twelve disciples to get me off of her."

She meant it too. I wish I knew why Tasha had a change of heart all of a sudden so I could tell my mama something that would calm her down, but I didn't. I could always assume, though, and my assumption was that Tasha was upset about me moving on with Savannah, or her side piece, Mike, told her I knew about them creeping.

"Do you hear me, Andre?"

"No, Mama, I didn't. I zoned out, trying to figure out what Tasha's problem was. What did you say?"

"I said you got a certified letter today, and the mailman said only you could sign for it. I don't know how they expect you to sign for it in jail."

That must have been my Maury letter. That was fast, but I guessed when they already had a blood and saliva sample processed, they moved quickly.

"All this stuff going on, and if I don't know shit else, I know the only people who are going to suffer over this is these kids. What happened to you keeping your word to me, Andre?"

"Mama, you gon' kick me while I'm down?"

"Over my grandkids, these innocent babies, I'll shoot you while you're down. What happened to keeping your word, son?"

She was cold for digging in her bag of tricks and pulling out this one to get me to think straight. My word was, and still is, *"If and when I have children, I'll never do them like my father did me. I'd never let money, jail, or anything else stop me from tucking them in bed at night, being the one to make sure they build a relationship with the Lord, and I'll let nothing stop me from doing what a real man is supposed to do, which is loving them through my own personal ups and downs."*

Those were the words I said to my mama when she tried to get me to understand what my father was going through and why he didn't always pick up a phone to talk to me. Her exact words were, "Baby, prison life is hard and being away from those you love makes it harder. Your daddy couldn't call you today."

"Why couldn't he? He called yesterday, and I bet he calls tomorrow. He hasn't even mentioned my birthday all month. Tell me why a man wouldn't tell his only son Happy Birthday?"

"Because it's easier for him to do his time without thinking about everything he's missing out on. He hasn't told me Happy Birthday, Merry Christmas, or Happy Anniversary in years. Now that you've gotten older and you know the truth, he's cutting it out and hopes that you understand."

I said those words as my response because I meant them, and nothing or nobody will ever be able to stop me from raising my kids. That's why I told my cell mate Tez that he needed to chop it up because regardless of whether he wants to admit the shit, he chose to commit the crime over being there when his child will be born. He might not have realized it at the time, but getting caught holds up to a seven-year sentence so you might as well say that he told his son fuck his first seven birthdays and holidays, but that doesn't give him the right to dodge them to make his situation better. It wasn't right for my father to do me or any other man who is serving time unless he is wrongly incarcerated, but even then, he should be busting his ass to try to prove his innocence.

"I meant what I said to you back then, and this is my last time talking to you from any cage. It's also the last time I'm going to allow you or anybody else to raise my kids for me. Fuck their mamas. Those are *my* kids. When I get out, I'll make you a believer in my word."

"I hope so, baby. Between Tasha, Savannah, and whoever this is trying to pin this new baby on you, all of them are unfit to raise my grandchildren in my eyes."

She had calmed down enough to have a civil conversation with me, so I stayed on the phone with Mama Dee until Ryan buzzed in.

"I know you said you'd call back after you snatched her up from work, but that was quick."

Ryan was speed talking, and I couldn't make out his words. However, I could hear Savannah in the background clearly crying.

"I couldn't hear you, say that again."

"I said that guy Amir is a real problem. He just shot at Savannah as she walked out of work. I shot back at him, but he got away. Savannah said he's been calling and threatening her since he found out she returned, and Mike said he had handled it, so she didn't tell me. Shit is getting real down here, fast. How did it go from one person trying to get her to four?"

Ryan had fucked up, and he knew it as soon as the words came out of his mouth. I could hear Savannah's sobbing stop, and she ask, "Four? What do you mean four people are trying to kill me? Ryan, who else is trying to kill me?"

I got his attention before he answered her question.

"Tell her the truth, Ryan. If she's been trained, you'll need the extra help for eyes and ears. Why didn't she have her gun on her today?"

Ryan asked Savannah why she hadn't carried her gun with her to work, and in a small voice, she said, "I forgot to get it registered."

I told Ryan to handle her and to call me when she was out of earshot or asleep. Not knowing what else I could do from in here, I hit the floor and did some push-ups, and then I prayed again but cut it short. I had murder on my mind and didn't need to disrespect the Lord by making him an accomplice to it.

Ryan never called me back, but that was fine because I was released three o'clock Friday morning. The walk from Antioch to my mama's house was a stroll, but when you're ready to tear some shit up, it felt a yard a way. When I got to her house, I ate a good breakfast, took my son to school, grabbed some cash she had tucked away for me, then hit the road in my Monte Carlo to Atlanta. I tried to call Ryan and tell him I was on my way, but he still didn't answer. I hoped everything was all right.

Around nine o'clock my time, ten o'clock Atlanta's, Ryan called me back.

"I didn't want you stressing, but after I told Savannah who all was looking for her, she dipped. I've been searching for her all night, and I can't find her anywhere. I traced her ATM transactions to Alpharetta, Ga., around eleven o'clock last night. She withdrew $800 and hasn't used the card since. She didn't have clothes with her, and she left her purse in the car. If she doesn't trust anybody to drive her around, I take it she's getting around on public transportation. I put a lookout at the bus and train stations and got with TSA at the airport. Nobody has heard or seen her yet."

"I'll be there in an hour. Meet me at the Houston on Peachtree downtown."

I hung up on him and started blowing up Savannah's phone, but there was no answer. As I started dialing the number I had on Amir, another call came in.

"Hello?"

"Guess where I'm at, my nigga? About forty-five minutes away from your bitch's house. Seems she's out sick from work today. Think I'll give her something to help her feel better before I put one in her head. I'll call you while I'm fucking her."

Mike hung up, and I hit the gas. The way I was driving, I'd be at Savannah's place in thirty minutes as long as traffic didn't pick up. As I swerved from one lane to another, I got Amir on the phone.

"Is this Amir?"

"Who's asking?" he shouted in the phone.

"I'm asking. My name is Dre, and I'm Savannah's fiancé—"

"I'll kill you, and I'll kill her too. She keeps playing with my heart like it's a toy. One minute she's making love to me. Then the next, she's telling me she's in love with you. I'll kill you. If you want her to live, make her love me, or I'll kill her. Where is she, huh? She's not at work, not at the gym. Is she with you? Is she making sweet love to you like she makes love to me? I'll find out where she lives, and I'll kill her. Do you hear me? I'll *kill* her!"

His crazy ass hung up before I did. There wasn't going to be any talking to him. I'd have to kill his obsessed ass too. I didn't bring a gun with me, but I was sure Ryan did, or else I'd use Savannah's. She never registered it anyway, which turned out to be a good thing. When I made it fifteen miles from the exit, my cell phone rang. It was Savannah calling me.

"Where in the fuck are you? You got Ryan driving around town looking everywhere for you. You know better than to go off by yourself."

She was silent, but I could hear her breathing hard. "People are looking for me, Dre. People want me dead, and you want me to sit around and wait for them?"

"I know, Savannah, but the only way we can protect you is by knowing where you are. I need you to tell me, baby, where are you?"

"Does it really matter where I am? No one can protect me forever. You can stop pretending now, Dre. I know the truth about everything."

What the fuck is she talking about? I thought. She was starting to sound like that crazy nigga she had been fucking.

"I don't know what the fuck you're talking about, Savannah, but now ain't the motherfucking time for this."

"You know what the fuck I'm talking about, bitch," she screamed her words into the phone. "You set me up. You set me up with Trisha to get my money. Why, Dre?"

I didn't know how she found out, but now wasn't the time to discuss it. "We can and will talk about this later. I need you to—"

"No, you conniving bastard, we will talk about this *now!*"

I wasn't about to go back and forth with her about this, so I answered the question.

"I found out you was fucking that lawyer nigga and a few other niggas. Trisha told me about Royce, and I found out about the others from following yo' ass. Just like I found out about this nigga Amir you fucked. Now, instead of breaking up with you for being the biggest ho I've ever met, I'm trying to make this shit work. So stop arguing with me and tell me where you are."

She was pissing me off. How was breaking my ass to protect her such a pain in the ass? She made me want to exit the interstate and change direction back to Nashville.

"That makes it okay to help her rob me, Dre? It's okay to rob your fiancée because she cheated on you, is *that* how you think? Get rid of all her money, and that will tame into being faithful? What kind of sick shit is that?"

I made it to the exit near Savannah's apartment, and Ryan was buzzing in. I put Savannah on hold.

"Change in plans. Meet me with heat at Savannah's spot. Mike is about ten minutes behind me on his way there, and Amir is trying to figure out where she lives now. I got her on the other line, and her ass is talking crazy. She's gon' fuck around, make me off her ass myself. I got to go."

I resumed my call with Savannah and asked the same question again. "Where are you, Savannah?"

She was sniffling like she had been crying while I placed her on hold. "I'm home, Dre. I needed to get clothes and my purse before I disappeared."

"Stay there. I'm on my way."

"You're on your way? I thought you were in jail. It's one lie after another with you, huh, Dre?" She got quiet, then said, "Hold on. I have a more important call coming in from somebody who *really* gives a fuck about me."

She clicked over before I could tell her not to. It must have been her daddy calling. If Ryan had everyone reach out to her, her daddy would be the only one she trusted. After holding on for five long minutes, she came back, and the weakness had left her voice.

"Were you even in jail with your lying ass, or do you have some more of your undercover work to do? Yes, I know that your ass is an undercover fed on the drug task force pretending to be that nigga in the drug game because you smoke a little weed." She laughed hysterically and then said, "Go ahead and do something you ain't never done before—like tell the truth."

"Savannah, your facts are off. We'll talk when I get there. Don't open the door for nobody but me."

"I'm not—not even for you. Remember, I'm the biggest ho you know. Ain't that what you just said? But I beg to differ because this little package Stephanie and my mama put together for me said otherwise. It was heartbreaking, but it made me finally realize that you ain't shit. I don't want or need you in my life. It's over, Dre."

"What package? What are you talking about, Savannah? It ain't over 'til I say it's over. All the shit I've taken from you, and you think you can just tell me it's over, and I accept it? Bitch, you crazy. When I get to that fucking apartment, you better unlock the door."

"No, bitch, you're crazy, and you're just as big of a ho as me." She laughed liked an evil villain. "Your son is cute, though, Dre. Andrew Burns, born January twenty-six, twenty thirteen. The bitch had y'all baby on my fucking birthday. Ain't that some shit. He's really cute too. Looks just like his sorry-ass Daddy. Congrats to you and Stephanie. Guess y'all want me to be the little nigga's godmother, right?"

"What the fuck are you talking about? Stephanie didn't have my baby. You're losing your mind, baby."

"I'm not your fucking baby." She was cried out. "Andrew is your baby. I'm your ex. Stephanie sent me another package with Trisha's help. I guess it was her response to the little Savannah box I sent her. Anyway, her letter said you didn't know about the pregnancy just like you hadn't known about mine. Unlike me, she was very happy to find out that she was carrying your child because she couldn't think of a better man to have a child with and the way you would cover her body in kisses as you nutted in her let her know how much you loved and appreciated her being there for you."

"What?"

"Stop the lies. You know what I'm talking about because you received a letter for DNA testing, and guess what the results say? She included a copy with this 8x10 of your youngest child. DNA says 99.9 percent all Andre Burns. The DNA was taken from the test you took in

Washington. You got that cutthroat bitch, Mrs. Jefferson, to get the DNA testing info you had done with Sade transferred for you, and she didn't even respect me enough to tell me. I'm over all this shit, but I have to ask you this . . . How could you fuck the only bitch that you knew I called my best friend? I thought you said you loved me?"

Savannah was crying in a way that I had never heard her do before. She kept saying, "Why, Dre?" over and over again. I had fucked up. I was fucking Stephanie, but just to get her to talk to me about Savannah. That first night I went to her house looking for Savannah high and drunk, I went into her raw. I could tell she hadn't had sex that many times by the tight grip she had on my dick. It felt so good that I released inside of her, not once, but every single time we had sex that night, which was three or four times. I took her to get a few of those morning-after pills from three different places before we went to church, but I didn't watch her take any of them. She came out with an empty container that stored the pill and a half-empty bottle of water. I assumed she'd taken them.

I double-parked in front of the apartment before I spoke. "I'm sorry, baby. I fucked up. I didn't want Stephanie, I swear. I was only fucking her to get information on you."

"Is that what they taught you as a detective, to fuck for information? So, when you came home telling me she sucked your dick and was trying to get you to sleep with her, you had already been fucking her, hadn't you?"

There was no reason to lie if I wanted to make shit right with Savannah. I had to tell the truth.

"Yes, baby. I had fucked her like three or four times before then, but all during the same visit, and I won't lie. I got some head from her a few times after that but never fucked her again. I saw you peeking in on us at the window right before I was about to put my dick in her. I was only going to fuck her again because it was her birthday, but when I saw you, I put on a show, so you wouldn't think I was unfaithful. I'm sorry, Savannah. You've fucked up, and I have too, but we can work this shit out. I forgave you for all those Wednesday and Sunday nights you were fucking that lawyer nigga and lying to me about your whereabouts. I need your forgiveness now. Together, we can get custody of my son from her and make something beautiful out of all of this shit."

I took a deep breath and shook my head. I couldn't believe any of this was happening, but it was. I knocked up Stephanie with the buildup from not fucking Savannah, but how could I fuck her, knowing she was fucking someone else? That didn't make it right I was fucking her so-called best friend in return, raw, but at the time, the shit felt right. Whatever the consequences were for my actions, I'd deal with them the best way I knew how. "What apartment are you in? Grab your gun and wait for me by your door. I got to get you out of here before Mike gets to you."

She laughed like I had said something funny. "I'm not going anywhere with you, Dre. It's over, and I mean it. If you or Mike come up here, I'm shooting to kill. I have real help on the way, and I'm getting far the fuck away from all of you. If you see me again, it will be in your dreams."

"This isn't the time to play stupid, Savannah. If you don't want to be with me, fuck it. I've taken way more of your shit than you have of mine, you selfish bitch, but I can't call Washington and tell our daughter I let you get killed. Let me get you to a safe place, and then we can go our separate ways. I'm done trying to be with a ho. I fucked Stephanie, and now I have another son to get custody of. I can't keep worrying about y'all hoes I've had kids with."

As I made my way in the doors, I almost knocked over two ladies who were checking their mail at the indoor mailboxes. I apologized, then turned on my feet to see who it was blowing their horn. It was Ryan. I rushed back out the door, and my phone was knocked out of my hands by another nigga rushing inside. Savannah had me fucking up. I picked up the phone in time to hear her last words.

". . . one son."

"What?" I asked.

"You heard me. You only have one son. Andre Junior is Mike's son. He told me, and that ghetto bitch you were fucking with confirmed it. Why do you think we were fighting at your mama's house? I didn't tell Ryan because I didn't want him to tell you, but now you know."

Shock was all over my face, and Ryan kept asking me what was wrong. I couldn't snap out of it. All I could manage to say was, "Bitch, stop lying. That ain't shit to play with. Yeah, don't let me in because I might put a bullet in yo' ass for lying. Andre Jr. *is* mine. I don't play when it comes to my kids."

"I thought you loved me? Now that I told you your best friend fucked your baby mama like Stephanie did me with you, I gotta die?"

She laughed until I had to stop paying her attention.

Ryan was pointing at a car parked in the parking lot that I passed on my way in. It was a burgundy Buick Regal. He was holding two guns but threw one back in the backseat of his car and grabbed another out of his trunk.

"I'll go to the back exit, and you take the front. She's on the twelfth floor, number 1208," he said and handed me the gun he had retrieved. The car he was pointing at had Tennessee plates and Davidson County tags. It was from Nashville. That could only mean one thing: Mike was already here.

"Fuck you, Savannah. I'm on my way up. Don't answer the door. I think Mike is already here."

I went to catch the elevator, but they were down, so I hit the stairs. I was climbing three steps at a time as Savannah continued to talk shit in my ear.

"You see, Dre, you're not the only person with secrets. How does it feel to know that I played your ass from the very beginning? I never wanted shit with you. That's why I gave up our daughter. That's why I kept fucking whoever I wanted to."

"Shut up, bitch. You're a ho. You didn't play nobody but yourself."

"Is that why you started following me and even gave me a rose when you saw me looking good as fuck in the club in Vegas with Big Ant?"

"That was a rose for your grave, ho, and if Big Ant's baby mama doesn't put you in it first, I will if you keep talking all that loose shit. You don't know shit about me—don't forget it."

Savannah didn't know a damn thing about me or what I was capable of . . . because I didn't. As I shouted my threats at her, they didn't feel like lies to scare her off, and I felt comfortable that they didn't. I was about to call her a bitch, but I thought I heard Ryan's voice in her background talking to her. It almost sounded like she had him talking to her on another cell phone and had accidentally hit the speakerphone button. I fell silent to listen, but she killed it by talking.

"Is that all you got? I'll be your bitch like you were Mike's. You've raised his child for seven years and even had your mother break her broke, raggedy ass to get custody of him. But guess what else, Dre?"

I had made it to the eleventh-floor staircase and had one flight of stairs to go.

"You like playing with your life, don't you, bitch? Who put you up to pissing me off? I heard them in the background. Tell them hoes it's working."

"Is it? You ready to shoot me now, or should I tell you more?"

I was too busy focusing on hitting the steps to respond. Push-ups were the only exercise I had been getting. The cardio was fucking with my breathing. Savannah took my lack of response as it being a yes for her to continue.

"The night you told me to take Mike out for his birthday . . ." I could hear her fumbling with her keys. "I took him to a strip club here, and we fucked in the men's bathroom. I brought him home, sucked his big black birthday dick, and let him fuck me on my kitchen counter until he couldn't get his dick back up. I completely understand why Tasha had to keep on getting dick from him while fucking with you. He might be the uglier ghetto friend, but your dick is garbage compared to his. Even his nut felt better going down my throat and wiped across my lips. It was too damn good not to keep fucking him, and the only reason he tried to rape me was that I wouldn't give him the pussy again. That was a huge mistake that I made. There's no way in hell that I should have chosen waiting for you over fucking him every day until you got out of jail."

I made it out the door on the twelfth floor, and Savannah was walking out of her apartment door with this cocky smile on her face. I didn't get a chance to see what she'd do or say next because the door flew open across the hall, the elevator doors opened at the same time, and somebody was coming from behind the tall tree at the end of the hallway. Shots were fired from every direction simultaneously. The people in the elevator, who had apparently pulled the emergency stop button, causing it not to work earlier, flew back in it. The man down the hall froze in his steps, and I watched two bodies hit the floor at the same time. One of them was Mike's coming out of the apartment in front of Savannah's, and the other body on the ground belonged to Savannah.

Ryan came from the staircase on the other end of the hall, where the man was standing near the tree. He snatched him up and brought him down the hallway with him. I ran to get the people from the elevator. To my surprise, it was Stephanie, and I assumed the other woman was Melinda because she was wearing Anthony's college basketball jersey. As a matter of fact, they were the two women I had apologized to by the mailboxes. They were unarmed, and they both looked at me, scared.

Ryan was holding Amir, who was only carrying a pocketknife in his hand. That was the same nigga that bumped into me and caused me to drop my phone on my way to Ryan. That's when the story told itself. Savannah had shot Mike in his head before he could point his gun at her, and I had shot and killed my beloved Savannah.

Damn!

Chapter Eleven

If the Apples Are Rotten, It's the Tree

There was no time for me to stomach what I had done, nor did I get to see her lifeless body because Ryan was already working the crime scene. He covered Savannah from the neck up with the shirt he had on before I could see where I had shot her. That confirmed it was a head shot. I had executed the woman I swore I loved. I went rushing over to her to kiss her, but that fool Amir smiled at me, so I tried to crack his jaw with the butt of the gun I was holding.

"Calm the fuck down, Dre," Ryan said as he snatched the gun out of my hand, ran over to make it Mike's, and sent me driving back to Nashville at full speed.

I couldn't have stayed if I had wanted to because I violated my probation for even being there. That didn't mean I left without putting up a fight, but in the end, Ryan's words held too much truth for me to continue the battle.

"Dre, you *got to go,* man. Everyone here thinks the bullet that killed Savannah came from Mike's gun. I have to make that true, and adding another gun holder causes too much suspicion. You just got out. Are you ready to go back to jail and say, fuck your daughter? You got to go, Dre. You *know* I'm right."

Ryan was right, and I got confirmation of it as I walked past Stephanie to the staircase.

"Dre, please don't be hard on yourself," she managed to say between sobs. "You tried to save her, you really did. His bullet was just faster than yours. I'm so sorry." She broke down crying like she had really lost her best friend and reached out to grab me so we could mourn together, but I snatched away from her. I hadn't forgotten why she was here.

"If he wouldn't have killed her, you bitches would have."

Stephanie pulled herself together quickly and looked at Melinda for help. When none was offered, she started back speaking without it. "No, we . . . We didn't come to kill her . . . just to shake her up some, Dre. We hate her for everything she is, but we both forgave her. You don't have to believe us—"

"You don't know me, Dre," Melinda spoke up, "but I did forgive her. I didn't know it, but we fucked her up with the shit we did to her as kids, and because of it, she ruined all of our adult lives. How can I not forgive her for doing us like we did her? Hell, it's a lot of stuff that we did to her that I'm sure she never knew we did."

"And, Dre, you knew that I loved her and that I would never—"

I kept walking at the sound of Stephanie's voice but needed to make sure I said one more thing to her while I had her face-to-face. "I'm coming for my son. Lawyer up."

I snatched the letter Stephanie and Melinda tried to stuff in Savannah's mailbox to avoid the eyes of the couple walking in the building. I knew Ryan said he had everything, but I thought of the surveillance camera and went into the security office. It was empty, and there wasn't a tape being recorded on. It was a live feed, but it wasn't being stored. Savannah just lay there still on the floor as Ryan gathered everyone up and forced them inside of Savannah's apartment and closed the door behind them.

"Savannah, baby, I'm so sorry," I cried.

I knew I had to go, but it felt like I couldn't leave without her. Snot mixed with tears, and anger flipped into a hurt that I've never known. When I looked back at the live feed on the twelfth floor, the screen had gone black. Ryan was doing his thing, and I knew he had to, so I got up and left.

I made it back to Nashville just in time to get the telephone call from the detective in Atlanta at my mama's house informing me that a body they had might belong to my fiancée, but that they needed a family member to identify the body before they could confirm it. After pleading for more information, the only information he gave me was she had been shot and killed by a single bullet to the head. He also said he was told I was her fiancée by Ryan. I wasn't legally her husband yet, and he couldn't release information to me. I didn't want to be the person who called her father or brother with the bad news, so I gave the detective their telephone numbers.

Mr. James, Savannah's father, had her body shipped back to Washington a week later. He felt like California had brought her too much pain for her to be buried there. He asked for my input on it, but I didn't have one because I was numb.

"I know you're sad, Dre. No man should have to bury the woman he loves."

"No, you don't. How could you understand when you've never had to bury the woman you love? I'm not sad."

I wasn't sad at the time. I just didn't have feelings about anything that was going on around me. It took Mama Dee to get with my PO so I could be granted permission to go to Washington to lay Savannah to rest and tie up any loose ends there. She would have come along with me, but once I told her that there was a chance Andre Jr. wasn't mine, she wanted to get that handled first. She wanted me to help find some peace in my life and closure to the drama I had been plagued with for years.

On my flight to Washington, I finally opened the letter that I brought back from Atlanta with me. It was from Melinda.

Hey, Nana,

I only called you that because I heard you hate it now. I just wanted to share with you a day in my life. Thanks to you, everything is different now. I woke up this morning and tried to get dressed. I didn't know if I should put on something short and tight for sex appeal or a dress for easy access. Big Ant liked them both, and then I realized it didn't matter what he liked anymore because if I put on either outfit, I wouldn't be wearing them for him. I can't get sexy for my man ever again, but that's okay. It was his choice to pull that trigger to take his own life. Thinking about how stupid his ass was to do the shit, I went back into my closet to find something else to put on.

It was Saturday, kinda chilly, but the sun was out. I could throw on some distressed jeans, a wife beater, and sandals and meet my bitches so we could spend the day getting fly for the night. You know, a trip to the nail shop, shopping, and, of course, we'd find somewhere to all eat together because that's what Keisha, Christina, and I always did.

We kicked it hard, and if Big Ant wanted to take his own life, fuck him. I'd find somebody else to fuck with while I was out with my girls, but you know what, Savannah? That isn't going to work either, and you know why it wouldn't, but just in case your good-ass job and fat-ass banking account made you forget about the shit us little folks are battling, let me remind you. I can't chill with my girls because they are in prison because of you. I can't kick it with my homeboys because they are in prison because of you. I can't hop on a plane and get away from the constant reminders that I'm out here alone because I'm on house arrest because of you. I can't even sit back and say fuck all of them, I got my freedom, and move on with my life, but how free am I really now that I'm living with HIV? And guess what? That's because of you too.

You have to be a very sick bitch to get revenge on adults for the dumb shit they did as kids. We didn't know better, nor did we think that we were really hurting you. I can't speak for anybody else, but if you would have picked up a phone after you left California and said the kid games we played on you had been fucking with you as an adult, I would have apologized and would have done anything to help. You might not believe me since it's obvious that you think me and everybody around me are hoes, but I'm a mother first. My baby deals with bullying, and it breaks my heart. Big Ant even spent time helping our baby deal with it, but that can't happen anymore because the bullying we did to you made you come back and fuck up all of our lives.

I can't even be mad at you anymore for it. I can't change the past, and what's done is done, but I have to know one thing. If you hated us for being hoes as kids, why did you become one as an adult? I've made a new friend in Stephanie, thanks to you. Her guilt from being involved in it all is so honest that I had to forgive her, and we hang out almost every day. The stories she tells me about you and your pussy scare me. If I didn't know about the prostitutes you hired, I'd assume everyone caught the virus from you. It's sad that after all these years that you claimed to hate us, you've become us, and the cycle almost repeated itself between you and Stephanie. She hated you so much that she woke up one morning and realized she was becoming you, and that thought alone almost forced her to take her own life. I'm glad she didn't because the revenge she's getting on you trumps anything me and my friends could ever do to you, and her revenge is legal. How does it feel to know your soon-to-be-boss, ex-best friend, ex-girlfriend, and the closet woman you've ever had in your life has given birth to the baby of the only man your evil ass will probably ever love? Not just his baby from what I've heard, but his first biological son as well.

I have no choice but to forgive you and move on with whatever life I have left because I feel sorrier for you than myself. No friends, no family, and even your mama reached out to me to work against you. Your mother actually offered me money to kill you since she has a million-dollar policy over your head and had me meet with a lawyer that you used to fuck on how if I committed the crime, I could get off by pleading insanity. I declined because I truly feel sorry for you.

You have plenty of enemies out here. I'm just waiting for your funeral information because I wouldn't miss being there for the world. That day that you lay in your casket will be the day you pay off your debt to me and Big Ant. You took him from us at the peak of his career and at the start of a new chapter in his life. I wouldn't miss the opportunity to be on the page where the last chapter of your painful life ends. Karma is a bitch, but Kismet is the

only bitch Karma backs down to. You better figure out which bitch is coming for you, then beg for forgiveness—twice!
—Melinda

On the day of her funeral, I had overslept from spending the night before in a bottle of Rémy with beer as the chaser. If it weren't for the limo service picking the family up from our house, I wouldn't have woken up. One by one, the family of Savannah piled in, dressed in all white as previously agreed. The Jeffersons and Sade only planned on attending the church service so they could get back here and prepare the food for the repast. I filled up the largest flask I owned with Rémy, then made my way to the limo that trailed the coffin in the hearse with Savannah's family.

"Good morning, family, friends, and loved ones. Today, we come together in celebration of a beautiful woman who was blessed with a beautiful, but short-lived life, our sister, Ms. Savannah James. Due to embalming issues, the family has requested a closed casket service, but we don't need to see her face to remember what we felt for her in our heart . . ." the pastor said as he took his place next to her casket.

I was listening, but I wasn't feeling anything, and the truth is, no one else seemed to be feeling anything either.

Even though it was a funeral, everyone looked more relieved by Savannah's death than saddened. I don't recall seeing tears fall from anyone's eyes except Sade's. It almost pissed me off that Savannah's death didn't sadden anyone, but look at the woman she was and the life she had lived. She had to have been a sweet and innocent girl before she chose her direction, this I had to believe. It just had been so long since anyone had seen that side of her that they must have forgotten it. I didn't expect any of her childhood friends to attend because Savannah had wronged them, and none did except for Melinda for the reasons she had written in her letter, and Will.

"Hey, Dre, I didn't want it to end like this for her. Man, my heart is with you and your baby girl. We are family. If you need anything, I'm right here like I've always been. Security." He smiled at me, and I pulled him in for a hug.

"I appreciate it" was all I said in return.

Besides the blood-related family, no one else came to pay their respects besides her colleagues and ex-lovers that remained friendly. I was surprised to see Stephanie at the service, but I think she was only there because she was a partner at the firm since she didn't make it to the cemetery or the repast. She didn't cry, but the way she rocked as she held my son, I knew she was hurting.

"Can you introduce me to our son, please?" It took everything in me to walk up to her, but I wouldn't be in the same place as my child and pretend I didn't see him.

"Andrew, this is your father, Mr. Andre Burns," she said as she handed him to me. If he was born on Savannah's birthday, he was now six months old and a big boy for his age. Looking into his face, it took everything in me not to let a tear fall. He was my twin. He didn't look like Stephanie, not one bit. I tried to find one thing that would make him hers, but there wasn't anything there.

"Hey, big boy, look at you. You're handsome, just like your daddy. Your mama and I have some stuff to work out, but I want you to know I'm never leaving your side. Where you live, Daddy will live nearby, and if I can't, then you will just have to come live with me."

"Dre—"

"Don't 'Dre' me, Stephanie. You didn't take those morning-after pills for a reason, so you will have to deal with the consequences that come with it. I love kids, and I'm a damn good daddy."

"I know you are. You know I do, but you can't just sit here and think I'm going to give him up because of the games that were played around him."

"Come up with something to make it right. I can't leave Nashville for four years. Tell me what we are going to do to make it work. You still have my number?"

"Yeah, I still have it."

"Then use it every day so that I can talk to my son, okay?"

"Okay."

"When do you leave Washington?"

"Tomorrow night at 7:00."

"Can I keep him until you and I can meet for breakfast in the morning?"

"Dre, I don't think—"

"You don't have to say it," I said, cutting her off. "Well, after this stuff right here is over with, can I swing by your hotel with Sade so she can meet her brother and maybe come back later and stay the night with him? I won't touch you nor will I try to. It's all about him."

"Let's see how it goes when you and Sade come, and I will decide from there, okay?"

"Cool."

The rest of the day was filled with joy as we listened to Savannah's father, uncles, and brother recall her childhood before all the bullshit began. As I had previously assumed, Savannah was once her father's angel. As he told story after story, all I could think about was preserving my daughter's innocence's to the harsh reality of the world as long as I could. The day flew by fast, and I never had the urge to reach in my coat to take a swig of my flask. I was drunk from all the love and support that filled the house.

Like all good things, they come to an end as the doorbell rang. Dressed in all black with a veil over her face,

Savannah's mother, Peaches, walked in. No one knew who she was, but being the only one in all black caused her to stand out and get the guests whispering around the house until she had grabbed the attention of not only Savannah's brother, Memphis, but of his father as well. The three of us must have asked her in unison, but all I could hear was the sound of my own voice.

"What the hell are you doing here?"

"Fellas, what kind of question is that to ask a grieving mother? I'm here for the same reason as everyone, and that's to mourn the death of my baby girl, Sa . . . Savannah. Oh my baby girl, Savannah."

She fell on her knees and pretended to be bawling her eyes out, crying. For half a second, I thought Mr. James was falling for it as he made his way to her side. Instead, he snatched her up by her left armpit and starting pulling her to my bedroom.

"Dre and Memphis, come on."

He wasn't asking us to join him in the back; he demanded it. All the guests in the house went silent without a clue of what was going on, and I could hear the Jeffersons wrapping up the gathering as we entered my bedroom. Mr. James released his grasp on her by slamming her onto my bed.

"What the fuck are you up to now, Trisha?"

She snorted like an overweight pig at the man she should have been addressing as husband. "Don't call me Trisha, Dwight. I prefer Peaches."

She unruffled her clothes and sat up tall. After months of being around Peaches, I had finally figured her out. She was in a huge identity battle with herself, and the name Trisha vs. Peaches belonged to two different women. Both of the women were snakes in the grass, but Peaches was supposed to be the calmer one of the two. This identity crisis she was going through meant nothing to the rest of us.

Memphis spoke up. "Peaches or Trisha, it doesn't matter what we call you, because a dog of a different breed is still a dog, and you're still a bitch."

Mr. James looked at his son as if he was going to correct him for disrespecting his mother, but he snatched off Peaches's veil and repeated himself. "What the fuck are you up to now, Trisha?"

She removed her black glove off her hand, revealing a wedding ring with a rock the size of a quarter in it. "I don't have to respond to you anymore, Dwight. You're not my husband. Like I told you in my letter, I've married me a *real* man."

"How could you have married a real man when you're not even a real woman? And you *will* respond to me if you want to make it out of this house alive."

So much pain and anger blazed in Mr. James's eyes that I took his threat to be serious, so I intervened. "Stop the bullshit, Trisha, and tell us what you want. You don't come around without panhandling."

She looked offended by my words, but we all knew they were true, and she did too. She went straight into her spiel.

"I came for my piece of the insurance money that's coming to you, Mr. Andre Burns, sole beneficiary listed on all of Savannah's insurance policies, and from you, Mr. Dwight James, owner of a $300,000 policy that you paid off on Savannah and Memphis by their twenty-first birthdays. I also was lucky enough to get a million-dollar policy going once I tracked her down in California and saw the lifestyle she was living. The problem I'm running across with that policy is that the United States still has us listed as married, Dwight, so the company wants us to come in together and sign some papers. Don't worry. I'm not that selfish. I'm prepared to give you $25,000 for whatever trouble that causes you to help me get it done, although I am the only one who paid those premiums. The way I see it, between the two of you, I should be 1.5 million dollars richer before I leave Washington again."

"Even in death, you only see your daughter as a cash register," I yelled as Trisha began pulling paperwork out of her purse and sorting it out on the bed like she hadn't heard me.

"You know my original plan was to have Savannah kill myself and then blackmail Dwight for his insurance payout." She nodded her head toward Mr. James. "I thought I could get you to do it for me for free, Dre, and then you let me down. I watched your drunken ass break the lights over the door at Royce's hotel room, plotting to get him but hoped you waited and decided to kill them both instead. I called your phone from the parking lot urgently asking you to meet me down the street to go over our plan. If I hadn't, you would have killed him, and my backup plan wouldn't have worked." She then nodded at Memphis as to say he was the backup plan.

"You see, when we all met up at the hotel, Savannah wasn't supposed to sign over the money to me, which would have pissed you off and caused you to kill her and Royce. My idiot of a son here was supposed to come in the room and kill you, avenging his sister's death, but his scary ass sent me a text from the car saying you were still in the hall when he got off the elevator, and he had changed his mind. The little bitch went walking off."

"Fuck you, bitch!" Memphis snapped at her, this time hushed by his father.

There wasn't a need for me to say a word about anything that she had said because Mr. James had directed me differently. "Andre, make sure the house is clear for me, will you, son? I want you to get my son, Memphis, here, and y'all head over to the police station. Report what you heard here tonight and everything else you know she's a part of, like that big wire transfer from Savannah's account, and how she had you break in your sister's house by blackmail, Memphis. When y'all are done reporting it all, tell them the reason why y'all are telling them everything."

It wasn't just Memphis who was lost by his father's last words, because I felt confused by them too. Mr. James snatched Trisha's purse that she had tightly at her side and retrieved a gun from it.

"Tell them you gave them all of that information because you needed to report a homicide. I'll be outside sitting on the curb when the police arrive." He pointed the gun at Trisha's head.

I grabbed Memphis by his shirt, tugging him out of the room.

"Let me go, Dre. Let me go. She isn't worth it, Daddy. Please, no!"

I couldn't protest against Mr. James's choice, especially not after committing homicide on my own future wife. He had enough information on the evil that Savannah's mama was running around committing to get off with manslaughter, and I knew just the lawyer we'd hire to ensure it, that's if they didn't force Royce to be a witness. Before I left him to commit one of the biggest sins we as flesh could commit, I said my last few words to him as a free man.

"I'll make sure to tell them how she held us at gunpoint trying to get the money we are getting from the insurance companies, Mr. James. So, try not to get blood on all those papers Peaches took the time to dig up. Memphis and I will have your lady friend waiting on you at the house when you get released. After I tell Royce about what went down with Savannah, I know he'll get you off your charge."

"Thanks, son, and one more thing. I'll need you to be at my side when I bury my wife. I guess I will know what that feels like after this."

"I'll always be there when you need me to be. Let's go, Memphis." Mr. James smiled at me in understanding, and I got Memphis into the hallway without any more hassle. He knew his dad would be all right after this, and the way he looked at his mother as he soaked up one last look at her alive said he wouldn't miss her, nor would he be holding anything against his father for deciding to lay her down. As I closed the bedroom door behind us, I said, "Rest in piss, Trisha."

Epilogue

It had been weeks since leaves had fallen to the ground, and snow now covered them and their deaden tracks. It was freezing out, but Sade had made a pact with herself that no matter where she found herself in the world or what she was going through, she'd return to her parents' graves every year on Valentine's Day. The day itself had no significance to her parents' relationship, but she enjoyed the irony of it. It helped coat the pain that was already disappearing and acted as a reminder on why she'd never allow herself to fall in love. It had been sixteen years since she had heard her mother's voice and three years since she felt her father's last loving embrace.

Although her parents weren't the ideal couple, she felt a bond with them both, so she had them buried side by side. It was hard for her to place flowers on her father's grave after being a daddy's girl for so many years. But that all changed on Sade's eighteenth birthday when her father confessed something that she wasn't ready to accept, and she didn't. Just thinking of his words made a tear fall from her eye, which she was sure had frozen before it would make its way down her cheek. After checking her surroundings for other mourners, Sade began talking to her parents.

"Hey, you two, it's been a year since our last visit, and I can't pretend that I've missed you, but I'm here. It's our third anniversary all together as a family and my third therapy session. I'm sure if I were ever to tell anyone I came out here and did this every year, they'd swear I was crazy, but, honestly, what did they really expect me to be with the two of you as parents? All my life I was told of my sex-crazed mother who had given me up to foster care to prevent my father from raising me properly, and how she died of an accidental shooting trying to prevent her plotted-out death. Your story, Mama, always sounds like something you'd read in a fiction book or see on a daytime soap opera to me. I mean, what kind of bitch screws her child's life up to pursue a life of meaningless sex?

"I'm sure if you could speak up, you'd be trying to defend yourself right now, but I wouldn't listen. I'm a daddy's girl. Always have been, always will be. It broke my heart, Mama, when Daddy sat me down on my eighteenth birthday and smoked that blunt with me. He knew I had been sneaking and smoking weed, just as I knew he smoked heavily, but he had never asked me to join him in smoking. I guess we needed to, huh, Daddy? Or else, you wouldn't have been able to tell me how you were the one who had killed my mother and calling it an accident was just an alibi for the truth. You told me you wanted her dead because, in a split second, you realized you wouldn't want to spend life without her. Oh, don't mind these tears that fall. They fall at the memory of hearing you confess, Daddy, not because I'm hurt from your death, Mama. I know it had to have taken you years to decide when the perfect time to tell me was, and even though you thought eighteen would do, you were still wrong. It hurt me to hear that my daddy and hero was a cold-blooded killer that my mama had fallen victim to.

"But I got over it.

"As I watched you drink that whole bottle of poison that I dressed up as punch, I felt the forgiveness flow right through me. I didn't think I could pull it off. I had to get the bottle of poison in your hands, then get five hours away with my foster parents and make sure I called to check on you, Daddy. After a day or so of you not answering my calls, my other daddy, or Mr. Jefferson, as the two of you liked to call him, called the police and asked them to check on you. My God, Daddy, Ryan, being the good friend that he was to you, took his time to tell me in person that you were found dead after committing suicide. I was so heartbroken and had told the police of your confession the day before you took your own life. You were saddened by what you had done to my mother that you killed yourself on her death date to make the shit symbolic. You see, the two of you weren't meant to procreate, because the combination of DNAs created a monster. While other twenty-one-year-olds are planning their futures, I'm already living mine. Don't worry. I'm going to school, and my grades are fine. It's what I do in my free time that should worry you. All I'll say is I'm definitely my mother's child and a daddy's girl for life. Happy Valentine's Day, you lovebirds."

"Are you coming, or do you plan on moving out here with them? Just let me know so I can drive off," her oldest brother, Andre Jr., yelled at her from his car. They weren't siblings by blood but had been raised together at her father's wishes. Although he believed his sister was completely out of her mind for making the annual trip, he always volunteered to make it with her because he knew why she had to, but that wouldn't make him join her at their graves.

"Yeah, hurry up, sis. It's cold out here. I'm ready to get back to Nashville, where it's warm. My nuts are freezing."

"What nuts, little nigga? You still got balls until you turn sixteen. You got at least three more months before you get some of these Big Burns nuts, boy," Andre said jokingly to his little brother.

"Ask yo' bitch about my Big Burns nuts. She'll tell you ain't no balls hung down there in years," he snapped back, and both brothers began laughing.

"Don't nobody want to hear about your Big Burns nuts, Andrew, and please leave him alone, Andre. You know he's going to tell Auntie Stephanie that you were messing with him, and then I'm gon' have to cuss the bitch out again," Sade said, turning her attention back to her parents' graves. Andrew wanted to check her about her constant disrespect toward his mother but knew better. So did Andre. If he and Sade ever had beef, he made sure to chew it up and swallow it before she knew it existed.

Sade wasn't right in the head, and it became more noticeable with each year that had gone by. Her maternal grandfather said she had inherited many of her ways from her grandmother, and her paternal grandmother pushed the blame on her grandfather, but those who knew her parents had known the truth. She was all the bad in Savannah and Dre combined into a beautiful woman with extraordinary looks and intelligence but plagued with a very dark side that she loved to feed. Her dark side didn't resemble anything seen from her parents, and those who had known them assumed she was the seed of some demonic creature that didn't have a soul. If this weren't true, Sade did all she could to make it seem as if it were.

"Well, I guess this is goodbye until next year," Sade said as she moved into her exiting position. She always concluded her visit in the same manner, which was spitting on both of her parents' graves, and why wouldn't she when she knew both were empty. . . .